Greasy Ocker

Derek Pratt

enigma
publishing

Also published by enigma publishing

Getaway with Murder

Death in Little Venice

Kiss and Tell

Devil in the Detail

by Leo McNeir

enigma publishing
PO Box 1901, Milton Keynes, MK19 6DN

First published 2005
© Derek Pratt 2005

A CIP record for this book is available from the British Library.

ISBN 0 9531742 3 9

Typesetting by *specialist* publishing services ltd, Milton Keynes

Printed in Great Britain by The Baskerville Press, Salisbury, Wiltshire

Derek Pratt has been associated with inland waterways ever since a happy fluke led him at the age of 18 to his first solo photography job working on the Blue Guides of British Transport Waterways. He lives in west London with his wife, twin daughters and four cats!

As a leading waterways photographer, his wanderings along Britain's towpaths have accumulated the collection of photographs that form his Waterways Photo Library. He has written and illustrated several books on inland waterways, the most recent being books on canal architecture and London's canals. He has also collaborated with waterways historian and author Anthony Burton on a whole series of books, including the recent trilogy, *Anatomy of Canals*. Derek Pratt writes and illustrates a regular monthly feature in *Canal Boat and Inland Waterways* magazine.

Acknowledgements

I would like to thank the following people who have contributed to this book:

Cassandra and Leo McNeir, Fred Barter, John Saxon, Tony Burton, Emrhys Barrell, Hermione Sacks and Janet Sacks.

The author would welcome any comments on *Greasy Ocker*. Please address them to him by e-mail at: derek@greasyocker.co.uk

Derek Pratt, May 2005

Christmas 1940

Santa Claus was late on Christmas Day. At the village hall, he looked at the anxious faces of the boatmen's children and told them that war restrictions had forced him to leave his reindeer and sleigh in Lapland. A group of watching boatmen knew by the smell of his breath that the delay had originated at the pub.

The children received modest presents as Santa distributed his seasonal goodwill, bid a merry farewell to all, and disappeared rather unsteadily back in the direction of the ale house.

Lines of boats stretched along the canal bank with smoke curling lazily in the still frosty air. Cooking smells drifted from the tiny cabins, where boatman's wives worked to produce a Christmas dinner despite the wartime shortages. A group of men sat on boxes smoking roll-up cigarettes. As they passed around a water can filled with beer, their talk was not festive but of the war and its effect upon their future. It was also about the demise of a boatman who had been killed five weeks earlier in the big raid on Coventry.

More than 500 people lost their lives that night and another 900 were injured. One of the dead was Joe Collingham, a hard-working boatman who was standing on the towpath, close to the canal basin, when a bomb exploded behind him. The blast threw him across the canal and he ended his life spread against a wall of a warehouse. His death passed without mention in the newspapers, but was vividly recalled by two boating colleagues who witnessed the event.

Ocker sat on the cabin roof, looking down at the group and listening to the story. At five years old, his experience of the war was restricted to watching processions of planes crossing the sky above the canal and his father saying reassuringly, "They be all right, they be all ours."

This Christmas story was nearer home for one of their own people had been blown to bits alongside the canal.

Ocker understood a little better his mother's fears for their next trip down to London, but his immediate concern was for his Christmas dinner in the cosy warmth of the cabin and afterwards a film show for the boat people's children in the mission hut.

He was born in the winter of 1935 in the back cabin of butty boat *Quebec* at Ocker Hill in the Black Country. The canal was frozen solid at the time and, what with one thing and another, his parents, Dolly and Reg, were never quite sure the exact day the birth took place. Reg remembered slipping and sliding along the towpath to fetch Old

Missus Wormold, a local woman whose midwifery skills were renowned in that area. She had no medical training and the local authorities frowned on her natal achievements, but it was to her that the local poor turned at the time of delivery. She asked no payment except for a bottle of gin, most of which was consumed during the confinement. There were many lurid tales about Missus Wormold, including one where, after attending a long protracted birth, she lurched drunkenly along the towpath carrying a bucket full of afterbirth, tripped over a mooring ring and fell into the canal.

The newly born baby was named Terry but, because of his place of birth, Terry Hill soon acquired the nickname of Ocker. In later life, his dishevelled appearance and reluctance to bathe earned him the nickname Greasy Ocker, after a slimy fleet of soap tallow boats that worked in the Black Country.

After Christmas dinner, his father ushered him out of the cabin and pointing to the mission hut said, "Now you'm go to the pictures while yer Mam and me lie down for half an hour. I heard they've got Laurel and Hardy and Charlie Chaplin."

As Ocker crossed the wharf towards the black mission hut, a scruffy boy stepped in front of him, placed a finger and thumb into his mouth, produced a large sticky sweet and said, "I'll bet yer don't know what this is?"

Ocker shook his head and the boy said, "That's a gobstopper! It changes colour as you suck it."

The boy replaced the sweet and sucked enthusiastically. After a minute he extricated the sticky mess and exclaimed, "See, it's turned pink – it was yellow before."

Ocker was impressed. At that moment he would gladly have swapped his Christmas dinner for a gobstopper.

"What's yer name?" the boy asked.

Ocker could hear the gobstopper clattering around the boy's molars like a ball on a pintable machine.

"Terry, but everybody calls me Ocker," he replied.

"That's a daft name, why do they call you that?"

"It's where I was born – Ocker Hill."

The boy suddenly made a sucking noise like water disgorging from a drain, removed the gobstopper and proudly proclaimed, "Look, it's gone green now."

Ocker examined the diminishing sweet and then looked at the boy. He was a couple of years older and a few inches taller. He had dark curly hair and shifty eyes.

Ocker plucked up courage and asked, "So, what's your name?"

"They call me Tom."

"I'm off to see the pictures at the mission. Are you going?"

"No," Tom said contemptuously, "I'm going to the spunk bag tunnel."

"What's that?"

"It's a tunnel under the railway. We go and count the spunk bags. There was six last time we went."

"What's a spunk bag?"

"You know, it's what blokes put on their thing when they're doing it."

"Doing what?" Ocker queried.

"Doing it with the lasses."

"What do they do with the lasses?"

"You know, they shove their thing into the lass's thing."

Ocker was even more puzzled. "Why do they want to do that?"

"I dunno, but they do it," Tom said, and added, "Anyway I'm off down there to count them. Are you coming?"

Suddenly Charlie Chaplin had lost his magic to the mysterious lure of discarded contraceptives, so Ocker followed his new companion along the canal towpath for some distance, until the last boats had disappeared around a bend. Ahead, crossing the canal, was a railway viaduct where Tom led Ocker down a track beneath the arches lined with hawthorn and elder bushes.

"It's just a bit further," Tom said. "Hey, I think there's somebody in there."

The two boys paused before the track, then turned towards the viaduct arches, where they heard rhythmical grunts amplified by the tunnel's acoustics.

"Hey up, there's somebody in there doing it," Tom said, eagerly edging his way forward to peer into the tunnel's depths. Two figures silhouetted by the light from the tunnel's exit were coupled together against the curved wall. As Tom leaned forward to get a better look, his foot slipped on the gravel path and he was catapulted down the slope, sliding on his bottom in full view of the startled couple. The man yelled a stream of obscenities and Tom, picking himself up, rushed up the slope past Ocker, shouting, "Run like hell, it's me Dad!"

Joe Raggett returned his attention to his companion. "Sorry about that, pet, it was our Tom."

"I hope he won't tell tales to your missus."

"He'll keep his trap shut 'cos he knows I'll tan his bloody hide."

Back at the wharf, Reg Hill was feeling concerned. He'd looked into the mission hall, where children and adults sat in the darkness, heartily laughing at the antics of Charlie Chaplin. He peered through the flickering gloom but there was no sign of his son anywhere.

A foul-smelling boatman, known as Bo Brummie, stood at the back of the hall watching the film. The boatmen would jest that you could always tell when Bo was around by the acrid stink that wafted from him. Bo Brummie, who worked with sewerage boats, seemed supremely unaware of his rancid stench.

"Owdo Bo. Have you seen young Ocker around?" enquired Reg.

Bo Brummie's hand slipped from his belt to scratch the deep recesses of his crotch. "Aye, I saw him off down the towpath wi' Joe Raggett's lad."

"Which way did he go?"

"Back towards the railway."

Reg strode purposefully across the wharf towards the canal and then saw Ocker and Tom Raggett running along the towpath.

"Oi, come 'ere yer young bugger," Reg shouted.

Ocker had an idea what was coming and his predictions proved correct when he received a substantial clout around the ear.

"Where the bloody 'ell have yer been?"

"I went off for a walk wi' Tom," explained the tearful Ocker, who decided further explanation might be necessary. "We went to look at a magpie's nest."

"Magpies don't nest at Christmas."

"It was one of last year's," Ocker snuffled.

"Who was that lad you were with?"

"His name's Tom."

"Aye, Tom Raggett. He's one of Joe Raggett's lads and yer not to play with him ever again."

"Why not?"

"Because we have nowt to do wi' Raggetts. It goes back a long way. Raggetts mean trouble and don't yer ever forget that. If I catch yer wi' a Raggett again, I'll give yer a belting you'll never forget."

At this point, Ocker's Christmas day came to a premature end. Banished to his bed in the back of the little boat cabin, he looked around the familiar warm interior with the stove, lamp and curtains edged in lace. Beside the table was a cupboard door painted with an intricate design of roses around an inlaid panel, a fairytale castle, lake and mountains to the rear. Crochet lace covered every shelf from which hung lace plates, some bearing the legend 'A Present from Blackpool'.

His mother had bought him comics and for a while he followed the antics of the cartoon characters, wishing he could understand the words inside the little speech bubbles. The creaking of ropes rubbing against mooring bollards and the gentle ripple of water against the boat's hull were soothing familiar sounds that gradually induced drowsiness.

He soon fell asleep, oblivious to the raucous voices singing popular boatman's songs clearly audible from the pub across the wharf.

****

They loaded 50 tons of coal at the colliery and headed south, with Reg steering the motorboat *Vancouver* towing the unpowered butty boat *Quebec*. It was a fine, cold day and a dusting of frost on the cabin roof soon melted under the rays of a weak, winter sun. Ocker spent most of the day sitting on the step near the stove, playing with his crayons and lead soldiers.

At a flight of locks, they met a horse-drawn boat travelling in the opposite direction. The boatman allowed Ocker to fill the horse's bucket with fresh water from a tap next to the lock cottage. Every time boatmen met at the locks, the talk was of the war and dire warnings of what might befall London in the air raids. Several boats travelling northwards carried grain, stone or metal ingots. Reg and the approaching boatmen greeted each other with the conventional greeting "Owd'yer do" and might exchange a shouted few words over the noise of the engines. Ocker enjoyed the long tunnels, waiting for the moment when the boat passed underneath the ventilation shafts and he would hear Reg's curses as water poured on to his head.

The coal was unloaded at a factory wharf on the western outskirts of London. It was always a dirty, dusty job and Reg usually ended up looking more like the miners who dug up the coal in the first place. Ocker went with his mother to stock up provisions from nearby shops. This was an onerous task for, although they had ration books, many shops wouldn't serve them because they were itinerant and their stocks were reserved for regular customers. Sometimes Reg would do a deal with a butcher, exchanging a secreted bag of coal for sausages and bacon.

After unloading, they travelled to the depot where the Canal Company had their offices. Here there were mooring places for dozens of working boats opposite a bridge leading to central London.

Ocker's mother went to a washhouse, which had basins and the luxury of running water. Here, over steaming tubs, was one of the few places where boatmen's wives could meet to gossip while doing the family washing. She would hear the other women's difficulties in obtaining provisions and the latest scandals involving people working on the canals.

Early next morning, Reg entered the office where a tall, skinny company clerk, suffering from an active skin disorder, was poking a ripening pustule on his chin with a pencil.

"Hello Reg, what can we do yer for?"

Reg shoved his shirt under the belt of his trousers and straightened his shoulders. "I want to load up, what yer got?"

The clerk replied, "All I've got is timber from City Road up to Northampton but they won't take it." He jabbed a thumb towards a trio of boatmen lounging in the corner. Despite the early hour, the boatmen were already drunk.

Reg spun round to confront them, "What's yer problem?"

The tallest boatman who wore a green shirt and blue overalls pointed a grimy finger at Reg. "Anyone who wants to carry timber in the Blitz is a bloody lunatic."

Reg turned back to the clerk. "Bugger the war, I've got to get some money on the table."

The clerk poked an ink-stained finger into his left ear, shook it vigorously, withdrew and examined the results of his excavations. "The job's yours if you're sure you want to go, but it can get a bit rough down there if there's a raid."

Reg shook his head. "If my name's on one of them bombs, then so be it."

The journey into London was uneventful and they arrived at a wharf near the City Road Canal Basin soon after midday. It was late afternoon by the time the timber was loaded. Reg had been advised to stay at the wharf until morning, but he'd refused saying he wanted to get clear of the city in case of a raid. As he steered into the gaping mouth of the tunnel, he heard the sound of the air raid warning siren. In the eerie darkness, all he could see was his light reflecting back from the tunnel roof and all he could hear was the thumping roar of his engine. He emerged at the other end of the tunnel into a scene from hell. Parachute flares were dropping over the railway and lighting up the darkness with a green light that cast brilliant shadows over the grubby townscape.

Reg shouted back to Dolly, who had brought the butty alongside the motorboat, "Jerry's after the marshalling yards!"

The boats were surrounded by incendiaries falling in groups and exploding with instant fire, hissing as they hit the water and sending clouds of steam high into the air. The sky was veiled by thick smoke blotting out the full moon. Reg cut the engine to tick over and went cautiously through to the next bridge.

"Bloody bombers' moon!" Reg muttered as he steered the motorboat towards the towpath. He gestured to Dolly on the butty, "Get it over, and get the kid out of the way."

The first high explosive bombs hit the gas works. They descended from the sky, screaming like a thousand banshees, followed by a sound like tearing sheets. A gasholder exploded and seconds later began burning furiously, sending a huge plume of fiery gas in a mushroom cloud of smoke and flame high into the sky.

Searchlights pierced the sky, frantically guiding the air defences in retaliation as wave after wave of enemy bombers dropped their payloads.

"You don't hear the bomb with your name on it," someone had remarked. "Poor old Joe Collingham, did he hear the one that killed him?"

Ocker, fully dressed, had been asleep when he heard the first bangs. He rushed up the cabin steps to hear his mother exclaim, "Oh my God! We're in for it this time."

The night sky was alive with livid colours of red and yellow, and people were running along the towpath yelling and shouting. There was a loud metallic clatter on the boat and Dolly screamed, "We've got a fire bomb on the butty!"

She steered the boat to the edge of the canal where Reg grasped the mooring rope, shouting, "Get the kid off the boat!"

Ocker jumped off the boat and stood transfixed as the load of timber began to burn furiously. The next moment a running man, who in his panic never saw the little boy, knocked him flat on his back.

Reg picked him up and pointing to a pile of sandbags, shouted, "Get behind them bags, lie down and don't move."

Ocker ran to the shelter and hid behind it as an enormous explosion collapsed a warehouse on the other side of the canal. A huge sheet of flame shot across the sky and burning debris flew through the air, pattering to the ground like falling autumn leaves. He could feel the heat on his face burning like a midsummer sun, and the sky had turned the colour of a tropical sunset. Fire engine bells and burglar alarms sounded above the exploding bombs, and he watched with horror as a warehouse's wall slowly disintegrated and dropped with a great splash into the water.

Reg and Dolly were thrown backwards and stunned by the blast that hit the warehouse. When he recovered, Reg saw the butty *Quebec* burning furiously and drifting side on across the canal. It was in imminent danger of colliding with the motorboat, whose stern end was not secured to the quayside. Dolly lay unconscious, face down under a pile of smouldering beer-crates.

Reg frantically threw the crates to one side, shouting, "Dolly! are you OK?"

He picked her up and cradled her in his lap, gently slapping her face, "Dolly, for God's sake, don't die on me."

He was reassured by a low moan as Dolly opened her eyes.

"Thank God you're alive."

"Where's Terry, what's happened to Terry?"

"He's OK, I put him behind them sandbags."

"Where's the boats?"

Reg looked over to the canal where the blazing butty boat was threatening to ignite the motorboat. He jumped aboard and started the engine, cast off and moved out towards the lock. He looked back to see *Quebec* sinking into the canal, hissing like an angry snake under an incandescent cloud of smoke, and Dolly lying against the smouldering crates, trying to remove something burning from her hair.

Then came hundreds of rats, running wildly across the quayside and over the sandbags where Ocker lay hidden. The little boy screamed as they swarmed over him and one of them became entangled in his woolly pullover. He could feel its bony feet sticking into him as he tried to dislodge it, and once it had gone, he ran in panic to escape the overwhelming noise, the choking smoke and the disgusting rats. He ran away from the water, stumbling over wharf gates blown off their hinges. An ambulance with a screaming siren appeared through a pall of smoke, then swerved to avoid the little boy, who was dashing across the road. He turned into a narrow street, running through acrid smoke that made his eyes water and, as he relieved the irritation with his sleeve, he saw yet more rats scurrying along the pavement.

Panic-stricken, he ran from the alley into a wide street and collided with a blonde-haired woman, who picked him up and then bent down to look at him face to face.

"Now then me darlin' are you lost, or do yer live round here?" Ocker shook his head.

"Do yer know where yer mummy is?" Ocker shook his head.

"Oh dear! Did the cat steal yer tongue?" Ocker shook his head.

"If yer don't live around here, then where did yer pop up from. I'll bet yer dropped out of one of them airyplanes." Ocker shook his head.

"Well, I'd best take yer to somebody who can look after you."

The blonde-haired woman took him by the hand and crossed the road to a building with an ambulance parked outside. A steady stream of people passed in and out of a door upon which was chalked in large letters: Women's Voluntary Service Station. They took him in, sat him on an upturned box and gave him a sticky bun to eat. Wide-eyed and shaking, he saw a procession of blitz victims, some covered in dirt and dust and bleeding from glass splinters. A large lady in a green tweed suit and a bright red jumper gave them tea and tried to calm them.

The raid seemed to be over, but a steady stream of people with minor injuries came in for treatment. One old lady with violently shaking hands tried to drink from a mug of tea, while another sobbed out a story about her husband buried in the basement of their home, now destroyed by a bomb.

Someone gave Ocker a mug of sweet tea and soon exhaustion overtook him and he fell asleep, still sitting on the upturned box.

"Now then, what are we going to do with you?"

The large lady in the green tweed suit was shaking Ocker's shoulder. "Now then young man, do you know where you live?"

Ocker at last found his voice, "On a boat."

"What, on the canal?" Ocker nodded.

"Right, we'll try to find your boat as soon as it gets light."

In the cold, grey light of dawn, the tweedy lady took him back to the canal through devastated streets, where buildings still burned and ambulances picked their way through piles of smouldering debris.

Reg and Dolly were giving Ocker's description to a tired-looking policeman when they were reunited.

The morning sky was covered with smoke like a grey fog and there was an acrid smell of charred wood. The butty boat, partially submerged and still steaming, lay sadly forlorn in the middle of the canal.

"Well, at least you've got your lad back in one piece," said the tired policeman, "which is more than I can say about your boat."

"I haven't just lost my boat," Reg said with a grim smile. "I seem to have lost me ration book as well."

October 1950

They were all exhausted after three days of rain, travelling south to the paper mills with fifty tons of coal. For fifteen hours they worked without stopping, steering through drizzling rain and cursing on the sodden, slippery lock sides. Reg steered the motorboat all day with Ocker or Dolly handling the butty. The last lock had a broken paddle and took ages to get through. It was dark, cold and wet, and Reg's patience was at an end.

"That's it, I've had enough! Let's have some snap and we'll get a couple of hours sleep."

Reg pulled the motorboat over and used the snatcher rope to pull the butty alongside.

Ocker wasn't too sure. "Shouldn't we get through the top lock and then tie up? The Raggetts are not too far behind us."

Reg was exhausted and was snuffling with a cold. He knew he should get below the last lock in case the Raggetts came along, but hunger and tiredness had got the better of his judgement.

The Raggetts' boats, on the same run, were waiting to load when Reg left the colliery. If they worked through the night and got ahead, they could unload first at the mill, leaving the Hills waiting half a day or more. Standing around meant a loss of earnings as the Hills did not receive a weekly wage but were paid by each ton of cargo delivered.

"You sleep and I'll stay up and watch out," Ocker volunteered. "I'll wake you if I hear the Raggetts coming."

He was used to staying awake and preferred sitting up at the cratch taking short cat naps, avoiding the deep sleep which often brought on the recurring nightmares of the Blitz.

At fifteen, Ocker was already a skilled boatman and was adept at handling a pair of loaded boats. He knew all the boatman's rope techniques and took great pride in passing on his knowledge to his younger brother, Raymond. The family was completed by two little sisters, seven-year-old Lucy and five-year-old Brenda.

None of the four Hill children had ever attended full-time school. Ocker's meagre education was restricted to a few days a month in a mission school where, for most of the time, he had very little idea of what was being taught and couldn't wait for the call to get back on the boats for the next trip. Consequently, Ocker at fifteen could barely write his name and could read only the most basic of children's books. His personal freshness left a lot to be desired and Dolly would often say to him, "For goodness sake, Terry, go and wash yourself, they can smell you coming a mile away."

To which Ocker would reply, "What's the point in washing when you're gonna get dirty again?"

His brown corduroy trousers were held up by a worn, wide belt and usually had a windlass tucked into it. In winter, he wore an old green woollen jersey and a tattered green beret topped his greasy dark hair. The term 'water gypsy' was normally an insult to boat people, but in Ocker's case the term was visibly justified.

****

The moored boats were wreathed in a grey mist rising from the water. The only noise breaking the silence of the night was Reg's rhythmic snoring and the distant hooting of an owl. Falling leaves pattered down into the canal and occasionally an acorn dropped with a loud plop into the water. Ocker, curled up in the cratch of the motorboat, had nodded off into a dreamless slumber. He didn't hear the lock paddles being cranked or the curses of the boatman trying to work the broken machinery. It was the sudden movement of the displaced water underneath his boat that finally woke him.

"Christ, it's the Raggetts!" he yelled, hearing the throb of their motorboat. He leapt from the boat and ran along the towpath, banging his fist on the cabin roof.

"Wake up, Dad, the Raggetts are coming."

Reg rushed out of the boat cabin, rubbing his eyes and swearing, "Them bloody night-owlers, I'll fix the bastards this time. Terry, gimme your windlass, I'll set the lock, you start the bloody engine." He pulled on his boots and limped off into the darkness, still cursing loudly.

Three o'clock in the morning in mid-October is a bad time to start a cold engine. There was moisture everywhere and the damp motor refused to obey the frantic demands being made on it.

Ocker clutched his head and kicked the engine, then he tried again and again. "Start, you rotten bastard!" And now he could clearly hear the put, put, put, of the approaching boats. The recalcitrant engine coughed, spluttered into life and then faded once more. The Raggetts' boats loomed out of the mist, breasted up together, with Tom Raggett steering the motor.

"Having a bit of trouble, Ocker? Serves yer right for sleeping on the job," Tom Raggett shouted, passing close to the moored boats. The excessive wash caused the crockery to tinkle in the cabin and woke up little Brenda. The Raggetts' boats disappeared into the gloom and Ocker tried once more to start the stubborn engine, before accepting it was now too late to get to the lock.

Reg waited by the lock, windlass in hand, but the boats that appeared out of the mist, belonged to the Raggetts. He made a futile gesture with his hands to stop the pair entering the lock. Joe Raggett leapt off the boat, poking Reg in the chest with a grimy finger, "This is our lock, now push off before you get hurt."

Reg ran up the lock steps in a vain attempt to push the lock gate against the boats, but slipped on wet leaves. At the top, members of the Raggett clan, who had swarmed out of the cabins, surrounded him. Alf Raggett, wielding a beer bottle, pushed his unshaven face an inch from Reg's nose. "Joe told you to push off and now I'm telling you to push off."

Reg could smell his foul breath and shouted, "Don't you tell me what to do, Alf Raggett."

Alf Raggett shoved a hand into Reg's face and sent him sprawling, then turned and shouted, "OK. Tom, bring 'em into the lock."

Reg picked himself up and, seeing Tom Raggett steering the boats into the lock, yelled, "That's our bloody lock."

"How many more times do yer need telling to push off," Alf Raggett shouted. Then he grabbed Reg by his collar, spun him around and kicked him hard in the small of his back.

Reg, flailing his arms, tried to stop himself falling, pirouetted at the edge of the lock, then slipped over the top into the gap between the boat and the lock side.

Joe Raggett pushed his eldest son aside and peered down into the lock chamber. There was a ghastly scream as the advancing boat squashed Reg into the wall of the lock crushing his chest.

Joe shouted at Tom, "Go into reverse, he's in the lock."

Tom Raggett put the boat into reverse, but it was too late.

Ocker heard his father's screams as he rushed along the towpath. "What's happened, who's making that noise?"

Joe, running down the steps to help Tom reverse the boats out of the lock chamber, replied, "It's yer Dad, he slipped into the lock."

Ocker waded into the lock as soon as the boats were clear and found his father floating on his back with blood trickling from his nose and mouth. Reg screamed in pain as Ocker picked him up and took him back to the towpath.

Young Ronnie Raggett standing open-mouthed, with eyes as wide as an owl, said," Is he all right?"

"Course he's not all right, you silly bugger," Ocker growled, laying Reg on the towpath.

Tom Raggett jumped off the boat, took one look at Reg and said, "Oh bloody hell, I'm sorry Ocker, he fell in the lock and I never saw him."

"You're a murdering bastard, Tom Raggett."

Joe Raggett intervened. "There's no point in fighting, we've got to get him into hospital. Where's the nearest phone?"

Ocker looked around in desperation "There's nothing around here, not even a house."

"There's one in the village," Tom said. "Come on, Ronnie, let's run to the phone and get an ambulance."

"The village must be a mile and a half away," Ocker said, watching Tom and Ronnie disappear into the mist.

Joe bent down and began to lift Reg by his shoulders. "Come on, Alf, we'd better help make him comfortable on the boat."

"You leave him alone, you've done enough damage, you rotten bastards," shouted Ocker.

"Well, get some blankets and keep him warm."

Dolly came running along the towpath, screaming, "What's happened – is Reg hurt?"

"I'm sorry Missus, but he fell into the lock right in front of our boat," Joe Raggett replied. "You'd better get a few blankets to keep him warm until the ambulance comes."

A distraught Dolly made Reg as comfortable as possible, but it took over an hour for the ambulance men to reach the remote place, by which time Reg had died.

****

June 1953

A small pub next to the canal had organised various celebrations for the boat families on Coronation Day. In front of the pub was a disused wharf with a rusty crane festooned with flags and bunting. On the quayside, trestle tables and chairs were arranged for food and drinks. Inside the public bar was a television set, where the boat people watched flickering black and white images of the Coronation ceremony with amazement. This was the first time most of them had ever seen television.

The rain held off until mid-afternoon, by which time the tea, buns and sandwiches had been consumed and the children had finished their organised games. Ocker, uneasy with crowds of people, prowled up and down the canal bank where lines of boats were moored in pairs.

When the rain started, most people went back into the pub, except for a group of young men and women, who sheltered under an awning outside the public bar. The deserted wharf now filled with puddles, where earlier it had been filled with revellers, and the festooned crane looked damp and forlorn.

Since Reg's death, Ocker had been working as mate to Uncle Billy, while his cousin George was doing National Service. Now George was back from the army ready to resume his place on the family boats and Uncle Billy could no longer afford to pay Ocker's wages.

It was a happy time for Ocker, working boats between the north-western ports and the Potteries. They carried felspar one way and returned with finished pottery that was packed for export. The locks were narrow and could only accommodate one boat at a time, unlike the more familiar wider locks on the London Road, where a pair of boats fitted side by side. One of Ocker's jobs was bow-hauling the unpowered butty boat at the locks, while Uncle Billy went ahead with the motor. Pulling a boat laden with twenty tons of cargo in and out of locks every day soon hardened up his muscles and put an edge on his appetite. Fortunately Auntie Rose was an excellent cook and her pies were renowned by everyone who had tasted them.

Ocker was eighteen years old and powerfully built. Some people said that underneath the scruffy clothing and long unkempt hair hid a good-looking young man. Many of the girls had noticed him, but his shyness and his disreputable appearance always kept them away.

Over the past few months, Ocker had become more aware of the opposite sex. He realised that there was more to life than canal boats and a belly full of beer, but so far it hadn't occurred to him that changing his appearance might improve his chances of getting closer to girls.

Most of his attention was focused on Kitty McCann. She was the voluptuous daughter of Wilf McCann, a well-respected boatman whose family had been friendly with the Hills for many years.

Kitty McCann had spent the early part of her life on her father's boats, but then her mother, Gracie, insisted that she should have a proper land-based education and packed her off to live with her aunt. Attending school every day was difficult for a young girl, who was used to being continually on the move, and for a while her aunt considered sending her rebellious niece back to the boats. Kitty's academic achievements were not great, but she was popular with her girlfriends and admired by the boys.

During her holidays, she would return to the boats to help her mother, father and younger brother Corky, but as she became a teenager, the boating lifestyle with its omnipresent mud and coal-dust gradually lost its appeal.

She went to live with her mother in a council house when Gracie also became disenchanted with the boating life, leaving Wilf McCann to carry on working the boats with his young son and whatever hired help he could find. Kitty would frequently visit a wharf or waterside pub to socialise with old friends, who may be moored there for the night, but afterwards she would return home, appreciating her freedom from the restrictions of the tiny, cramped cabin, smelling of cooking and sweaty clothes. No longer did she have to lie on her bunk, trying to ignore her little brother squatting on the jerry pot just a few inches away. She no longer had to suffer the indignity of having to strip off her clothes so that the fleabites on her buttocks could be dabbed with disinfectant. At home now, she could sit on a proper toilet with soft toilet tissue instead of pieces of old newspaper. She had the privacy of a locked door with no need to keep shouting, "Don't come in, I'm using the pot."

Now she lived in a home with a proper bathtub and electric light, neither of which she had on the boat, or with her aunt, who had only primitive facilities in her old house. When she left her home, she stepped out on to a pavement instead of sinking ankle deep in mud and horse manure. Despite all this, there was still a part of her that yearned for the canal life.

Many of her old friends had gathered at the pub on Coronation Day and she was enjoying the attention that she was receiving from a good-looking young boatman. She was quite aware of Ocker, crouched against the wall of the bridge on the opposite side of the canal, and wondered when he would pluck up the courage to speak to her. Ocker, peering out through the lashing rain, miserably watched the object of his lust and affection flirting with a young man under the awning outside the pub's public bar. He saw the light reflecting off her hair as she tilted her head to laugh and he wondered if she was aware of his lonely vigil under the bridge.

As darkness fell, the lights inside the pub cast an inviting glow over the saturated wharf and Joey Boat Johnson began to play a medley of popular songs from the twenties and thirties on his accordion.

One song was a familiar tune, loved by the boat people, whose voices joined in with the chorus:

"She's a nice girl I know and she squeezes absolutely so
You can do just what you want, with any other fellow's wife,
But keep your hands off, that's mine."

Under the lamp, Kitty McCann and her admirer were locked together in an embrace, while Ocker gloomily peered through the rain from his shelter under the canal bridge.

****

January 1954

"It requires not only courage but mental resilience for those whose youth lay in the calmer and more slowly moving times in order that they adjust themselves to the giant outlines and harsh structures of the twentieth century."

Winston Churchill

"The days of commercial carrying on the narrow canals are finished, and the sooner you lot wake up to that fact, the better your future will be."

Ben Barnwell placed his pint of beer on the table, wiped his moustache with the back of his hand and looked at his audience with the bearing of a politician about to commence a speech.

Revelling in his status as soothsayer and prophet, he predicted gloom and doom to anyone who would buy him a pint. His awesome physical presence generated respect among the disciples, who gathered to listen to his pronouncements from his favourite chair next to the fireplace in the Anchor Inn. He was a large man with a flowing nicotine-stained white beard that often retained some evidence of his last meal. His florid complexion was a result of not only years of boating, but also of years of imbibing his favourite mild beer and whisky chasers.

Ben once owned a canal-carrying business and boatyard on the edge of the Black Country with contracts with the nearby coalfields. He designed and built special boats that were able to carry large tonnages of coal to factories and power stations on the lock-free sections of the northern Black Country. His entrepreneurial schemes made him a notable local figure, but his business collapsed after he failed to pay his government dues, and he was subsequently arrested for tax evasion. His only option was to sell his boats and his business to pay his debts and avoid imprisonment. Now he spent his day sitting in the Anchor Inn, dispensing wisdom and drinking vast quantities of local ale.

Some of the young boatmen, tired of Ben's doctrinal preaching, finished their drinks and left. Ocker acknowledged their departure but Ben, in full flow, didn't seem to notice his audience had reduced.

"The powers that be are not interested in investing in canals," he said, waving his hands in a sweeping gesture that made Ocker grab for his beer before the glass disappeared off the end of the table.

A group of men entered the pub and looked across at Ben, waving their hands in greeting. One of the men shouted, "Are you having your usual?"

"Thanks Bert, I'll have a pint of mild."

Turning back to Ocker, he resumed his diatribe. "Most of the canals will be shut down in ten years unless there's some money invested in 'em soon."

"But you'll always need boats to carry bulk cargoes," Ocker said.

"Don't kid yourself, lad," Ben replied. "The future for bulk cargo-carrying will be by road on specially built freightways with enormous lorries pulling trains of trailers. No cars will be allowed, just these big lorries carrying all the stuff we took by water."

"What'll happen to the canals?"

"They'll keep a few open for pleasure boating and shut down the rest."

One of the newcomers brought a pint of beer to Ben, but there was none for Ocker, who went to the bar and replenished his glass. When he returned with his drink, Ben was engaged in deep conversation with the group of newcomers who had now commandeered the table. His interview with the great man was obviously over so Ocker, grunting an unacknowledged "Cheerio," took his drink and sat on his own in the corner of the bar.

A tall, thin angular man with a large bony nose and pale blue eyes entered the bar. He looked around and saw Ocker at a corner table.

"There you are, I've been looking all over for you, I should have known you'm be in the pub."

"Hello John, I thought you'd finished with me for the day."

John Farden owned a boatyard on the opposite side of the canal from the pub. It was an old family concern going back several generations, but trade had slumped to the point where John was beginning to wonder how much longer he could stay in business. He couldn't afford to pay wages to full-time employees any more, so enthusiastic part-time workers like Ocker were a godsend.

"Old Jack Bromford's been taken off to the hospital, sounds like he's ruptured himself."

"Where was he?"

"He was loading down at the steelworks and tried to move summat that was too heavy for him. There's a load of tubes to be brought back, so I want you down there. I'll drop you off in the van."

The huge steelworks were bewildering and noisy. Cranes rumbled back and forth on overhead gantries, loading and unloading boats that waited in lines at the quayside. Mud-spattered lorries picked their way between stacks of sheeted steel piled high on the open storage area.

John Farden dropped him at the loading quay where dozens of empty boats stretched five or six abreast across the canal. The single motorboat was already loaded and, after a quick check of the sheeting, John Farden handed Ocker the keys, saying with a grin, "Off you go then lad – and don't get lost."

It was the first time Ocker had ever worked in this part of the Black Country and it felt good to be on his own with a loaded boat.

It was a cold January day with frost in the air. The light was beginning to fade as he steered the boat out of the steelworks through a short tunnel and then he was alone. Factories lined the canal and jets of steam hissed out of hidden outlets. Smoke hung around the bridge holes, then wafted on the surface of the water, which crackled as the boat fractured slivers of ice, shattering them into thousands of tiny pieces. At one point, the canal ran along an embankment and Ocker could see the wintry sun setting in a sky tinted with shades of pink and mauve by the pall of smoke from silhouetted factory chimneys. Lights began to appear in the windows of terraced houses, which crept up a hillside in front of a wasteland of cinder tips and worked-out quarries. Behind the terraces stood the gaunt remains of derelict engine houses, their defunct, crumbling chimneys pointing towards the darkening sky.

It was dark when he stopped the boat by the entrance of a long tunnel. He went into the cabin, lit the fire and brewed some tea. He sat on the bench and ate old Jack's sandwiches and a piece of cake. Jack's cabin smelled musty and looked dirty. Peering into the gloomy interior, Ocker thought he saw something moving in the bedding – he shuddered, took his tea and sat outside.

After his snack, he switched on the headlight and entered the tunnel. No other boats were inside so he was able to relax and listen to the booming echo of the engine. When he reached the end and emerged into the open air, he tied the boat up by the toll office island, locked the boat and walked to a canalside pub popular with boatmen.

He entered the bar and he saw his cousin George drinking with a group of men by the window.

George, a young man of medium height with a round freckled face and a shock of sandy coloured hair, stood up when Ocker entered the bar.

"Hey up, Ocker, haven't seen you for a while."

He went to the bar, bought Ocker a drink, and they joined the boisterous group of boatmen.

"So what's new, are you still working for Johnny Farden?" George asked.

"Yeah, I've just brought a load of tubing up from the steelworks. I'm moored up by the tunnel."

"Wow! Has Johnny Farden let you out on your own? Whose boat have you got?"

"Old Jack Bromford had an accident when he was loading. They think he's ruptured himself."

"It's easily done 'specially when you're getting on a bit like him," said young Corky McCann, swilling down the contents of a pint glass. Corky was the fifteen-year-old younger brother of Kitty McCann. He had opinions on most subjects and it mattered little whether he had the knowledge to back up his arguments. Corky was loud mouthed and his views irritated Ocker, who at the same time envied his confidence.

"I'll tell you something," Corky continued, "I won't be boating when I'm Joe's age. As soon as I see something better and easier, I'll be off. It's a mug's game slogging yer guts out every day in all weathers. Now who's gonna buy me a drink 'cos that barman knows how old I am and won't serve me?"

"Any excuse to get out of buying your round," said George.

Joey Boat Johnson scratched his long bony nose and said, "How do you feel about staying on the cut, 'cos things are getting worse. Young fellers like you could do better for yourselves working in a factory or in an office."

"I worked in a factory for one day and that was enough," said Ocker.

George intervened, "I haven't heard this story – so what happened?"

Ocker cleared his throat and wished he hadn't brought up the subject. "The bloke I was supposed to be helping sent me to another part of the factory to get the long stand from his mate. He kept me waiting for over half an hour until the foreman asked me what I was doing. When I told him I was waiting for the long stand, he told me they were pulling me leg and kicked me up the arse. Everybody was laughing at me so I packed up and left and never went back."

George laughed, "C'mon mate, that's one of the oldest tricks in the book. They usually catch out new lads with summat like that."

Corky leaned back on his chair, placed his feet on the table and said, "Why don't we go and look for Two-Bob Doreen?"

Two-Bob Doreen was the local prostitute who hung around the pubs and boatyards. Ocker was aware of her exploits from lurid tales in Black Country bars.

"I bet she won't turn out on a cold night like this," said George.

"Doreen's not fussy," said Joey Boat Johnson, "but her prices have gone up. She charges ten-bob a time these days."

"Bloody inflation everywhere," George said grinning. "Go on, Joey, you know where to find her. She's probably cadging drinks in The Swan."

Joey left the group, who started to tell stories about their experiences with Two-Bob Doreen. A boatman, called Spotty Harold, explained with graphic detail how she had taken his virginity over a pile of beer crates behind the very pub they were sitting in at that moment. Ocker squirmed in his chair while the others roared with laughter as the descriptions became more blatant and personal.

Corky McCann took out a tobacco tin and expertly rolled a cigarette. He winked at George and Harold, then turned to Ocker, "Hey Ocker, have you had it up with Doreen?"

"No, no, not me."

Corky struck a match on the side of the table and lit his rollup. "Well then, who have you had it up with?"

"That's my business," Ocker replied.

"You know what I think," Corky persisted. "I don't think you've had it up with anybody."

"You mind your bloody lip or you're gonna get thumped," Ocker shouted, his face colouring up in anger.

Conversation in the bar ceased for a few seconds and all eyes turned expectantly to the group in the corner.

George intervened, "Come on Corky, leave Ocker alone."

Corky grinned, "Alright, alright, my dad always told me to have respect for my elders."

"One of these days you'll go too far and somebody will give you a right going over," said George.

Joey Boat Johnson returned. "Come on lads, she's outside. Get yer money ready, there's enough of us to make it worth her while."

Ocker's stomach churned when he realised that he was expected to contribute to Doreen's expenses. The men quickly gulped down their drinks, followed by a loud scraping of chairs as they rushed towards the door with Ocker reluctantly trailing in the rear. Some of the other drinkers in the bar shouted ribald suggestions as the group disappeared though the door.

Two-Bob Doreen strode purposefully along the towpath towards the railway bridge with her entourage trailing behind her. As soon as she reached her destination, she turned to face her customers and Ocker saw her illuminated by the lights from the nearby marshalling yard.

She was a big woman in her early forties, still good-looking in a tarty sort of way, with her red hair combed in the style of her movie heroine, Rita Hayworth.

As a young woman, Doreen would entertain her clients at home, but now she had three teenage children and space in the tiny terraced house was at a premium. With middle age fast approaching, she took her clients wherever opportunity and a modicum of privacy permitted.

"Right now, which of you young gennulmen is going first."

Ocker was pushed forward to be confronted by Doreen, who had removed her coat to display a formidable bosom.

She smiled and he could see the crows-feet wrinkles around her eyes. "Come on then, me darling, it's a cold night so wotcha waiting for?"

Ocker tried to retreat, but was restrained by his companions.

"My word, we've got a shy one, but take no notice of them, me darling, and you come with me."

Doreen took Ocker by the hand and led him around the back of the bridge out of sight from the others. She lifted up her skirt and Ocker was horrified to see she wasn't wearing knickers. The last time he had seen a female's private parts was years ago when his younger sister was being bathed in the boat cabin. What he saw now was quite different and, while Ocker's brain told him to run, his body stood paralysed and rooted to the spot. Doreen was fumbling with his fly buttons and saying, "Come on, I haven't got all night."

It was all over in a few seconds of acute embarrassment for Ocker who, in his haste to get away, forgot his trousers were around his ankles, tripped and fell full length on to the towpath with his bare bottom exposed to the moonlight.

"Well, that seems to be that. First time was it?"

Ocker grunted, pulled up his trousers, fixed his belt and then buttoned his flies.

"You've still gotta pay me, but I'll tell you what I'll do."

Ocker handed over a creased ten-shilling note, which Doreen shoved into her purse. She then took out a two shilling coin and offered it, saying with a laugh, "'Ere you are – after that, I'd better give yer some change."

Ocker took the money and slunk away into the darkness with his companions' laughter ringing in his ears.

****

The year's first brood of ducklings left their nesting site underneath a clump of reeds in the shade of an old brick wall. They followed their mother across the blackened, oily water of the canal. It was early spring and buds were just appearing on bushes growing from the brickwork of a decaying wharf. A burnt-out car with its wheels missing was all that remained of a once busy factory. Most of the windows facing the canal had been smashed and the roof had been stripped, leaving wide areas open to the sky and nesting pigeons.

Tom Raggett remembered once loading aluminium from that wharf on to the family boats and mused on how things had changed.

He was born in his grandmother's terraced house next to the canal in Coventry. His mother left the boats after his eldest brother, Alf, had been born, and stayed away from the canals, taking a job in a factory and leaving her children in the capable hands of their grandmother. Joe Raggett paid fleeting visits when his boats were nearby, resulting in the birth of Tom and younger brother Ronnie. Joe was a notorious philanderer, who had numerous illegitimate progeny dotted around the map of the inland waterway system.

As soon as the boys were old enough to make themselves useful, they joined their father on the boats. It was a hard life and he remembered arguments with his brothers when they started to outgrow the limited space in the two tiny cabins.

Tom and his brothers grew up looking like their father. They were all muscular men of a medium build with dark curly hair and swarthy good looks. His father wore a distinctive red handkerchief tied around his neck. When he was working, he wore a greasy waistcoat and old corduroy trousers with half of the fly-buttons missing. Joe Raggett usually had a cigarette fixed between his lips, which over the years had stained his moustache. The Raggetts worked hard, often fifteen-hour days, six days a week, mostly carrying coal from the Coventry collieries to factories in London. They would try to pick up return cargoes of timber from Brentford to the Black Country, returning along the 'Bottom Road' back to the collieries to begin the cycle all over again.

On Sunday they rested, when Joe Raggett would shave, change into his best clothes and disappear for the day, visiting various lady friends, leaving his sons to their own devices.

A regular Sunday stop was at the big oak tree on the Jackdaw Pound where Joe was friendly with a farmer's widow. In the evening, he would return from the farm with a broad smile on his face and enough farm produce to keep them eating for the rest of the week. Tom enjoyed Sunday at the big oak tree where the three brothers roamed the woodland, catching rabbits with a ferret and their Jack Russell terrier.

On a winter's afternoon, Tom would stay for hours in a cinema near the colliery until a diligent usherette would have him thrown out. Afterwards, he would strut back along the towpath, pretending to be John Wayne, or Randolph Scott, firing imaginary guns at passing wildfowl.

Pubs were a favourite meeting place, where Joe would swap stories with boating cronies like smelly Bo Brummie, who played the harmonica and worked with the manure boats. Giggetty Jim, the 'Number One', and Wheelock Joe would often be there with members of the McCann and Randall boating families.

The demise of the Raggetts as a boating family began after the death of Reg Hill. The inquest absolved the Raggetts from blame, although the coroner ended the proceedings with a verbal addendum that only the lack of independent eye-witnesses had got them off the hook.

The truth of what really happened that night was common knowledge throughout the waterway system and afterwards the Raggett family found themselves ostracised. They hung on for a year trying to make a living before finally giving up the boats. Joe Raggett left his wife and went to live with a widow in Nuneaton, taking a job as a maintenance man on the local canal. Alf Raggett was convicted for armed robbery of a bank in Wolverhampton and was serving a long term of imprisonment. Tom went to do his National Service and then went back to live with his mother and his younger brother, Ronnie, in Birmingham.

He was now in his mid-twenties and worked as a motor mechanic. Years of boating, then as a mechanic in the army, had left him with a powerful physique. Girls found him attractive with his smart suits and his dark curly hair combed forward in the style of the popular film star, Tony Curtis.

Tom picked his way around puddles of rainwater on the crumbling towpath. In front of him stretched the canal, its grimy waters hemmed in by lines of old factories and, in the distance, the first of a flight of locks, which climbed between a concrete canyon of office buildings towards the city centre.

He paused by the lock and looked into the chamber. Leaking gates allowed water to seep in sluggishly and debris floated backwards and forwards in the bottom of the lock. The flotsam was proof that no boat had navigated the lock for some time.

Tom was meeting Vince Rothwell, who was a regular customer at the garage. He regularly serviced his car and would deliver it to his club, or occasionally to his home in the city's southern suburbs.

To all outward appearances, Vince Rothwell was a well-dressed, successful businessman whose accent betrayed his East London origins. The neighbours, who saw him leave his home in his maroon Jaguar every day, assumed he had an office in the city. In fact, Vince drove to a club called the Maple Leaf, located in an insalubrious street south of the city centre, where he conducted his dubious business deals.

He was born in East London and spent his teenage years working in the markets before leading a gang of youths in housebreaking and thieving from shops. After a few years, they progressed to armed robbery and eventually a payroll job, which yielded several thousand pounds. Vince's entrepreneurial villainy upset some of the established local criminals, who informed on him to the police in return for a few custodial favours. He managed to avoid arrest and decided a change of scene would be better for his health.

Arriving in Birmingham with plenty of money, he discovered the Maple Leaf Club, which soon became his headquarters for his criminal exploits. June Rollins, who managed the club, formed a liaison with the gregarious Londoner, and they lived together in a large house in the suburbs. After a year, Vince bought the club, making the previous owner an offer he couldn't refuse.

Tom pushed open a door and walked down a flight of stairs into the club. Prints of hunting scenes adorned the walls and red tassels hung from the wall lights, casting a warm glow around the room. June perched on a high stool, smoked a cigarette, and watched the customers seated around a dozen tables in front of the well-stocked bar. At first glance everything seemed respectable, but closer examination of the clientele soon destroyed that illusion. Some of the customers were playing cards and judging by the amounts of money lying on the table, the stakes were high. Vince Rothwell sat alone at a table in the corner, drinking a glass of whisky and reading a newspaper.

He was in his mid-thirties with slicked-back black hair already showing a hint of grey at the temples. When he escaped from London, he grew a moustache and lowered his sideburns to alter his appearance. June said he resembled Clark Gable. He gestured to Tom, "Sit down lad, June will get you a drink – what's your poison?"

"Oh, I'll have a pint of bitter," Tom said, looking across the room at the card players.

"Do you like to gamble – play cards or bet on the gee-gees?"

"No, not really. I've played rummy and had a bet on the National."

"Good for you, lad, betting's a mug's game unless you're the bookmaker or running the game."

"What about drinking – do you like to get drunk?"

"I'm not that keen – I like the odd pint," Tom replied.

"Good," said Vince. "The last guy who worked for me was as pissed as a fiddler's bitch most of the time. Drink loosens the tongue and I don't like guys discussing my business in every public bar in Brum. Do you understand what I'm saying?"

Tom nodded and then greeted June who brought him a bottle of beer from the bar.

"Hello, you're the young man from the garage?"

"Yeah, I delivered the Jag to your house a few weeks ago."

Vince lit a cigarette and continued. "Let's get down to business. I'm looking for a new wheels man and they tell me you're a hot driver. I'm also looking for a bloke who can handle himself and sort out the other geezer when the occasion arises. I'm looking for a bloke who is discreet about my business and keeps his nerve when the Old Bill's around. Now am I talking about you and do you want the job? If not, drink up and there's the door."

Vince put the cigarette in his mouth, placed both hands behind his neck and looked at Tom through a haze of smoke.

"What happened to the last bloke?" Tom asked, nervously.

"He fucked up on a job and nearly got us all nicked."

"Is he still around?"

"You must be joking. I gave him twenty quid and told him to piss off. So, do you want to think about it?"

"No," Tom answered, "I'm your man. When do I start?"

"Good, I like doing business with a man who can make a quick decision, especially when it's the right one. You look like a geezer I can get on with so I'll take you on. Give your notice in at that poxy garage and start working for me as soon as you can."

****

A Number One came a backering by, and they say so, and they hope so.
And we said "Oh Mam, that horse will die, oh poor old horse."
From Atherstone to the Hartshill length, and they say so, and they hope so.
'Twas there that poor beast broke his strength, oh poor old horse.

Traditional Boatman's Song

It had been a long winter with weeks of miserable cold, wet weather and Ocker was glad it was over. He rolled up his shirtsleeves, feeling the warmth of the spring sun on the arm that lightly gripped the tiller. With the help of his brother Raymond, he was taking an empty pair of boats back to the boatyard for urgent repairs to their battered hulls. They were travelling on an old canal that had seen better days when fleets of boats regularly carried coal from the local collieries. Many of the mines had closed down and now much of the remaining business was going by road. Maintenance of the canal's infrastructure was suffering from lack of investment, underlined by crumbling banks, leaking locks and overgrown towpaths.

All around them were old quarries and disused pit spoil heaps being reclaimed by nature. One of the heaps had formed a conical summit, giving it the appearance of a green alp. Hawthorn and buddleia clung on to precipitous slopes, which would be ablaze with rosebay willow herb later on in the summer.

They rounded a bend and saw a crowd of people congregated by a bridge with a pub on the side of the towpath. Several lunchtime drinkers had left the pub and were watching a collapsed horse kicking and snorting in its death throes. A boy had his arms around the horse's neck and was sobbing uncontrollably. The boatman was detaching the unfortunate beast from the boat and removing its harness and spreader. Its decorated nose bowl now lay discarded at the edge of the canal.

Ocker and Raymond moored their boats and rushed up to the bridge to see an old boatman they knew as Giggetty Jim explaining to the spectators, "We've 'ad the 'orse since 'e was a foal."

He turned to face Ocker and Raymond, "Hello lads, this is a bad business."

"What happened?"

"It was that last bridge 'ole. There's so much bloody rubbish in there I had to whip the poor old booger to get through."

The prostrate horse had become still and its tongue hung out of its mouth. The boy howled in anguish, pressing his face into the horse's neck, which was soaked in sweat and flecked with foam dribbling from its mouth.

"What are you gonna do now, Jim?" asked Ocker.

"That's finished boating for me. I've 'ad enough, I'm packing it in."

"Why don't you get yourself a motorboat?"

"No lad, I can't get on with them new-fangled motors," he explained. "I've spent all me working life with 'orses, but these days I spend more time pullin' the 'orse out of the cut than driving 'im."

"Yeah, I suppose it's hard working a horse when the towpath is so overgrown and dropping into the cut."

"It's taking twice as long to do the job than it did a few years back," Jim replied.

The pub's landlord brought Jim a pint of bitter. "Here, get this down you. I've phoned the knacker's yard, someone will be coming to take the horse away."

Jim swallowed the pint in one draught. He prodded the horse with his boot, but the life in the poor animal had finally gone.

The drama was over and the lunchtime drinkers drifted back into the bar. The boy sat snuffling by the dead horse and Giggetty Jim stared blankly into the distance.

Ocker decided he should remove his cap in respect for the deceased and patted Jim's shoulder as a gesture of sympathy.

"Mebbe you'll change your mind after a few days."

"No lad, it's time to retire," Jim sniffed.

"Sorry about the horse, but we've got to move on," Ocker said.

"That's OK lad, I'll see you around," Jim replied, accepting another pint of beer from a sympathetic bystander.

Later that day, Ocker and Raymond moored up for the night by a wharf near the centre of a small town. Ocker left his brother to secure the boats while he crossed the nearby bridge and walked up a side street, where he knew there was a butcher's shop on a corner.

It was late Friday afternoon and the shop was full of local women buying provisions for the weekend. Reuben Fuller, the butcher, was in a foul temper. His supplier had been late delivering and because of meat shortages, half his order had not arrived. Customers had complained all day and now ten minutes before he was about to close with a shop full of gossiping women, who should walk in but a scruffy boatman from the canal.

"I'd like a pound of sausages," Ocker said pointing to the glass-fronted counter where the meat was displayed.

Fuller raised himself to his full height and hooked his fingers into his blue striped apron, "Would you? Well, I haven't got any and I'm closing, so good afternoon."

"So what are they supposed to be?" Ocker said, jabbing his finger on the glass counter.

"That's for my regulars, not for scruffy boatmen, so be on your way."

Fuller had a reputation for being quick tempered. He was a large, red-faced man, who was fond of his drink and it was rumoured he kept a bottle conveniently placed behind his counter. During the war he had been a 'Desert Rat' in the Seventh Armoured Division and he would regale his drinking pals in the pub with endless stories about slaughtering 'them bleeding Eyeties'. Reuben Fuller hated all foreigners, especially Italians, Germans and Arabs, and he included boat people in the same category.

"I'm going nowhere, there's no law against me buying sausages and my money's as good as anybody else's," Ocker persisted.

"Oh! We'll see about that," said the red-faced butcher, moving around the counter at surprising speed for a large man. "I told you to get out, now go before I throw you out."

"I'm not going without them bloody sausages," Ocker said, emphatically.

The women customers screamed abuse at Ocker as Fuller stepped forward. He grasped Ocker by the shoulder and threw him across the shop towards the door. Ocker hit the door jamb, bounced back, struggled to keep his feet and then straightened up and hit the onrushing butcher full in the nose with his right fist. It was a powerful blow delivered with all Ocker's weight behind it.

There was a sickening crack as the butcher's nose was broken and he crashed to the floor. Ocker dragged open the door and ran out of the shop, closely pursued by two of the women.

He ran down the towpath, shouting to his brother, "Quick Ray, cast off and let's get these boats moving." Ocker started the engine, but before the ropes were untied, a policeman accompanied by two of the women customers appeared at the bridge.

"That's him there, that's the booger who did it."

"Which one did it?" demanded the constable.

A large woman wearing a headscarf over an impressive array of curlers was the spokeswoman. "It was him – the big scruffy one – he done it." She brandished a clenched fist at Ocker.

The policeman strode down the towpath with one arm raised, as if he was about to stop the traffic on the road.

"Don't give me any trouble, you've done enough for one day," said the policeman.

"It was self defence – he went for me 'cos I wanted to buy some sausages."

"You can tell that to the magistrate on Monday morning," said the policeman, sternly. "I'm arresting you for assault."

Raymond intervened, saying, "You've got to be joking."

"Were you involved in this fracas?" the policeman asked.

"Well, no, I was looking after the boats."

"Then keep your nose out, otherwise I'll have you down the cells as well."

"So, what am I supposed to do until Monday morning?" asked Ocker.

"You'll wait in a cell and behave yourself."

"Serves the booger right!" screamed the woman with the curlers.

Ocker spent the weekend locked up in a cell. He looked even more untidy than usual when he stood unshaven before the magistrates. Wearing an impressive plaster across his nose, Reuben Fuller gave damning evidence, describing Ocker as an aggressive intruder, who manhandled his female customers before launching an attack upon himself.

"I never touched any of those old biddies," Ocker shouted.

The magistrate was unimpressed by Ocker's outburst, saying, "You will please be quiet."

From the back of the court a well-dressed lady stood up and said, "Excuse me, I would like to say a word on behalf of this young man."

"And who are you?" enquired the magistrate

"My name is Myra Ashby."

"Are you related in some way to this young man?"

"No, I had never seen him before last Friday."

"So what is your interest in this case?"

"I was a customer in the shop where the incident took place."

The magistrate peered over his spectacles, saying, "Are you in the legal profession?"

"No, I'm the crime reporter on the Gazette."

"Ah yes, I thought the name was familiar."

She explained that she had witnessed the incident, stating that although Ocker had struck the butcher, he was nevertheless provoked in his action. She also added that as a reporter for the local newspaper, she intended to print the story in the next issue.

Up on the bench the magistrates went into a huddle like the front row of a rugby scrum. They eventually emerged to pronounce sentence. Ocker received a fine and was told to report to a probation officer.

His lady benefactor met him in the waiting room. "Mister Hill, as you heard in the court, my name is Myra Ashby and I work for the Gazette. I intend to make an issue of this incident in the next edition.

Don't worry about the fine – my newspaper will pay that for you."

Ocker grunted his appreciation and followed Myra to another part of the building, where the probation officer resided.

"I've already spoken to the probation officer. You sit here and wait until your name is called and I'll be in touch later."

Myra Ashby left him in a waiting room, staring at a floor strewn with discarded magazines and newspapers.

"Hello, are you Terry Hill?"

He looked up to see a pretty young woman standing in the doorway opposite.

"Please come in."

He shuffled into the office and sat down in front of a desk covered with books and papers.

"My name is Jennifer Stroud. I'm your probation officer and I require some personal details before I can assess your situation."

Ocker looked apprehensively at this attractive young woman. He became acutely aware of his unkempt appearance.

Jennifer Stroud regarded this wild-looking man with his long black hair and unshaven tanned face. She noted his dark brown eyes with their ridiculously long lashes and his broad, muscular shoulders under a sweat-stained shirt.

"You look like a strong man, no wonder you broke his nose."

Ocker shuffled in his seat and felt a trickle of perspiration down the back of his neck.

"I need some personal details. Where were you born?"

"At Ocker Hill, on me Dad's boat – that's why they call me Ocker," he stammered.

"I'm sorry, I don't know where that is."

"It's next to a big power station in the Black Country."

"In the Black Country?" she repeated. "That would be in what town?"

Ocker shrugged, "I dunno miss, I only know the canal."

She wrote something down on her note pad and continued, "And when were you born?"

"When! Oh, I think it was nineteen thirty five."

"You think – aren't you sure when you were born?"

"I think it was nineteen thirty-five," Ocker repeated.

"And what's your birthday?"

"Well, we reckoned it was the first of February, but it was cold so me Dad was busy with the boats and me Mam couldn't be sure."

Jennifer paused and regarded Ocker with some curiosity. "What date does it say on your birth certificate?"

Ocker frowned, "What's a birth certificate?"

"Haven't you got a birth certificate?"

"Me Dad couldn't be bothered with official things, he said they wasted too much time." ·

Jennifer did a quick calculation, "You're twenty-two, haven't you been called up?"

"What's called up?"

"You know, National Service, in the army."

"No, but I know some blokes who have."

Jennifer tried another angle. "Where do you live, do you have an address?"

Ocker was feeling very uneasy about where these questions were leading him. "I live on an old butty boat in the boatyard. It's part sunk."

Jennifer tapped her front teeth with her pen. "Have you ever had a proper fixed home – I mean on dry land, not on a boat?"

"I've never slept in a house, only on a boat or sometimes out in the open in the summer."

"Tell me Terry, have you ever been properly employed?"

"I takes me work where I can get it."

"What I mean is, have you ever paid income tax?"

The trickle of sweat had descended lower and was now inserting itself between his buttocks.

"I dunno, what's income tax?"

Jennifer stared at him, then smiled. "How wonderful – a man who doesn't know what income tax is!"

Ocker shrugged, but said nothing.

"Presumably you don't pay insurance and you are not registered with a doctor?"

"I've got nowt wrong with me, I don't get sick, what do I wanna doctor for?"

Jennifer sighed. "I don't believe this. Where did you go to school, what education did you have?"

"I was never a scholard, I learned me numbers and me letters at the mission school." He thought hard for a moment and added, "That was when me Dad was unloading or waiting for orders, then we were off up the cut."

"In other words you can't read or write."

"I know me letters and me numbers." Ocker's gaze left the floor and for the first time looked directly at the young woman. "No, I can't read or write."

"And I have to admit it, Terry, that you are the first person I have ever met who doesn't exist – officially that is."

Ocker desperately wanted to scratch the itch on his backside.

"What happens now, miss?"

"You'll have to stay out of trouble and come and see me from time to time. Meanwhile, I'll get you some books and we'll try and improve your reading."

"Thank you, miss. Am I gonna get into more trouble for not having those papers you were asking me about."

"No, I think we'll keep that a secret between us," she replied.

"Thanks, miss."

Jennifer smiled and sniffed the air, "I understand you've been locked up all weekend so I'm sure you'll be wanting a bath – the public baths are at the end of the street."

****

Summer 1957

"Ah'm in a love – Oooh! – Ah'm all shook up."

A group of teenagers stood around a juke box playing Elvis Presley's hit tune for the seventh successive time. They clicked their fingers and chanted, "Oooh!" in the appropriate places.

Vince Rothwell growled. "Oh Gawd, not again. I reckon they'll know that bloody tune backwards before they go home."

Frankie Bowers threaded his way between the chairs with a tray of drinks. He was a small man with a thin, wiry body that earned him the nickname, Frankie the Ferret. There was little that Frankie couldn't climb up, over or into, and he was an expert peterman, capable of finding his way into most safes and silencing most security systems. He was equally adept at silencing adversaries with a flat cap studded with broken razor blades, that he called his chiv.

Frankie placed the drinks on the table and inclined his head towards the bar. "I see they've got some new tits behind the bar since we were last in here."

Vince grinned, "I had noticed – the best pair I've seen all week."

The barmaid pulled pints of bitter for a group of men sitting in front of the bar. Each time she bent over the pumps, the men's conversation would stop as they peered down her cleavage like a row of budgerigars looking into their seed trays.

Tom laughed and drank his beer. He felt a familiar twitch in his stomach as his nervous system came into conflict with his digestion. This usually occurred before a heist.

Tonight's mark was a large detached house in the southern suburbs, whose owners were on holiday in Bermuda. Tom would wait inside a van that had a deceptively powerful souped-up engine, while Vince and Frankie robbed the house.

Vince had done his homework and discovered that the neighbour who watched the house went to her fitness class every Tuesday evening. The security system would present little opposition to Frankie Bower's skills. All they had to do was to wait in the pub until dark.

Vince's team was working well, creating an Aladdin's Cave out of the lock-up garage behind the club. Tom's job was to show professional 'fences' the accumulated loot and then bring them to Vince in the club to finalise the business. Sometimes he would deliver the goods to the purchaser's premises, especially if the buyer seemed nervous of interception by the police.

The music stopped and the teenagers left the room. A roar of motor cycle engines announced their departure from the car park and a faint smell of petrol percolated into the bar through the open door.

"Thank gawd for that," Vince said, "I was beginning to get a bit pissed-off with the Elvis appreciation society."

"I'll put something different on the juke box," Tom offered.

Vince put a restraining hand on Tom's arm and said, "Leave it alone mate, the first rule when you're going out on a job is to keep a low profile. Remember not to draw attention to yourself. Keep a low profile and merge into the background."

Vince finished his drink and placed the empty glass in front of Tom. "That doesn't stop you buying the next round, but keep your hands off that barmaid's tits."

Outside the house, Tom glanced anxiously at his watch and tapped his fingers on the van's dashboard saying, "Come on – you're taking too long."

The neighbour, who had now returned from her class, was standing by her garden gate looking suspiciously at Tom and the van. Then Vince and Frankie appeared by the entrance of the house, beckoning to Tom to pull into the driveway. Tom reversed the van into the drive, where it was quickly loaded.

Vince and Frankie jumped into the van and Tom slowly pulled out into the road, looking out for the suspicious neighbour, who by now had gone indoors to phone the police.

Tom rammed his foot down on to the accelerator and speeded down to the end of the road.

"What kept you?" Tom yelled.

"We knew there was a safe but it was well hidden and then Frankie had trouble blowing it, so we made a right bleeding mess of their carpet. Anyhow, it was a good tickle – well worth the wait, there must be more than a 'monkey' in cash."

He turned into a main road leading towards the city centre. After a while, he saw a police car pull out of a side road and begin to follow them.

Tom peered into the rear view mirror and said, "We've got company."

Vince looked back. "It's the Old Bill and he's on the radio, probably checking out our registration."

"That old cow's clocked us," said Tom, increasing his speed.

The police car switched on its blue lights and siren, then flashed its headlights.

"Hold on, he's trying to overtake us, I'm gonna try and lose him," yelled Tom, smacking his foot down on the accelerator. There was a loud screech and smoke from burning tyres as the van leapt forward, forcing the police car to return to the left side of the road.

"Can you get rid of him?" Frankie shouted over the scream of the engine.

Tom didn't reply as he glanced at the speedometer registering sixty miles an hour and then saw traffic lights at red in the distance. A line of stationery vehicles waiting at the lights grew rapidly closer and the police car became larger in the rear view mirror.

Three large goods lorries approached on the opposite carriageway. The second lorry pulled out to overtake the leading one and Tom saw his chance of escape. Just at the point where the two lorries were abreast, Tom swung the van across the central reservation. It leapt into the air, landing a few yards from the lorries in a grinding sideways skid, with Tom struggling to correct the steering. With the leviathan vehicles looming above him, Tom smashed the van through bushes dividing road from pavement, scattering pedestrians.

The overtaking lorry skidded, hit the other vehicle and then bounced across the central reservation broadside on, hitting the police car. The third lorry, totally unaware of the incident until he saw the smoking tyres of the ones in front, ran into the back of the lorry on the inside lane with a sickening crunch.

Vince, watching the entire scene as it receded through the back window, pursed his lips, blew and said, "Bloody hell, what a mess!"

****

"Most of us have never had it so good"
Harold MacMillan, Bradford, July 1957.

A grimy black locomotive, enveloped in a pall of steam and black smoke, pulled a long train of coal wagons from the direction of a distant colliery. Ocker stood on a canal bridge adjacent to a railway viaduct, looking at a derelict pub. Its windows were boarded up and tattered fly-posters advertised long-forgotten wrestling bouts and a local dog show. Beyond the pub, a long flight of narrow locks stretched up a bleak, open windswept hillside towards a forlorn cottage at the top. The locks were derelict too, with decaying wooden lock beams. Crumbling brickwork supported a wild garden of weeds and grasses, and water-filled hollows full of reeds dotted the hillside on both sides of the canal.

The canal had once been a vital connection between the Black Country and the waterways of the northwest, but now the locks were about to be demolished.

For years, Ocker's father and boatmen like Giggetty Jim had carried coal to Midland industry and beyond, working twenty-four hours a day with artificial lighting on the wharves to allow night loading. The gradual decline in trade and the difficulties in working boats on a crumbling canal system had forced many boatmen to leave the waterways. A unique way of life with its own peculiar traditions stretching back several generations was coming to an end. Boatmen, who knew little of life beyond the 'cut', were shunted into repetitive factory work or were queuing for the dole. Families were split as the younger members headed off to the big cities.

He stood at the top lock looking down the slope, imagining the lock flight busy with boats, horses and boatmen. He remembered his father saying how cold and windy it was in winter on this bleak hillside.

John Farden had said, "You'm better 'urry up if you want to see 'em, they say them bulldozers are coming in any day now."

Some of the lock structures and their attendant side-ponds had already collapsed into the ground and young shrubs and trees were thrusting eager roots into the resultant marshy rubble. Subsidence had reached an advanced state on this doomed hillside, soon to surrender itself to the scarring of opencast mining. At the top of the locks, a canal junction was surrounded by slagheaps from mining activities soon to progress down the slope. Three sunken boats almost blocked the channel that led to the colliery, and reeds encroached from the edge of the canal. A long-discarded bicycle frame broke the surface where duckweed left a green scum across the water.

The windows of a derelict cottage were boarded up and in the garden an old greenhouse was in imminent danger of collapsing. Ocker pushed open the garden gate and looked into the greenhouse. Its floor was covered in shattered glass and he shuddered as he saw a large grey rat scuttle under a bench.

Next time Ocker came this way, the canal and its locks would be totally obliterated.

****

Ocker's adventures at the butcher's shop and his subsequent weekend in jail had been widely reported in the Black Country newspapers.

John Farden rushed out of his office waving a copy of Myra Ashby's report, when Ocker and Raymond arrived at the boatyard.

"Look Ocker, you'm got your photo in the paper."

Ocker recalled the embarrassing day when a press photographer spent more than an hour taking dozens of pictures of him steering the motorboat.

Raymond grabbed the newspaper, pointing to the photograph, "You could have combed your hair before you had your photo done."

"I did comb me hair – well, sort of. I didn't have a proper comb so I used me fingers."

John Farden spread the newspaper out and, remembering Ocker's reading problem, handed the copy to Raymond.

"Come on Ray, read us what it says."

"NO SAUSAGES FOR THE BOAT PEOPLE? by Myra Ashby

Terry Hill, a canal boatman, was attacked by a local butcher, following a dispute over a pound of sausages. The magistrates fined this hard-working young man after he had spent an entire weekend in jail. His only crime was to defend himself against a brutal attack by a tradesman highly prejudiced against boat people."

"Does it say Ocker broke his nose?" asked John.

"No," Ray replied. "She goes on about prejudice against minority groups and how that should have been wiped out after the war."

"Anyway you can read that later. You lads have got to get yourselves up to Manchester and bring back a pair loaded up with flour."

"What pair?" asked Ocker.

"*Hanwell* and *Whitwood*," John replied.

"They're Harry and Sid's boats."

"Harry and Sid are in the nick."

"Blimey, what have they done?"

"Got drunk and then had a fight arguing about football."

"What's wrong with that?"

"They took on a bar full of blokes and smashed the place up. The landlord didn't like Brummies beating his regulars over the head with the furniture."

"They'll probably be out by the time we get up there."

"It doesn't matter. Grayson's don't want them on their run any more, so they're fired. That contract runs until the end of the year, so you two could pick it up if you play your cards right."

The previous boatmen had neglected the boats, so when Ocker and Raymond arrived at the wharf, they found a disreputable looking pair of craft with flaking paintwork encrusted with dirt.

Harry Bannerman's personal appearance reflected his attitude to his boats and he showed little interest in looking after them beyond basic maintenance to keep them on the move. The last time Ocker saw Harry, he had expounded his philosophy about boat maintenance: "Them boogers belong to the company so they can bloody well look after 'em."

When time permitted, Ocker and Raymond set about cleaning the boats. Priority was given to the engine room where oil had seeped out beneath the engine and had permeated into the hold, where it would soak into cargoes of bagged flour or sugar. They cleaned and polished the engine until it shone and its copper and brass work glistened for the first time in years.

Then began the business of clearing out the wildlife inhabiting the cabins. On his first night aboard, Raymond, sleeping in the butty *Whitwood*, had been almost eaten alive by bugs. Ocker persuaded the boatyard to issue and fit new side cloths with the company name stencilled on the sides and, at the same time, he began the painstaking restoration of the cabin's decorated paintwork. Raymond started work on the butty cabin, repainting the carrier's name and a colourful panel showing a medieval castle with a hump-backed canal bridge. He rubbed down the faded tiller and then painted it in red, blue and white like a barber's pole. The rope stern fenders were replaced with new ones acquired from a retired boatman, who made them as he sat outside his canal-side cottage. Raymond turned his attention to the cratch, removing peeling paint and repainting the surface in a series of diamond shapes coloured red, blue, white and yellow. He rubbed down the battered drinking water cans and painted them with red and white roses.

In just a few weeks, *Hanwell* and *Whitwood* looked resplendent in their fresh paint and the cabins were at last fit for human habitation.

****

Christmas 1957

The hotels on the Hagley Road had Christmas trees festooned with colourful lights in their entrances. Tom Raggett had plenty of time to admire the festive adornments as he slowly drove the van in heavy traffic. It was always the same at this time of the year with desperate last minute shoppers and drunks leaving office parties. Two cars had collided at an intersection and were blocking the road. A police car arrived and a policeman began to sort out the congestion.

The driver of the police car remained in his seat and Tom became aware that he was showing some interest in the van. Tom felt uneasy and with good reason, for the van was packed with stolen merchandise. It was with some relief when at last he was able to move past the entangled vehicles and carry on his journey to Kidderminster.

At Kidderminster, there was an antique dealer who owned a shop that often saw more business leave by the back door than went out through the front. Vince and the dealer had spent four hours haggling and negotiating in the lock-up on the previous day. The Kidderminster dealer would only pay cash on delivery so Vince warned Tom to be on his guard because, as he put it, "There's a lot of bleeding villains around that would kill for that sort of money."

Tom was looking forward to a few days off in Blackpool with his new girlfriend. He had left the sleazy bed-sitter, with its thin partitioned walls, which had been his home for most of the year, and now rented a flat at Acocks Green. Doris had moved in with him almost immediately and now the two enjoyed an unrestrained love life without nosy neighbours hearing every sound through paper-thin walls.

Bing Crosby was singing *White Christmas* on the van's radio as the traffic began to thin out and Tom was able to increase his speed.

After a while, Tom noticed a police car was following a short distance behind, so he signalled correctly at a roundabout and saw the car was still following him. At the next roundabout, the police car switched on the blue flashing light, overtook at some speed and swung across in front of the van. Tom jammed on the brakes and screeched to a halt. A uniformed sergeant jumped out of the car, wagging an accusing finger at Tom.

"Get out of the van." His voice then took on a sarcastic tone, "If you don't mind, sir."

Tom protested, "What's the problem officer – I wasn't speeding was I?"

The other policeman opened the passenger door and began feeling around in the glove compartment.

"Is this your vehicle?"

"No," Tom replied.

"Does it belong to your employer?"

"No."

The sergeant now addressed the other officer, "Found anything in the front?" The reply was negative.

"Will you open up the back?"

Tom was feeling dizzy, but was trying desperately to appear calm. He went around to the back and opened the doors.

The sergeant seemed very happy. "Well! Well! What do we have here? I do believe we've found Santa's grotto. I hope you fed your reindeer before you came out because I think Santa Claus will have to accompany us to the nick and answer a few questions."

Tom looked stunned as he was led into the back of the police car. The driver ignored him and said to his companion, "Let's get this face back to the nick before the party ends."

Only one person was on duty at the front desk when they arrived at the police station. Tom was shown to an interview room with a young constable to watch over him, while the arresting officers went down the corridor to join the office party. Ten minutes later, they returned to interrogate Tom. It was quite obvious that this was the last thing they wanted to be doing with a party going on in full swing down the corridor.

"Can I have a fag?" Tom asked the officer.

"Maybe, when you've answered a few questions."

It was a bare interview room with a table and three chairs. There were dark stains on the white-painted walls where greasy heads had leaned against them. It was warm in the room and the detective removed his jacket, rolled up his sleeves and loosened his tie. The uniformed sergeant, who had arrested him, had taken off his cap to reveal close-cropped ginger hair. He stood behind Tom, impatiently tapping the wall with a walking stick.

Sounds of laughter drifted up from the party and there was a loud bang as someone burst a balloon. The ginger-haired officer was unhappy to be missing the festivities.

"You have been arrested for being in possession of what appears to be stolen property. You say the vehicle is not yours, nor belongs to an employer." The officer looked up at Tom, "OK. So who does it and its contents belong to?"

"It belongs to a bloke I deliver for occasionally."

"His name?" He picked up a pen and looked expectantly at Tom.

"Don't know his name. I meet him in a pub in Brum, and sometimes he asks me to do a delivery for him."

The detective leaned back in his chair, grinning at the ginger-headed officer and sighed. "Fancy that! Would you believe it, it belongs to a bloke he met in a pub."

The ginger-haired officer was standing behind Tom. "Very plausible, I'm sure, and tell me what does this bloke in the pub look like?"

Tom opened his mouth but the officer leaned across the table and placed his index finger in front of his nose, "Don't tell me, let me guess. He was an old man with a long white beard, twinkly blue eyes and he was wearing a bright red coat and trousers."

"And I bet he has a hood with bits of white fur round it," said the ginger-haired officer. "Do you know I think I've seen him working that big store in Corporation Street."

The door opened and a uniformed officer entered the room. He placed a sheet of paper in front of the detective, who glanced at its contents and thanked the constable.

"Mister – what's your name again?"

"Raggett, Tom Raggett."

"Oh yes! Mister Raggett, do you realise I'm missing a good party while I'm sitting here listening to your fairy stories."

"I'm sorry about that so I'll be on my way and leave you to your party," replied Tom. He stood up and pushed back the chair. The ginger-haired officer stepped forward and cracked the walking stick hard on Tom's right collarbone. Tom howled with pain and the officer then whacked him across his kneecaps. Tom collapsed on to the floor, sending the chair spinning into the corner. The ginger-haired officer replaced the chair, picked Tom off the floor and shoved him back into his seat.

"Now, don't mess us about any longer. Tell D.S. Milner where you got the van and the stuff from."

Tom grimaced from the stinging pain in his shoulder. "I told you it belongs to this bloke I see in a pub."

"Which pub, where is it and what's it called?"

"Its near New Street Station – I can't remember the name."

"And where were you going?"

"To see a bloke in Kidderminster."

"And what's his name?"

"I don't know his name."

"Don't tell me, let me guess – you were meeting him in a pub."

"That's right."

"If you don't know his name, how were you supposed to recognise him."

Tom paused for a moment, then said, "He's looking out for the van in the pub car park."

"So, what's the name of the pub in Kidderminster?"

Tom gulped and said," I think it's the Navigation Inn – it's by the canal."

"You think," said the detective, picking up the sheet of paper. "Well, I think we've already identified some of that property as being the proceeds of a robbery at Knowle in August, where a neighbour identified a white van. The description of the driver fits you well enough and although the registration plates have been changed, I reckon your van was the one which was responsible for a multiple pile up later that evening, when being pursued by the police."

Tom's mouth had suddenly gone very dry, "Can I have a glass of water?"

"I don't see why not, Mr Raggett. In fact I think you'll be on the proverbial bread and water for some time."

****

It had been a bad year for Giggetty Jim. His wife died from pneumonia after repeated warnings by her doctor that living on a boat through the winter would eventually kill her. On New Year's Day, she discovered an infestation of bugs in the boat cabin, stripped out all the bedding and burnt sulphur candles. Giggetty Jim explained at the funeral, "She went mad 'cos I knowed them little boogers were in there, but they don't bother me."

The bedding was spread over the cabin roof and examined in minute detail for signs of insect life. On replacement, it absorbed dampness from the January air from which she caught the chill that eventually led to her death.

Giggetty Jim was born on the family boat at Wombourne in the last decade of the nineteenth century. He had been a boatman all his life, working with horses throughout the Midland canals. He spoke with a strong local accent, which made him almost incomprehensible outside the Black Country. Despite a life of hard work, his only regret was, in his own words, "I wish I'd 'ad some edification and learned to read an' write like a scholard."

In 1914, just before war began, he married a boatman's daughter. Most of their courting was conducted around various Midland colliery basins, while their boats were loading. He fought in the trenches on the Western Front, being gassed and twice wounded at the Somme.

Later in the war, his experience with horses enabled him to get a safer post, working with transport animals behind the lines. When the war ended, he returned to the Midland canals and continued working with horse-drawn boats.

They had six children, three boys and three girls, who all worked with the boats. Over the years, his children left the waterways for land-based jobs, all except for his youngest son, who stayed until April that year. The death of the horse, coupled with diminishing trade, operational difficulties and advancing old age, convinced Jim to retire. His son, disillusioned with canal life, eventually emigrated to Australia to get an outdoor job where he could work with horses. The rest of his family was scattered around the Midlands.

Jim was forced to sell the boat he had owned for some years, but not trusting banks, he hid the money in a box under the floorboards of the little terraced house he lived in. He spent a lot of time in the local canal-side pub drinking with old cronies, telling the old tales and recalling how much better things had been in bygone days.

Sometimes his audience consisted of local youths, who poked fun at the old boatman. When a group of unscrupulous young men plied Jim with even more drink than usual, they elicited information about his hidden treasure. They split into two groups and, while two men kept Jim talking and drinking in the pub, the other three broke into his house and ransacked it. The floorboards eventually revealed their secret and five young men were rich for a few days until the police caught up with them.

Myra Ashby, who was now becoming increasingly interested in the lives of the boat people, covered the story of the robbery and she saw the possibility of a good human-interest story for her newspaper. She met Ben Barnwell and, between them, they decided to organise a surprise party for Giggetty Jim on Christmas Eve. The newspaper agreed to finance the party at the Anchor Inn and Ben contacted as many of Jim's friends as could be found to turn up for a grand celebration. Ben also asked for a generous contribution from all the guests towards the public collection already donated by the newspaper.

"Are you going to Jim's party?" Raymond said.

"Oh, I dunno, I don't like parties," Ocker replied.

"Kitty McCann will be there."

"What's that got to do with me?"

"C'mon, Ocker, I know that you're keen on her."

"What gives you that idea?" Ocker said, his cheeks flushing a bright shade of pink.

"'Cos you start blushing every time I mention her name."

"Bollocks!"

"It's true, so you get some smart new clothes and see what happens. She likes you, but she's put off 'cos you're such a scruffy git."

"I dunno, I never know what to buy when I get in them tailor's shops."

"I'll come with you and get you fixed up."

"Well, I'll think about it."

On the night of the party, Ben Barnwell stood by the door of the pub, extending a huge hairy fist in welcome.

"Come on in, Ocker me lad, and get yourself a drink. It's on the house tonight, the Gazette is paying."

The Anchor Inn had two separate bars and, on this Christmas Eve, one of them had been reserved for the private party. A large hand-written notice pinned over the door bore the legend, 'A Merry Christmas to Giggetty Jim', and underneath in smaller lettering, 'From all his friends on the Cut'.

Above a roaring fire in the fireplace, another hand-written notice proclaimed the same greeting. Paper chains hung from the tobacco-stained ceiling and the bar in the corner was draped with silver and gold tinsel. Stan the barman pulled pints of beer and totalled the amounts off on a list that had already grown to an impressive length. The Gazette faced a hefty bar bill for the room was already quite full.

Ocker helped himself to a pint of bitter and looked around the room. Judging by his florid complexion, Giggetty Jim had been in the bar for some time. He nodded a greeting to Joey Boat Johnson, who unclipped his accordion and blew the dust off the bellows. Ocker saw his brother Raymond with a new girlfriend by his side, standing by a trestle table full of sandwiches, sausage rolls and mince pies. They were laughing loudly at a joke with Cousin George and Ocker fervently hoped it wasn't the story about him and Two-Bob Doreen. He shook hands with Giggety Jim and then went over to greet his Uncle Billy and Aunt Rose.

"Nice to see you, son, are you still on the Northern run?" Uncle Billy asked, spraying Ocker with mince pie crumbs.

"We just finished the last load," replied Ocker, brushing the crumbs off his jacket. "A load of sugar from Manchester. We lost a day with engine trouble at Audlem."

Aunt Rose looked approvingly at Ocker's appearance. He was wearing a new shirt, trousers and a neat dark green jacket. "My word, Ocker, you'm looking very smart. I'll bet there's a young lady somewhere?"

A hand slipped around Ocker's waist and right on cue a voice said, "Oh yes, I see you've noticed how well he scrubs up."

Ocker turned to see Kitty McCann smiling at him, with a blue ribbon pulling her long hair into a ponytail. The ribbon matched the colour of the very tight sweater she was wearing. Ocker also saw his brother and his cousin George watching the proceedings with some amusement. Raymond made an obscene gesture that Ocker chose to ignore.

He felt himself colouring up and said, "It's getting a bit warm in here."

"Come on, Ocker, you can get me a drink," Kitty said, pulling him away to the bar,. "Did you know I've left home and I'm a shop girl now?"

"No – where's the job?"

"I'm selling children's clothes in a shop at Wolverhampton right by where your mum lives."

"Where do you live?" Ocker asked.

"I've got a bed-sitter just around the corner from my job."

Joey Boat Johnson began to play the accordion, accompanied by Birdy Finch on the harmonica. The first song was a sentimental Victorian ballad and Kitty, placing one arm around Ocker's waist, gently swayed to the music.

"I don't suppose you've ever learned to dance?"

"No, I've never had any call for it," Ocker replied.

"Now's the time to learn," she said, turning to put both arms around his neck and fixing him with her large brown eyes.

Ocker found it embarrassing to return the stare and glanced over her shoulder to see George and Raymond grinning broadly. Raymond made another obscene gesture that Ocker again ignored.

Kitty began to move her body to the music. She pressed herself close to him and Ocker suddenly felt with horror the first stirrings of an erection. The music stopped and Ocker with some relief excused himself. "I've gotta go to the lavvy, I'll be back in a minute."

Joey Boat Johnson pulled out a heavy oak table into the centre of the bar shouting, "Come on, Jim, give us a dance."

The tempo livened up and Giggetty Jim sprang up on to the table, showing a great deal of agility for a man in his seventies, who was already drunk. The audience clapped their hands enthusiastically and the dance ended with Jim falling backwards into the arms of the nearest bystanders.

After emptying his glass, Jim was back on the table, performing some intricate steps that brought applause from his audience. When the musicians were replenishing their glasses, Jim had the table pushed back to the wall and then demanded, "Now I wants a pretty young wench to dance wimme."

He selected Kitty McCann, the musicians were briefed, and Jim took her by both hands and launched into a whirling dance.

The audience squashed back to the perimeter of the bar, allowing maximum space for the dancers. Everyone was clapping and cheering as the couple twisted and spun at breakneck speed. At the end of the dance someone caught Jim and shoved him exhausted into a chair, where Kitty gave him a big kiss.

"Phew! That old man's got more energy than all the rock 'n' rollers down the Palais put together," Kitty's said, her face bright red after the exertions.

Outside the pub, Ocker was wandering up and down the towpath, desperately trying to control the bulge in his trousers. He tried thinking obscure thoughts unrelated to the source of his problem, but the image of Kitty's face and soft warm body refused to go away. Then he saw his brother furtively disappearing around the back of the pub, hand in hand with his girlfriend, and remembered the ticket drawer on the butty boat, which had recently become a receptacle for contraceptive packets. Ocker had never used what Raymond called 'rubber johnnies' and recalled the day when, out of curiosity, he had opened one of the packets to examine the transparent, slimy object, which he found impossible to replace in its container. Each time he tried to squeeze it into the packet, it would slip from his fingers, and finally he lost it completely and it fell into the canal. He watched it gradually unfurl, float to the surface and then wrap itself around the propeller of the motor boat. Ocker spent several minutes fishing with the boat hook before unravelling it from the propeller and triumphantly raising it from the water, much to the disgust of a passing grey-haired lady, who was walking her dog on the towpath.

After a while, Ocker decided it was safe to return to the fray inside the pub. The revellers had split into groups, some standing, others sitting, and all getting down to some serious drinking.

Kitty turned her attention to Ocker. "You've been gone a long time, I thought you'd found yourself another girl!"

She put her arm around his waist and once again Ocker was fixed with those mocking brown eyes.

"Did you find another girl out there?"

"No, I just went out to the lavvy," he replied, feeling his tongue beginning to stick to the roof of his mouth.

"There's a good rock 'n' roll group playing at the Locarno on New Year's Eve. Why don't you take me and let your hair down for a change? Your brother says he's going."

Ocker grunted, shuffled his feet and glanced anxiously at the door.

"Why are you so shy?" Kitty asked, with a mischievous smile. "You're not at all like your brother. I saw him sneaking out just now with that girl and I'll bet he's already getting his leg over."

George shoved a pint of bitter into Ocker's hand. "Get this down, you look as if you need it."

Joey Boat Johnson played a medley of old ballads on his accordion. Corky McCann and his friends wanted to hear modern and upbeat songs, but Joey said he couldn't play rock 'n' roll. Ben Barnwell was persuaded to sing, displaying a fine baritone voice, then invited everyone to join in the familiar choruses until Stan the barman reminded them that his extended licence ended at midnight.

Giggetty Jim downed another pint and announced, "I'll be orf for a pee – get me another one in before the bar closes."

Ben led the communal singing with a series of carols as the midnight hour approached, when Stan the barman yelled the time honoured cry, "Time ladies and gentlemen, please!"

At that moment Raymond burst into the pub, shouting, "There's a body in the cut."

They all dashed out to the towpath, straining their eyes in the darkness. George ran to his boat moored nearby and returned with a torch and a boat hook. The beam of light revealed a man floating face down in the murky water. George gave the torch to Ben and then pulled the body to the water's edge with the boat hook. Willing hands grasped the man's clothing and dragged him out of the canal, turning him over to reveal his face. A concerted gasp came from the onlookers as the torch picked out the features of Giggetty Jim.

George slapped Jim's face, but got no reaction. He turned to the onlookers and said, "I reckon he's drowned – there's no sign of life."

Now the only sounds were sobbing from Kitty McCann and the radio inside the pub playing the festive song, 'God rest ye Merry Gentlemen'.

Myra Ashby standing at the back of the clustered group was already composing a headline for the newspaper. She stepped forward and enquired, "I'm sorry to ask at a time like this, but does anyone know his real name?"

****

There was a stunned silence in court when Wheelock Joe Bates exposed himself in front of the magistrates. A few surprised giggles followed as he produced a harmonica from his coat pocket and began to play 'When the Saints Go Marching In'. The constable, giving evidence in a monotonous droning voice, stopped with his mouth gaping like a distressed goldfish. The senior magistrate peered over her glasses and said sternly, "For goodness sake, will someone please cover that man up."

Myra Ashby couldn't believe her luck with yet another good story unfolding about canal people. She had followed the exploits of this old boatman, whose mental condition had deteriorated since he retired from boating. At first he was known as that poor old flasher on the canal towpath and mothers would hurriedly hustle their children indoors. Joe sought a wider audience and began exposing himself to women in the main shopping centre and at the same time playing his harmonica. A strategically placed constable's helmet had brought an end to his performance and Joe was hauled away in a police car amid enthusiastic applause from the younger spectators.

Tom Raggett, waiting in line for his case to appear, remembered an occasion when Wheelock Joe and his own father had a drunken 'highest up the wall' contest in a pub urinal with a ten shilling bet on the outcome.

The magistrate, unimpressed by Joe's courtroom exhibition, ordered him to be detained for a mental report and Myra Ashby hurried away from the court to write her story, unaware that another ex-boatman was soon to take centre stage in the same arena.

Vince Rothwell furtively glanced through dark glasses around the waiting area, then sat down next to Tom.

"Look mate, I've got you a good brief so do exactly what he tells you. The odds are you're gonna go down, but he'll do his best for you and get you the lowest possible sentence. Do your bird, keep your nose clean and you'll be out before you've got your boots under the table."

"What happened, did somebody grass on me?"

"Yeah, there's two in the frame: Sammy Sissons and the guy from Kidderminster."

"Why would the antiques' guy set me up?"

"Sometimes these guys do that to keep in with the Old Bill."

Vince peered over the top of his dark glasses and surveyed the faces passing back and forth along the long corridor. "I don't think the antiques' guy is in the frame for this one 'cos there was a lot of nice 'tom' in that load and he knew he was getting some good gear."

"Sammy Sissons?" Tom queried.

"Yeah! I reckon it was him 'cos he didn't like you taking over his patch when he went inside. I told him I don't need piss artists like him, I want professionals on my team. There have been rumours that he's been seen talking with that ginger-haired bastard that nicked you. I'll make a few more enquiries and if it is him, me and Frankie'll give him a seeing to."

Vince peered nervously along the corridor towards the outside door where a posse of uniformed policemen had appeared.

"Look mate, I can't be seen here. I've gotta be on me way. I'll make sure you're not short of readies while you're inside."

Tom watched Vince thread his way through the crowded corridor until he disappeared into the street. He paused on the step, removed his dark glasses and coughed, his breath vaporising like a cloud in the cold air. Vince looked back and, with a brief wave of his hand, was gone. It would be some time before Tom saw him again.

****

The trees in front of the Locarno were bright with colourful bulbs reflecting their cheerful light on the front of the building. A partly torn poster advertising a concert by the City of Birmingham Symphony Orchestra hung from a notice board which also proclaimed 'Rock in the New Year with Bilston Bill, the Black Country's answer to Elvis Presley.'

Ocker stood next to Kitty in the queue on the steps, listening to the cacophony from the interior of the dance hall, and wished he were elsewhere. After he paid their entrance fee, Kitty grasped his hand and led him into the concert hall. The New Year's Eve celebrations were well under way inside the biggest room Ocker had ever seen. The band featured two saxophones, a trumpet and two over-amplified guitarists playing in front of a sweating drummer. Each time the drummer was presented with a solo spot, he seized his moment of glory and proceeded to hammer everything within reach in an orgy of percussion. The audience stopped dancing and stood in the dark cheering as the drummer worked himself into a frenzy, with his sticks blurring under the harsh spotlights. A mighty crash of cymbals detached one of them from its stand and sent it careering off the stage into the darkness. At that point, the rest of the band completed the number with a finale of such magnitude that Ocker felt the floor vibrate under his feet. House lights were restored as the band retired from the stage for a well-earned break.

Ocker saw his brother on the far side of the floor. He and Kitty made their way across the room through a haze of cigarette smoke, passing a long queue of girls waiting for the ladies' toilet. Ocker greeted his brother and noted that his partner was not the girl he was with at the

Anchor Inn party.

"Hi, Ocker, this is Margie."

"Pleestemeetyer, I'm sure," said Margie, who was pretty and petite with dark hair, a very tight skirt emphasising a well-rounded bottom and an equally tight woollen sweater. Margie's introduction to Kitty had produced an expression of scowling rivalry. He turned his attention to Raymond, who was wearing a new dark blue suit with narrow, 'drainpipe' trousers and a long two-button style jacket. His shirt was cream with a rain-check pattern and he wore a blue and green 'slim jim' tie. His dark hair was combed into a Tony Curtis quiff, bobbing on his forehead.

Raymond placed his hand on Ocker's shoulder and spun him round. "Hey Ocker, look who's here!"

Ocker turned to see a young girl wearing a blue dress with white facings.

She smiled. "Hello, Terry, you look surprised."

"Yeah, but..." Ocker spluttered trying to find the right word.

"What you're trying to say is I look so grown-up."

"Well yeah, I suppose I am," Ocker replied.

He stared at his younger sister Lucy in astonishment for he hadn't seen her for months. "Should you be here – who's looking after Brenda?" said Ocker. "I've forgotten, how old are you?"

Lucy laughed. She had a lovely tinkly laugh and her eyes were sparkling. "Well, elder brother of mine, believe it or not, I was invited. Mum is looking after Brenda and I'm fifteen."

Raymond nudged Ocker in the ribs. "You'll have to ask Jennifer to give you some maths lessons next time."

Kitty intervened. "Oh yes! And who is Jennifer?" She tilted her head and looked at Ocker, fluttering her eyelashes. "And here's me thinking I was your only love."

Right on cue, the amplified voice of a male singer boomed out, "No other love have I, only my love for you."

Kitty clutched her hands together in mock delight. "Oh, Ocker, what perfect timing, how did you arrange that?" She threw her arms around him and gave him a kiss full on the mouth. Raymond and Lucy howled with mirth, but Margie was not amused and excused herself, saying, "I wanna go forra piss."

"Charming! I don't know why I bother with her," Ray commented, as he watched her wiggling her bottom towards the ladies' toilet, then added, "Now I remember."

An overweight tenor sang an up-tempo ballad in the manner of Elvis Presley to an attentive group of teenage girls. Occasionally, he would remove the microphone from its stand and rotate his burgeoning beer belly in the manner of the King of Rock and Roll. Some of the girls jumped up and down, screaming their appreciation. A few couples began to jive, but most people just carried on talking.

"Oh, look! There's Brian," Lucy said, pointing to a thin, pimply youth clutching two bottles of Coca-Cola. With his blue suit and Tony Curtis curls, he was a skinny clone of Raymond. Ocker realised that this scrawny youth was his sister's escort for the evening.

Brian pointed towards the entrance foyer. "There's gonna to be some bother out there in a minute. Some Teds from Sparkbrook have just come in without paying and there's some real hard bastards among 'em."

There was a loud crash of broken glass and angry raised voices rang out from the foyer. A gang of truculent intruders burst into the main hall, scattering people in all directions. The outnumbered security men were left to call for police reinforcement.

One of the Teddy Boys, wielding a weighted cosh covered in rags, confronted a security guard, who had just detached himself from the mêlée. The guard, holding his jaw, already appeared to be dazed when the Teddy Boy swung his cosh and cudgelled him at the side of his head. The force of the blow spun him round twice before he plunged to the ground, spraying blood across the floor.

Up on the stage, a bemused singer was crooning, "Oh I lerve you gal, I lerve you Peggy Sue-o-oo," and then, forgetting the microphone was still switched on, shouted, "What the fuck's going on out there?"

Girls screamed as the Teddy Boy stomped menacingly across the floor towards the singer, swinging his cosh in circles around his head. The band stopped playing and watched open-mouthed like rabbits transfixed by a stoat. The singer stuttered into his microphone, "Now look 'ere sonny, let's not get violent."

The Teddy Boy, advancing to the front of the stage with malevolent intent, shouted at the singer, "OK, poofter, now it's your turn."

The singer gulped, threw down his microphone and rushed past the band, yelling, "Stuff this for a lark."

The band stampeded after him, as the Teddy Boy jumped on to the stage and began throwing instrument stands at the cowering audience. He picked up the drumsticks and battered the cymbals, before kicking the largest of the drums off the stage. Jumping from the stage, he held the drumsticks aloft like a victor's trophy and strutted arrogantly across the dance floor. The Teddy Boy smirked and shouted, "Anybody else fancy having a go?"

A dark-haired man stepped out of the crowd and confronted the Teddy Boy.

"You're a bloody nuisance and I think you should bugger off and take your mates with you."

"And who the bloody hell might you be?"

Ocker didn't get the opportunity to reply as police reinforcements arrived with the remaining security guard. The rest of the Teddy Boy gang scattered in all directions leaving their leader isolated in the middle of the dance floor without his weapon and confronted by Ocker. The Teddy Boy threw the drumsticks in Ocker's face and turned to escape, but Ocker brought him to the ground with a rugby tackle that would have graced Twickenham Stadium. He grasped the Teddy Boy by his hair and squashed his face into the floor.

"Thank you sir, we'll take this one," said a policeman, hauling the Teddy Boy to his feet.

The Teddy Boy rubbed a bloodied nose with the palm of his hand. He examined the red smear and howled, "'Ere, look what he's done to me nose – I'll 'ave him for assault."

Ocker suddenly found himself the centre of attention and became aware with some embarrassment that the crowd were giving him a round of applause. Kitty rushed up to him, gave him a big kiss and said, "Ocker, that was brilliant! I didn't know you had it in you."

Ocker shuffled his feet and muttered, "Neither did I."

Raymond slapped him on the back, saying, "I think you deserve a pint after that. What made you do it?"

"I dunno, I just felt that I ought to do something."

Kitty eyes were sparkling when she took his hand and said, "I've got a feeling I ought to do something too. You're coming back with me tonight."

****

His black leather jacket and blue jeans made the ginger-haired sergeant inconspicuous among the lunchtime regulars in the public bar. He sipped his beer and squinted through the cigarette smoke at his companion.

"No excuses, Sammy, I need more information about Rothwell."

Sammy Sissons squirmed in his seat. "I'm sorry Mister Milner, but I think Vince's sussed me out."

"That's your problem. Now, you get me something I can work on, or I'll be reopening your file."

"Please, Mister Milner, Vince can be a mean bastard if he finds out I'm grassing on him."

Sergeant Milner drained his glass, pushed the table back and eased himself on to his feet. "Get to work, Sammy," he said, slamming the glass down on the table.

Frankie Bowers, hidden behind a newspaper at the back of the bar, witnessed this tête-à-tête. The two men were out of earshot, but Frankie understood enough from their looks and gestures that Sammy was probably a police informant.

He slipped out of a side door and walked to the Maple Leaf, where Vince was seated at his usual table in discussion with a group of men. It appeared that their business was concluded and the conversation had now descended to telling dirty jokes. One of the men laughed raucously and slapped his thigh at the conclusion of the story.

Frankie bought a drink, sat down and looked around the room. The usual crowd was there, some playing cards, others studying the racing pages. June sat behind the bar chatting to a man in a grey suit, who had the florid complexion of a heavy drinker. Frankie recognised him as Peter the Punter, a man who specialised in fixing racehorses and had a notorious reputation around the racecourses. Peter had been involved in a big race scandal when he had, in his own words, "taken the bookies for twenty grand." Since that day, two years ago, he was having increasing difficulty in placing bets with suspicious bookmakers and had been steadily drinking his fortune away. Frankie and some of the other regulars would put a few bets on for him, making a few pounds for themselves at the same time. Frankie was rarely out of pocket with Peter's tips.

Vince shook hands with his customers, who finished their drinks and began to leave the building. The man with the raucous laugh looked unsteady and slipped on the stairs, much to the amusement of his companions.

Frankie sat down at the table. "I followed Sammy to the White Lion and guess who he met there?"

"How about that ginger-haired bastard, Milner?" suggested Vince.

"Go to the top of the class!" said Frankie. "So what're we going to do about Sammy – I reckon he's the one who grassed on Tom?"

"Then we'll sort out that little sod, once and for all," Vince replied.

****

Sammy Sissons shared a grubby bed-sitting room with several hundred cockroaches. Since his release from prison, he had tried without success to get a job driving mini-cabs, but now he was reduced to petty thieving and supplying information to the police for the price of a meal.

It was almost dark when he shuffled down the street to the pub on the corner. Floodlights, illuminating the sky above the nearby football ground, cast eerie shadows on the crowd scurrying towards the stadium's entrance.

There was a local derby match and a large noisy crowd was homing in on the ground like iron filings to a magnet. It was ten minutes to kick off and the pub was quickly emptying its last-minute drinkers.

Sammy stood outside the pub watching the fans rushing by in their brightly coloured scarves. He saw Harry the Dip mingling with the crowd outside the stadium. Harry originated in East London and was an expert pickpocket, specialising in sporting crowds. His usual attire was an old grey suit with a grey shirt and grey socks. He said this made him unobtrusive in the crowds, which provided him with his living. Harry's attendance was guaranteed when there was a game attracting a large throng of people. He was one of the regulars in the Maple Leaf, a friend of Vince Rothwell, and it was he who originally recommended Sammy as a driver.

Sammy slumped into a chair by the door and stared gloomily into his pint of bitter. The pub was almost empty, but the fans' recent occupation was evident by the discarded newspapers littering the floor and spilled beer swilling on the tables. The barman looked pleased. "We've done well tonight, we usually get a few more in for a derby match."

Sammy nodded trying to appear interested.

"I see Smith's back from injury and they've got Kinsey in the team tonight."

Sammy nodded again.

"Albion are on form – they're going to take some beating tonight," the barman said, trying hard to involve Sammy in his favourite subject. "Mind you, they're not Real Madrid or even Wolves."

Sammy decided to contribute to the discussion and said, "Yeah, they say Wolves are doing well this year."

The barman leaned across the bar, prodding the wet surface with his forefinger. "I grant you that Wolves have a good team with Wright and the others, but where would Man United be now if they hadn't lost all them lads at Munich?"

Sammy shook his head.

"I'll tell you where they'd be." The barman's Lancashire origins were becoming more pronounced. "They'd be up there at the top in front of your bloody Wolves."

Sammy abruptly ended the barman's tirade, emptied his glass and said, "I'm off to the bog."

The men's lavatory stood in a yard at the back of the pub, partially lit by the stadium's floodlights. As Sammy stood at the urinal, he heard a sudden loud groan from several thousand voices as one of the City players missed an open goal. The noise was almost tangible as it reverberated through the brick walls.

Then Sammy heard a different sound as he turned and saw two figures silhouetted in the doorway.

"Hello Sammy. So, who's been a naughty boy then?"

Sammy shaded his eyes, peering against the stadium floodlights, "Who's there?"

"Don't you recognise my voice?"

"Sounds like Vince."

"What a clever boy you are, Sammy." The voice had a menacing tone that sent a shiver down his spine.

"Are you going to the match?" Sammy tried to sound casual and unconcerned, although his legs were beginning to shake.

"Not tonight, my son. You see me and Frankie have a bit of business to attend to."

"Well, I'd better be off," Sammy said, making a move for the door, but then found his exit blocked. "I was just about to see Harry the Dip."

"No, no, my son, Harry says he doesn't want to see you 'cos since you grassed on Tom Raggett, you've become what he calls *persona non grata.*"

Vince Rothwell's Latin pronunciation was rather more akin to Peckham, but Sammy was getting the message.

"Please, Vince, that wasn't me, I swear." Sammy's voice had assumed a pleading tone.

"You're a lying bastard and it's time you had a mouthwash."

Sammy squealed with pain as Vince grabbed his arm and twisted it around his neck. He dragged him into the WC cubicle, forced him to his knees and pushed his head into a stinking lavatory pan.

"Oh, deary me, some people do have disgusting habits," Vince said, pulling the cistern chain and flushing the toilet over Sammy's head.

A sudden crescendo of anticipation from thousands of voices within the football stadium terminated in an ear-splitting finale, as the home team scored the opening goal.

Frankie grinned and observed, "I think we're one up."

Sammy emerged spluttering from the cubicle, frantically trying to wipe his face on his sleeve.

Vince leered at him. "Get up Sammy – you're a rotten, stinking little toe rag."

Cheers from the celebrating crowd subsided into excited conversation and the referee's whistle restarting the game could be clearly heard over the hubbub.

Sammy stared wild-eyed, trying to focus on his assailant against the brilliant stadium floodlights. "I didn't rat on Tom Raggett, honest to God, I swear on my old Mum's grave."

"You're grassing to that bastard Milner."

"I'm not, honest, I haven't seen him since I got out of the nick."

"You saw him this afternoon. Frankie was in the White Lion – he saw you with Milner."

"No, no – er, he just happened to be there when I was. He was asking me how I got on inside the nick."

Vince shoved Sammy towards Frankie and said, "Frankie, I think its time for him to meet the cheesecutter."

Frankie removed his cap, which had razor blades sown into the neb. "Here you are Sammy, this is for Tom."

The cap swung in an arc, catching Sammy on the neck below his ear. He felt an intense stab of pain as blood poured from a severed artery. A scream died in his throat as he slowly slumped to the floor, choking on his own blood, his fingers clutching at the gaping wound.

A long blast of the referee's whistle was clearly audible over the murmur of the crowd inside the stadium. "That sounds like the final whistle for you, my son," Vince said sarcastically, and the two men turned, leaving the building with Sammy Sissons grovelling on the floor in the darkness.

****

Ocker and Raymond toiled through the cold, grey winter months carrying cargoes on *Hanwell* and *Whitwood* between Manchester and Wolverhampton. They were guaranteed another six months of work until the new contract expired, but conditions on the canal were deteriorating every day. Leakages made locks difficult to fill and the mechanisms were often broken or so stiff that even strong men like Ocker and Raymond could barely move them. On top of all this, there was the seasonal freezing of the water and the omnipresent mud, which got into everything inside the cabins.

On his return to Wolverhampton, he would spend an evening with Kitty, eating fish and chips at a little cafe before going to a cinema. Afterwards they visited a pub, before quietly creeping back to Kitty's room, where Ocker was beginning to discover the delights of a night in her bed. Regular sorties between the sheets had begun on that memorable New Year's Eve at the Locarno and romance had transformed Ocker both in outlook and appearance, much to the amusement of his brother.

"You don't look at all like the Greasy Ocker I grew up with."

"Mebbe, but all these new clothes have to be paid for which means we have to work harder to get 'em."

"That's the trouble with partnerships," Raymond said, grinning.

Ocker and Raymond were moored at the end of a deep cutting, conveniently close to a remote canal-side pub. They were preparing a stew for dinner when there was a loud knock on the side of the cabin. Raymond went outside and came face to face with a belligerent gamekeeper, brandishing a shotgun and sniffing the air.

"That'll be one of my pheasants cooking in your pot."

Raymond frowned. "As it happens we're cooking rabbit stew. That's if it's any of your business."

"Look here, sonny, pheasants is my business and you've been poaching 'em. I heard you and your mate in the coverts not half an hour ago."

Raymond's response was predictable. "Now you look here, we haven't touched your bloody pheasants. We only stopped here a few minutes ago and we've had a hard day so you take your gun and push off."

The gamekeeper waggled his shotgun in Raymond's direction, saying, "Don't take that attitude with me, sonny."

Ocker remonstrated from the boat, "You heard what my brother said, we've not had your bloody pheasants."

The gamekeeper swung the shotgun towards Ocker, and Raymond, seeing the man off guard, jumped off the boat and grabbed at the shotgun barrel. There was a short violent scuffle with the two men fighting for the gun, until Raymond lost his footing on the muddy towpath and slipped backwards, pulling the gamekeeper towards him. A loud explosion sent Raymond catapulting across the towpath into the undergrowth clutching his leg. Ocker leapt from the boat through a cloud of gun smoke, wrenched the weapon from the gamekeeper's hands, grasped him around the neck and hurled him into the water. There was a large splash and the man emerged in the middle of the canal, waving his arms and shouting, "Get me out, I can't swim."

Ocker retorted, "Now's a good time to learn," and turned to help his brother, who was screaming in pain and holding his leg that was streaming blood.

"Ocker, you've gotta do something quick, I think he's blown me bloody knee away."

Ocker picked him up and, carrying him like a baby, ran down the towpath as fast as he could to the pub.

He crashed through the door, yelling, "Can you get an ambulance for my brother as quick as you can?"

A group of farmers sat around a table drinking pints of beer and playing dominoes. One of them observed, "That leg of his don't look too good – what happened to him?"

"He's been shot."

The barman looked startled and leaned over the bar for a closer look.

"Don't you have a phone?" Ocker pleaded.

"Oh, yes," stammered the barmen, "I'll ring for the ambulance."

One of the farmers left his game of dominoes and examined Raymond's leg.

"It's made a right mess of his kneecap, the bloody things hanging off."

He produced a large handkerchief from his pocket saying, "He needs a tourniquet round that afore he bleeds to death."

Raymond groaned in pain as the farmer tied the handkerchief tightly around his thigh.

"How did this happen?" asked the farmer.

"Bloody gamekeeper shot him."

An old man with white mutton-chop side-whiskers spoke up. "Oi thought oi heard a shot a few minutes back. Oi'l bet a pound it was old Simon the gamekeeper. He's a short-tempered old bugger."

"He's a wet, short-tempered old bugger now. I chucked 'im in the cut," Ocker said.

The old man slapped his thigh in delight. " Oi wish oi'd seen that. Is he still in there?"

"I dunno and I don't care," replied Ocker.

The old man grasped his glass of beer and held it up to Ocker. "Here you are young feller, have a drop of this."

"The ambulance's on its way," announced the barman, who then added, "Could you put him on the oilcloth, it's a real bugger getting bloodstains out of the carpet."

The barman gave Ocker a glass of beer and said, "Do you think he wants one too?" He nodded towards Raymond, who had passed out on the floor.

****

Summer 1959

The lights dimmed all round the stadium, leaving spotlights illuminating the track. The electric hare began its circuit slowly at first, then quickly accelerated. The crowd on the banked terraces yelled as the hare attached to the rail approached the traps where six greyhounds yelped and howled in anticipation. A bell rang loudly as the hare passed the traps and the dogs were released. There was a blur of movement and colour as the greyhounds pursued their quarry at a tremendous pace. The race was over in a few seconds and the stadium announcer's voice called out, "The result of the third race. First, Appenzell Beauty in trap five; second, Lichfield Leonard in trap one."

Vince Rothwell tore up his ticket and showered confetti over Frankie Bowers' head. "You really are a know-all bastard, I should have listened to you again. Did you get both of 'em?"

Frankie picked the shredded ticket from his collar and laughed. "I had five and one reverse forecast. It was Peter's tip, he's the one you should listen to."

Frankie went off to collect his winnings, leaving Vince to study form for the next race. Peter the Punter approached, counting a wad of banknotes. "Watcher Vince, did you get a result on that last race?"

"No, but Frankie did. He's gone to collect his money."

Peter shoved the banknotes into the inside pocket of his jacket and said, "Have you still got the rozzers on your neck?"

Vince grimaced, "Oh yeah! Every time I turn I've got that ginger-headed sod Milner breathing down my neck. It's over a year now since Sammy croaked, but he won't leave me alone. It's affecting business at the club 'cos the punters don't want to be caught doing a deal when the Old Bill barges in."

"Did you know he's here?"

"What Milner! What's he doing at the dogs? He's not still watching me is he?"

"To be honest Vince, I don't think he's interested in you tonight. In fact, I doubt that he even knows you're here."

Peter pointed towards the rear of the stands, where several private boxes provided rich and favoured punters with comfortable surroundings to eat, drink and have a steward place their bets.

"Is Milner a married man?"

Vince thought for a moment, "Yeah, I think so. I don't know much about his private life."

"OK, so if he's a married man, what's he doing snogging with a bird in a private box at a dog track?"

Vince agreed, "Yeah, why come out here when he can do that at home, unless it's an anniversary or something."

"Would he come out to a dog track with his missus on an anniversary?"

"It's not likely, is it?"

"I reckon your Mister Milner has got himself a bit on the side."

Frankie returned with a broad smile on his face, "I won a 'pony' on that race."

Vince interrupted. "Hey Frankie, go up to the boxes and have a shufty. Peter reckons Milner's up there with a bird. He knows my 'boat race' only too well but he doesn't know you. If it is him, see if you can borrow a camera with one of those telephoto lenses from one of your press-boy mates down there and get a shot of them together. Even better, do you know if Harry the Dip is in the stadium?"

"I'll find out." Frankie gave Vince a ticket. "I've backed a five and six reverse forecast for you on the next race."

Frankie returned twenty minutes later with Harry the Dip.

"I've got a photographer on the job for an earner, if he can get a decent compromising shot. She doesn't look much like his wife to me."

Vince turned to Harry. "Go up there with Frankie and have a 'butchers'. When they leave the ground, try and lift her handbag. All I want is her address, you can keep the rest – but just remember who she's with. If he catches you at it, he'll have your goolies for breakfast."

In the next race, trap five won with number six close behind. Vince smiled to himself as he turned to collect his winnings. "Maybe my luck is changing after all."

****

Sergeant Milner entered the Maple Leaf club like a bad guy in a B-movie Western. Conversation stopped and nervous faces turned to the entrance where Milner, accompanied by a uniformed officer, surveyed the room with obvious distaste.

Vince broke the silence. "Good evening, Sergeant, can I be of any assistance. Do you and the constable fancy a drink, or perhaps this isn't a social call?"

Milner strolled casually across the room, looking at faces that averted their gaze on his approach. He stopped when he recognised Vince's companion at the table. "Tom Raggett! When did they let you out?"

"Oh! They got so fed up with me they threw me out," Tom answered, and some of the customers laughed.

"You seem to be keeping bad company. If my memory serves me right, you said in court that you didn't know Mister Rothwell."

Tom assumed an air of innocence. "That's very true, we've only just met."

There were a few suppressed chuckles around the room, softening an atmosphere that crackled with tension.

"At least I know it wasn't you who slit Sammy Sissons's throat and left him bleeding to death at the back of that pub." Milner's voice suddenly raised an octave higher. "You were having a nice holiday at the tax payer's expense."

"Very enjoyable too, Sergeant," Tom replied." I was just saying how nice it was to my – er, new friends, when you came in."

"Don't get smart with me, Raggett, I'm not in the mood." Milner's voice had taken on a menacing tone.

Vince intervened. "Well, it's so nice to see you again, Sergeant. I must say how much we all enjoy your regular visits to this humble establishment."

Vince looked around the room where he had everyone's attention. "And how's your good lady these days?"

Milner hesitated and frowned. "What are you getting at? I don't see what business that is of yours."

"Oh! I'm delighted she's well, Sergeant. So, tell me how's the wife?"

Vince emphasised the last three words to loud guffaws from a fascinated audience.

Milner's fists clenched and for a moment he looked as if he was about to lunge at Vince. He took several deep breaths and said, "Very amusing Rothwell, and just what are you implying?"

"Oh! dearie me, Sergeant, what you do when you're off duty is your own business." He reached down to his briefcase and selected a black and white photograph. It clearly showed Milner, glass in hand, staring affectionately into the eyes of a female companion.

"I hope you enjoyed your evening at the dog track. Did you get a result at the end of it?"

There were further howls of merriment from customers, who were thoroughly enjoying the contest.

Milner picked up the print, looked at it and said, "This is an invasion of privacy."

Vince grinned, "If you say so, Sergeant, you know the law better than me. By the way, how do you define adultery?"

Milner tore the print into little pieces and tossed it back on to Vince's table.

"I can have more prints made – there is a negative," Vince said.

Milner turned defensive. "That was an evening out with my wife – a celebration."

Vince persisted. "A celebration. Well, well, I'm so pleased for you, Sergeant. Tell me, what was the occasion?"

"That's none of your concern."

Vince leaned forward and looked Milner straight in the eye. "It seems strange to me that a man, who lives in a flat in Kings Norton, should be out celebrating with his wife, who lives in Edgbaston. It's also very strange that the same wife has a different name and already has another husband working all week down in London."

Vince produced a wad of black and white photographs showing Milner entering and leaving a house in Edgbaston. Others showed him walking hand in hand in a park with the same lady as in the dog track photographs.

Milner spluttered with rage. "I was getting evidence for a case I'm working on."

There was hysterical laughter from all around the room and the uniformed constable, who accompanied Milner, turned to face the wall to hide his amusement.

Vince, now enjoying himself immensely, waited for the derisive banter to subside. "I accept your story, Sergeant, so perhaps I don't need to send copies of these photos to any interested parties, like the local press or your chief inspector."

"This is blackmail, Rothwell, I won't forget it."

"Just remember to close the door on your way out," Vince said, waving a dismissive forefinger towards the exit.

****

A steam engine, puffing energetically, pushed three coal-trucks to the top of an incline. Here they uncoupled and were nudged along a track leading to a ramshackle loading shed. The engine reversed into a cloud of its own steam and disappeared back into the colliery. A sweating brakeman stopped the leading truck adjacent to the waiting narrowboats and two men stripped to the waist began shovelling coal down a chute into the boat.

It was a hot day in the height of summer and the workers by the canal at the colliery were complaining of the heat. Ocker, covered from head to foot in coal dust, was evenly spreading the load as it spewed into the narrowboat's hold. Every few minutes, he would pause to drink from a grimy bottle of water that Wilf McCann refilled from a quayside tap.

Sharing the task of filling the hold was Wilf's teenage son, Corky, who kept up a continual banter of crude observations directed at Ocker and the other workers on the wharf. His father described him as "a good worker on the day, but a bit of a harum-scarum." Some of the men on the wharf had stronger opinions, but respect for Wilf McCann made them absorb his son's taunts.

After a few months scratching around for odd jobs at Farden's boatyard, Ocker had joined Wilf and his extrovert son on their boats, *Ferntree* and *Ballarat* at the beginning of the year. Raymond had returned to work after his knee injury and was working with the Randall's boats on the same coal run to the south.

Wilf McCann was regarded as one of the elite 'Number One' owner boatmen. Most of his cargoes were obtained by sub-contracting to bigger canal carriers, but recent failing health had left him with a problem only solved when Ocker joined him on the boats. It was many years since his female family members announced they were fed up with the boating life and were leaving for land-based occupations. This *fait accompli* had, in Wilf's phrase, "fair got oi flummoxed." Now he had resigned himself to the fact that his wife and daughter were never coming back to the canal.

Finally the boats were loaded, their contents evenly distributed and securely sheeted. Three exhausted boatmen covered in sweat and coal dust, washed under a tap in the mess room and then ate their sandwiches.

"This is the worst part of boating, getting rid of the muck after loading," Ocker said, squinting against the sun's glare.

Corky looked surprised. "I didn't think you worried about a bit of muck. Isn't that why they call you Greasy Ocker?"

"Well, mebbe I wash a bit more often than I used to."

"Yeah, thanks to my sister," Corky grinned. "She didn't like a smelly, dirty bugger like you cuddling up to her in bed."

Ocker rolled his sandwich wrapper into a ball and threw it at Corky's head, "You watch your tongue, you cocky young bugger."

Wilf removed his cap, scratched his balding pate, and remarked, "When you two boogers have finished mucking about, there's forty odd ton of black nuts to get down to Ricky."

Ocker and Corky rolled down side cloths over the load and tightly tied the strings. They laid planks end to end from the top of the cabins to a cross-bearing at the front, which made it possible to walk along the length of the boat above the hold. Then they mopped the wet coal dust from the cabin roof, stern counter and gunwales.

Two miles from the colliery, a waterside pub and public baths were conveniently situated close to the canal. After mooring, Ocker and Corky scrubbed coal dust from the boat's paintwork before retiring to scrub more dust from themselves. Wilf had already gone on ahead for a bath and the two young men could hear him coughing as he washed inside the cubicle.

"Your dad's doing a lot of coughing these days," Ocker observed.

"He says it's the coal dust getting on his chest," Corky replied.

"Yeah, I suppose it's bound to affect your chest when you've been carrying coal for as long as he has."

"That's right, you've got to remember the poor old bugger's not as young as he was," Corky answered, as he collected his soap and towel from the attendant.

Wilf McCann's health had been failing over the past year, and Ocker had joined him just at the time when he was seriously considering retiring and selling the boats. He felt he could cope for a while longer now he had two strong young men to do the really hard work, but the persistent cough and subsequent loss of weight was a constant worry and so far he had refused to visit a doctor.

Ocker awoke at five the next morning, reached across the cabin and lit the kettle on the stove. Corky was snoring and snorting loudly on the other bunk. Ocker shoved his foot against him and shook him vigorously, "Wake up, you lazy bugger."

Corky groaned, "Oh! Shut it, Ocker, it's not time to get up yet."

"Come on, you've got a day's work in front of you," Ocker said, pulling on his boots. "You shouldn't have drunk so much ale last night."

Ocker climbed the steps out of the cabin and breathed in the morning air. The early morning sun penetrated through wisps of grey mist and rose over a bridge adjacent to the pub.

He knocked on the side of the motor cabin where Wilf was sleeping. "Wake up, it's time to get moving! It looks like a nice day."

A sudden paroxysm of coughing confirmed that Wilf was awake.

Ocker insisted that they ate a decent meal before starting out, changing a tradition for Wilf McCann, who had usually settled for a 'boatman's breakfast', consisting of a cup of tea and a Woodbine cigarette. A long-standing agreement with the pub landlord allowed them to use the outside lavatory before moving off.

The sun was already quite warm when Ocker started up the motor. Corky cast off and took over steering the butty, while Wilf returned to the cabin to what he called 'doing his wimmin's work'.

Ocker was back on the familiar territory he remembered from his youth, travelling south, carrying coal from the Coventry coalfield to the paper mills near Watford. On this beautiful morning, he was steering the motor *Ferntree*, towing the butty *Ballarat* a rope's length behind.

Wilf, in the butty's cabin, was doing domestic chores, quite happy for once to be sitting back and letting the young men get on with the work. Each time that locks appeared, he would take over the tiller, allowing Corky to jump off the boat and run down the towpath, windlass in hand to set up the lock. The rattle of the lock paddles reverberated through Corky's skull as the effects of the previous evening's drink slowly wore off. Ocker, now very much the captain, berated Corky's lock operations, shouting instructions in a continual stream of invective.

Arriving at a flight of locks, they found the first evidence of boating activity since they started out that day. A motorboat with a distinctive 'pop, pop' sound from its engine waited for its butty, still engaged inside the top lock. The boats were on their way north to the Black Country, loaded with timber. While Ocker was speaking to the captain about the possibility of a return load, he saw another pair of boats nearing the bottom of the flight, also travelling southwards. Recognising the Randall boats and sure his brother Raymond was on board, he sent Corky running down the locks to find out where they intended to stop for the night.

Later that day, as the sun descended in an orange glow over a sheep-studded hillside, Ocker steered the boats into a mooring space behind the Randalls' pair, already tied up outside a canal-side pub.

After eating their evening meal on the boat, the three men entered the pub to be confronted by a notice asking boatmen to remove muddy boots. Ocker could see that the once modest car park had been greatly enlarged and now an extension had been added to accommodate a new restaurant.

He saw his brother sitting with Percy Randall in the corner of the public bar and greeted him, "Hey up, Ray, what's happened to the pub?"

"New management. They're after road trade, that's where the money is now."

"What's in the new building?"

"That's a restaurant for the motorcar folk," Raymond said. "There's no brass in a load of scruffy boatmen supping a few pints all evening."

"Do you think they'll serve me?" Ocker said.

"As long as your bloody boots are clean," Raymond laughed.

Percy Randall wagged his pipe and said, "I remember this pub when it was just for boatmen, which is why it was built in the first place."

Raymond sighed, "Here we go. Come on, Percy, I bet you can remember when beer was a penny a pint and that included a feel of the landlord's wife as well."

Everyone laughed, but Percy continued unabashed. "Don't you be so cheeky. I can remember boats moored up here two deep for half a mile along the cut in the evenings. And what nights we had when the boating lads let their hair down after a few pints." Percy sipped his beer and resumed his reminiscences. "There was a time when wimmin couldn't come into this pub. Old Zeke Dickinson was the landlord then and his missus was a right tyrant. If she saw a boatman with his wife in the bar, she'd be out telling the wimmin to get back on the boat and look after their kids."

"And what happened if they wouldn't go?" Corky asked.

"She'd be after 'em with her besom and chase 'em out of the door."

Wilf confirmed the story. "That's right. I can remember me dad telling the tale how he got into a fight with old Zeke and they both finished up in the cut after his missus threw me mother out of the bar." Wilf began to cough and turning his head spat into his handkerchief.

"What happened after that?" Corky asked.

Wilf cleared his throat and continued, "Old Zeke and me dad climbed out of the cut, shook hands, went back in the pub and got roaring drunk."

The group of men finished their drinks and Ocker and Raymond went to the bar to replenish everyone's glasses. Wilf coughed again into his handkerchief and then mopped sweat from his brow, remarking, "By gum, it's hot tonight."

Percy Randall leaned across the table, peering at Wilf with an expression of concern. "Are you sure you're OK, Wilf?"

Wilf dismissed the suggestion, "Oh! I've just got a bit of a cough, you know how it is with the coal dust."

"Well, mebbe so, but you don't look too well to me. You need to look after yourself and don't work too hard." Percy poked Wilf in the chest with his pipe, "There'll still be plenty of work left when we're dead and gone."

Percy puffed contentedly at his pipe, while the three younger men engaged in conversation.

"Did you know Tom Raggett has been in prison?" said Raymond.

"I heard his brother Alf is in Winson Green for armed robbery, but I hadn't heard a thing about Tom since he went in the army," replied Ocker.

"Caught with a van load of knocked-off gear," said Raymond. "I've heard Alf has been moved to a nick down in London – Wandsworth, I think – and Ronnie Raggett's been on probation for thieving."

"They sound like a right bunch of villains," Corky remarked. "Me dad often talks about them. Rumour has it that Joe Raggett did some time in gaol when he was younger. I remember me dad saying he was one of the biggest villains on the cut."

Raymond drained his glass and replaced it on the table. "I remember stories that Joe Raggett was the randiest bugger on the canal. They say he's got bastard kids spread along the canal from Brentford to Birmingham."

"Aye, that dirty booger was after my Gracie," Wilf said. "That were years ago, but we came to blows over it."

"You had a fight with Joe Raggett?" Raymond asked.

"Aye, he said he hadn't touched her and I called him a bloody liar."

"What happened then?"

"He broke me bloody nose," said Wilf, tapping his finger on the side of the offended organ.

"What did Gracie say?" asked Percy.

"She said I was daft getting into a fight over nothing."

Wilf continued sipping his drink and sweating profusely. Presently he stood up and made his way unsteadily to the lavatory.

"Looks like me dad's had enough for tonight," observed Corky.

Ocker shook his head. "He's only had two pints."

The three young men carried on talking, while Percy stared out of the window reflecting on distant times. After a few minutes, a well-dressed man with a southern accent ran into the bar saying to the barman, "There seems to be a drunk passed out in the toilet."

Ocker grabbed Corky's arm. "Come on, that's no drunk. I reckon it's your dad."

They found Wilf lying unconscious on the floor of the toilet, with his shirt stained with blood. Once again, Ocker had to ask a pub's manager to call for an ambulance. Wilf stayed in hospital for a week while tests were made and then he returned home. Gracie was told that there was nothing anyone could do for him. Ocker and Corky carried on working the boats until Wilf's death six weeks later.

****

The rebellion at Cochinos Bay, now called the Bay of Pigs, has been totally quashed by Cuban Government troops. Most of the fifteen hundred invaders are believed to be Cuban exiles hostile to Fidel Castro. The Cuban leader today accused the United States of plotting a coup to overthrow his government. In Moscow, President Khrushchev still smarting from the U-2 spyplane incident, denounced the US government and demanded an apology from President Kennedy.

The latest world crisis made little impact on the Maple Leaf's regular customers. Flickering television pictures in the corner of the bar broadcast news of imminent global destruction between the two bickering superpowers as the cold war deepened. The impending apocalypse was lost in importance to more mundane matters, such as berating the favourite at Market Rasen that had lost that afternoon.

Vince Rothwell, seated at his usual table, was the only person in the club that evening who seemed interested in the news.

He surveyed the room, waving his hand in a dismissive gesture. "Just look at 'em. If old Khruschev drops one of them H-bombs on Birmingham Town Hall, they'd still only worry if their bleeding horses had gone down."

He threw a beer mat at Harry the Dip, who was deeply engrossed in his poker game. "Oi, Harry, have you built your nuclear shelter yet?"

"Do me a favour, I'm just about to earn me week's wages," said Harry, whose eyes never left his opponent's face.

Vince shrugged his shoulders and turned to Tom and Frankie. "While we're on the subject of wages, I reckon we could be on to a very nice little earner, providing everything works out and Kennedy doesn't get us all incinerated."

Picking up his briefcase, Vince produced a newspaper article, headed by a photograph of two men shaking hands and grinning at the camera. He prodded a finger at the large man on the left of the picture. "Do you recognise this geezer?"

"He looks familiar, but I can't think who he is," replied Tom.

"I know him," Frankie said, "I've seen him on television. He's a toff on that quiz show – usually wears a horrible pink shirt and a bow tie."

"Right, and his name is Lord James Crantock," Vince added. "Sit back, gentlemen, and I'll give you a short biography of our next mark because he's going to make us all rich."

Vince delved into his case and produced more papers. "It pays to know who you're dealing with, before you turn him over." He handed his glass to Tom. "Get us a refill first and ask June to turn that television off."

Tom stood at the bar watching Harry the Dip.

"An' I'll raise you a tenner." Harry dropped the crumpled five-pound notes on top of an impressive pile of notes already in the centre of the table. His opponent, a middle-aged man with thinning hair, was now having doubts about his cards and a bead of sweat ran slowly down his forehead.

Harry felt confident. "It'll cost you twenty to see me." The man opened his wallet and produced the money, tossing it on the table. "OK, I'll see you. What you got?"

Harry spread his cards face up on the table. "Full house, Kings on sixes."

The man sighed, "Three tens and that's me out."

Harry scooped up his winnings, saying, "Well, gents, don't they say the sun shines on the righteous?"

Vince grinned. "I'll bet he's had those Kings up his sleeve all evening."

Tom returned with the drinks and sat watching Vince with an expression like a hungry dog waiting for its bone.

Vince sorted his papers and began, "James Crantock was born with the proverbial silver spoon in his mouth. His old man was Luke Crantock, the ointment king from Liverpool. He made his fortune from all the silly buggers who ever cut their knees playing football in the back yard."

He selected another sheet of paper and read, "James went to Eton and Oxford and learned how to be a young gentleman. Later on he worked in the family business as accountant and dabbled in local politics as a councillor in Liverpool. He stood as a Tory in a safe Labour seat and lost his deposit. He eventually got elected when he went down south in what they call the Tory heartlands."

Vince scratched his head, sipped his drink and continued, "He was in the RAF during the war as an administrator and managed to avoid seeing any action. After the war he got a nice job as a parliamentary secretary in some poxy post-war department. He began writing articles on politics and the economy for some of the stuffed shirt papers and then began broadcasting on the wireless. He managed to get himself invited to the right sort of social gatherings, political dinners, film premieres and got his photo in the magazines and papers with royalty, politicians and film stars."

Vince paused. "At the same time he's making out with some of the biggest villains in London. He's been on the pay roll of one of the best known firms in the East End for years. He introduces them to respectability and provides under the counter information. In recent years we've all seen him on TV, when he was given a peerage to sit in the House of Lords."

Vince finished his drink and replaced his glass on the table. "There's one thing about his lordship that is generally not known by his adoring public." Vince smiled at his companions. "He's a raving queer."

"So, he's not married?" queried Tom.

"No, he never married although he likes having his photo done with all the models and actresses. That's good for his image, but it's the geezers that he's really interested in."

"How did you find that out?" asked Frankie.

"A bloke came to see me about a week ago. Turns out he used to work for his Lordship as a chauffeur. After a few weeks, he finds one of his duties is dropping his pants at his master's pleasure. So he ups and tells his Lordship to button up his flies and stuff himself."

"So what happened then?" asked Tom.

"He got the rocket, but before he left he got some information about the gaff which he has passed on to me – for a percentage of the action."

Harry the Dip wandered past, waving a wad of banknotes to the group. "Like taking candy from a baby. Do you fancy a drink, lads?"

Vince nodded," Thanks, Harry, but we're talking business."

Returning to his story, Vince continued, "Now this geezer, who was the chauffeur, says that his Lordship keeps a lot of cash in a safe at his mansion near Oxford. He takes cash 'cos he doesn't want the taxman nosing into his affairs and most of it is hot money from our mutual friends down in London."

"How much are we talking about?" asked Frankie.

"This chauffeur geezer reckons it runs into several thousands, but the problem is getting inside and then there's the safe."

"Any idea what sort of safe he's got?" Frankie asked.

Vince checked his notes. "Apparently, he has an Argent Disque with an anti-explosive locking bar. Does that mean anything to you Frankie?"

"Yeah! It means it's difficult to get into. Some of the best petermen in the country would have trouble getting into that one."

Vince continued, "He's also got security alarms all over his house and on the gate where you drive-in."

"So what do we do?" said Tom.

"We'll have to persuade his Lordship to open the safe for us, which means we have to get into the house without the Thames Valley CID boys joining us for tea. OK, so we find out when he does the recording for his next TV show and be waiting for him when he returns home. Instead of asking him for his autograph, we'll be in after him before his chauffeur switches the alarm on again."

Vince grinned at his companions, turned, and shouted, "Oi, Harry, where's those drinks you promised us?"

****

It was the first time Ocker had ever worn a tie and he felt as if an unseen assailant was slowly strangling him. He ran his finger inside the collar of his shirt, desperately trying to loosen the pressure on his throat. His new suit felt stiff and unyielding, and there was a faint odour of mothballs on the jacket.

His lunchtime sandwich and beer left a strange lumpy sensation in the pit of his stomach and he hoped he was not going to be sick. A familiar nervous trickle of sweat ran down his back, insinuating itself between his buttocks. He wanted to scratch his backside, but knew how embarrassing that simple action would be when you were the centre of attention.

Ocker was about to get married!

A flight of steps led down to a small garden outside the brick-built registry office, where the constant pressure of many feet had worn the grass into bare patches. A sweating photographer arranged a wedding group on the steps and was trying to hold their attention.

Raymond, acting as the best man, limped across the lawn from a nearby telephone box and said, "Sorry mate, but Lucy hasn't turned up this morning, so Kitty has asked Brenda to be her bridesmaid."

"Never turned up!" Ocker repeated. "What do you mean – what the hell is she doing?"

"She's been arrested."

"What! You must be joking."

"It's true, she was arrested yesterday on the Ban the Bombers march. She threw an egg at a politician." Raymond smiled weakly. "All down the front of his pin-stripes."

"Bloody hell, she knows I'm getting married today!"

"I know, but she's banged up for the weekend, unless they can arrange a special court seeing as there's so many of them in the nick. Whatever happens, she's not going to be here in," Raymond looked at his watch, "about fifteen minutes."

Ocker ran his fingers inside his collar, longing to rip off the tie that was choking him. He saw familiar faces appearing from the garden and mingling with the guests from the other wedding. The imposing figure of Ben Barnwell climbed the steps with his hand extended, saying, "Good to see you, lad. I never thought I'd see the day when you'd wear a suit and tie."

He grasped Ocker with a huge hairy hand and slapped his back. Ocker gasped for breath. "Thanks, Ben, it's good to see you."

The manic cameraman now tried to organise the wedding party in front of a clump of drooping shrubs. Some of his subjects seemed more interested in getting to the reception and were drifting away towards their cars.

Ocker greeted his Uncle Billy and Auntie Rose, now retired from boating and living in Lichfield. Cousin George, who was carrying his new baby, followed them. George had started his own motor business and boasted that since leaving the canals, he had acquired a wife, a baby and a Jaguar car.

His conversation soon took on a familiar theme. "Come on, Ocker, there's no future in boating. You're going to be a married man with responsibilities, let me fix you up with a job in my business."

"Thanks, George, but I reckon I'll carry on with the boat."

"I hear you're the new Number One since Wilf died, so what happened with the boats?"

"Wilf left *Ferntree* and *Ballarat* to Kitty, Corky and me, in his will."

"How come you're only working the motor?"

"Corky wanted to pack in boating and start up a haulage business with a mate, so I had to sell the butty to pay off his share."

"So what's he doing and who's he working with?"

"To be honest, George, I don't know. We hardly see him these days and he won't say who his partner is."

George pointed to the road where a black limousine was pulling into the kerb. Kitty emerged from the interior of the car, flanked by her mother and Ocker's sister, Brenda, who looked uncomfortable in Lucy's bridesmaid dress. Kitty, wearing a lavender coloured outfit, was smiling radiantly at friends.

Ocker's tongue felt as if it was welded to the roof of his mouth and he glanced hopefully towards the pub on the opposite side of the road. George nudged him in the ribs. "Here comes the blushing bride, no turning back now, Ocker."

Kitty and Ocker were directed into the marriage room and told to sit down before the registrar's table.

"How are you feeling?" Kitty asked with a smile.

"Scared," replied Ocker. "And this bloody tie's choking me."

"I've never seen you in a tie before."

"I've never worn one before."

Kitty examined his tie and straightened it. "There, that looks better. The knot was halfway round your ear."

"I'll never wear a tie again."

Kitty frowned, "Hey, you wore that shirt yesterday."

"So what," Ocker replied.

"You don't turn up to get married in a dirty shirt."

"It isn't dirty, I looked before I put it on."

"But we bought you a new shirt last week, what's happened to it?"

"Ray packed it in my bag for the holiday."

"You were supposed to wear it today."

Ocker shrugged and turned his attention to the guests filing into the seats behind him.

The registrar entered the room, sat down and began the ceremony by reminding them of the sanctity of the marriage room. He spoke in a rather condescending voice and stared almost accusingly at the chief participants. He spent several minutes writing in the registry book while the guests chatted and Ocker wriggled in his uncomfortable chair. The heat in the room had become oppressive and Ocker felt that every stitch of his clothing was sticking to him. He tugged at the recalcitrant tie until Kitty gave him a sidelong glance and shook her head.

Having completed his writing, the registrar stood up and motioned Kitty and Ocker to approach the table. There was a gasp, followed by sniggers and giggles from the guests, as it became obvious that the dark-suited official urgently needed to adjust his clothing. The registrar had forgotten to zip up his fly and an inch of pink shirt protruded from under his corpulent stomach.

The registrar began the ceremony. "I call upon these persons here present, to witness...," the official stopped his intonation as he saw Ocker staring at his trousers. His eyes slowly descended to the lower part of his body and made the humiliating discovery.

"Er, um!... Please excuse me for a moment."

The registrar retreated from the room to make the necessary adjustment, leaving behind an aura of stifled merriment. He returned to complete the formalities in a less reverential atmosphere.

Kitty and Ocker, now officially married, accepted congratulations from a red- faced registrar and departed to an assortment of raucous comments from Raymond and George.

"At least Ocker remembered to do his flies up," laughed George.

"Even if he forgot to change his shirt," said Kitty, sweetly.

The sweating cameraman took photographs of everyone before they left for an afternoon reception. He arranged everyone into a family group and then groups of friends. Afterwards, they left for a reception at the Anchor Inn.

They walked into the pub along an avenue formed by boat people waving decorated windlasses and showering them with confetti. Before entering the pub, Ocker and Kitty unveiled a plaque on an outside wall of the pub.

In memory of Giggetty Jim born in 1892
A Number One boatman drowned here at Christmas 1957
and sadly missed by his friends.

Afterwards, Ocker saw Ben standing on the towpath, staring at the spot where Giggetty Jim had drowned.

"You've got yourself a nice girl, lad, I hope you'll be very happy."

"Thanks, Ben," said Ocker, and asked, "Were you ever married?"

"No, lad, I've had a few lady friends, but I never got round to asking any of them – not that they'd have taken me on."

"Well, you seem to know what to say to people. I've always admired that. Women seem to like that sort of thing," Ocker paused. "Well, I reckon they do anyway. I've always had trouble saying the right words."

"You said the right thing today when you got married."

"All I did was repeat what the fat bloke told me to say."

"Yeah, but you said it like you meant it – that's important."

"I'll try to do what's right by Kitty."

"I'm sure you will, lad," Ben sighed. "The trouble is when you get past fifty, you realise there's more life behind you than there is in front, and it's then you get regrets. Looking back now, I wish I'd had a wife and a few kids – it would have been nice watching them grow up."

Ocker didn't know how to reply to this so he settled for a firm handshake.

"Thanks again, Ben."

"It's a pleasure, lad, now let's get inside. Kitty will be wondering where you've got to and I want a pint before I make my speech to the happy couple."

The landlord of the Anchor Inn had prepared one of his bars for the wedding reception. It was the same room as the ill-fated party for Giggetty Jim. A table, set for the close family, included George, who was paying for it all. The remaining guests were seated around trestle tables, overflowing with food.

Ben Barnwell was the only guest brave and articulate enough to stand up and make a speech. With the formalities over, people began to congregate in small groups and Raymond joined George at the bar.

"Thanks for paying for the party, George, it's much appreciated."

"It's a pleasure. I know Kitty and Ocker will need every penny they've got to start their home and as I'm not short of a few bob, so what the hell."

"We all know why Lucy didn't make the wedding, but what happened to Corky?"

George grimaced and drew Raymond away from the bar to a quiet corner. "Don't tell this to Ocker or Kitty or it'll spoil their day. You know Corky has gone into the haulage business with the money from selling his Dad's boat?"

"Yeah, Ocker was annoyed about splitting up the pair."

"Do you know who Corky's new partner is?" George asked.

"No, I haven't a clue."

George glanced around furtively and said, "His partner's Ronnie Raggett and Tom's involved somehow. Did you know Tom's been released from gaol?"

"Yeah, I had heard," said Raymond. "Any idea what business they're in – I bet it's not straight, if I know the Raggetts?"

"They're supposed to be shifting scrap metal and clapped out domestic items, like cookers and fridges. Tom said there's a market in doing 'em up and selling 'em to poor people."

"Have you seen Tom?"

"Yeah, I saw him about a week ago. He's mixed up with some dodgy types in Brum and he wasn't saying much apart from hints about big deals coming up soon. Well, I don't know about big deals, but did you hear yesterday's news?"

"No, I was too busy trying to get Ocker sorted out for his wedding and the holiday."

"There was a mass breakout at Wandsworth Prison down in London yesterday morning. Guess who's gone missing?"

"Not Alf Raggett."

"Yeah, he's over the wall."

"Do you reckon Corky's involved?"

"Why else would he miss his sister's wedding?"

"Bloody hell, George, Kitty'll go spare when she hears about this and so will Ocker."

"That's why we must keep quiet about it. They'll find out soon enough, but hopefully it won't spoil their day."

"Does Gracie know what Corky's up to?"

"No, she hasn't seen him for weeks and doesn't have any idea what he's doing."

"So he's moved out of home."

"Yeah, Tom said that Corky and Ronnie could move in with him until they sort themselves out."

"Sounds like a right thieves' kitchen."

"Especially if Alf's with 'em."

"My bet is they're sorting Alf out today and Corky's up to his neck in it."

Joey Boat Johnson began to play the accordion and, although his repertoire was limited, his choice of songs was popular with his audience.

George had promised to drive the bridal couple to the station in time to catch the train to Torquay, so Kitty had changed her clothes in the landlord's flat above the pub. She entered the bar wearing a green and yellow dress with her long dark hair hanging loose on her shoulders. Appreciative whistles and applause greeted her progress as she grabbed Ocker's hand and headed for the door.

All the guests followed them to the car park to see them off and someone had tied a piece of cardboard to the bumper of George's Jaguar, reading 'Just Married'.

George swung the car in a wide arc around the wharf with Kitty and Ocker waving out of the open window. Raymond picked up a newspaper that blew across the wharf from the draught of the car. A huge banner headline said LOCAL MAN AMONG MASS PRISON ESCAPEES and, underneath, a villainous looking photograph of Alf Raggett.

****

"For Chrissake, Alf, you'll never get away with it!" Tom Raggett shouted.

"It's gotta work, I need to be out of the country by the weekend," Alf Raggett replied.

"OK, let me speak to Vince. He's got contacts with some blokes who own a private plane. We'll get you out that way."

"It'll take too long – I've gotta get to Holland."

"Go later, we can hide you up here for a few weeks until the heat's off."

"I've gotta meet these blokes in Holland at the weekend or it'll be too late."

"What are you gonna do when you get there?"

"That's my business, so the less you know the better for all of us."

"Be reasonable, Alf, have you seen Ronnie's wagon?"

"No, but I'm sure it's OK."

"It's a rust bucket – he'll never get past the customs. It'll probably break down on the way there and do us all a favour."

"Ronnie says it's in A1 condition."

Tom laughed, "Obviously you haven't seen the A1 recently. It was full of road works when I was on it last week."

"What's Ronnie's mate like, can you trust him?"

"Yeah, Corky's alright. Anyway he's off to his sister's wedding tomorrow."

"Oh no, he ain't. I need both of 'em on that lorry. Apart from that, he knows who I am and I'm not having him getting pissed at a wedding and blabbing his mouth off."

"Be reasonable, Alf, his sister's getting married."

"Fuck his sister!" Alf roared and added, "Maybe you have, you randy bastard."

"No, I haven't, his sister is Kitty McCann. Do you remember the McCanns on the boats?"

"Yeah, I remember the McCanns and so does me Dad – he was knocking off Wilf McCann's missus."

"Bloody rubbish," Tom snorted.

"And I remember Kitty. She was a nice little dark-haired tart with big tits. I'll bet she's a looker now. Who's she marrying?"

"Would you believe, Ocker?"

"Not Greasy Ocker," Alf spluttered. "She's not chucking herself away on that scruffy bastard."

"Apparently he's cleaned himself up since he met her."

"What a bloody waste!" Alf said. "She's the sort of little tart you dream about when you're in the stir. By the way, thanks for fixing me up with that other tart last night. What was her name?"

"Marlene."

"She was OK, she did a nice turn."

"Yeah, Marlene's not fussy, she'll do a turn for anybody if the price's right."

"Sod off, Tom, how much do I owe you?"

"That's OK, Alf, you can have that one on me 'cos the way you're going, you'll be inside again before the weekend."

****

"I don't believe this," the bearded dockyard policemen said to his colleague. "We'd better have a look at that one."

A line of trucks bound for the continent were being scrutinised as they queued outside the docks. The policeman walked over to the old lorry with its badly secured load and spoke to the driver, "Hey son! Pull this old rust bucket out of the line and park it over there."

Corky nodded and edged the lorry out, followed by cloud of exhaust fumes. He moistened his lips and wished he had a drink. He glanced across at his companion, who looked apprehensive.

Ronnie Raggett smoothed down his long, greasy hair and climbed out of the cab.

"Where do you think you're going?" the bearded policeman asked, putting out a restraining hand.

"I gotta take a leak."

"Not before you've answered a few questions."

"But I'm desperate."

"Then use a bottle."

The policeman beckoned to Corky to leave the driver's seat, while his colleague suspiciously examined the outside of the trailer.

"Who is in charge here?" asked the bearded policeman.

"We're partners," replied Ronnie. "He drives and I do the business."

"I see, and what are you carrying under those sheets?"

"We've got a load of refrigerators," said Ronnie. "Export order for Holland."

"My word!" The policeman's voice took on a tone of amused sarcasm. "We shall have to tell the government about this, I'm sure Mister MacMillan will be wanting to honour you with an award for industry."

The second policeman, peering under the sheeted load, was looking thoughtful. He beckoned to his colleagues and was joined by the first policeman, who pointed a finger at Corky and Ronnie and said, "You two don't move until I tell you to."

The two policemen peered under the sheets, then emerged in deep discussion. One spoke into a walkie-talkie radio, while the other returned saying, "I take it you have the necessary export documentation for this load?"

Corky produced his passport. It was brand new and unstamped. "Is this what you want?"

"No son, that's OK for exporting you. What I want is your green card, your certificate of insurance, your registration documents, your letter of authority and, looking at the age of this vehicle, a certificate of road worthiness."

Corky looked helplessly at Ronnie. "You do the business, have you got these things?"

Ronnie shrugged and looked appealingly at the officer, "It's the first time we've done this."

The policeman sighed, "Let's see your passports then."

Two customs officers were asked to join the group and the four of them went into a huddle. Ronnie Raggett's passport was the subject of heated discussion and one of the policemen spoke urgently into his radio.

"Let's get this load stripped down."

The refrigerators strapped together in lines were uniform in size except for a single large unit at the end nearest the cab. Close inspection revealed a series of holes drilled in the top of the unit. The officers began to get excited and clustered around the refrigerator. One of them exclaimed, "I think we might have a result here."

"Gimme a hand to open this door," yelled the bearded policeman.

Eventually the door was opened revealing an unshaven man crouching in some discomfort with his nose pressed to a funnel that led to the airholes.

"Mister Alf Raggett, I presume?" said the triumphant police officer.

****

Vince stifled a yawn, "What time is it?"

Frankie switched on the car's interior light and peered at his watch, "Half past one, do you reckon he's still coming?"

"Yeah, I think so. He's probably boozing at the studio in the hospitality room. They call it the Green Room. It's where they all go to get pissed after the show."

Headlights illuminated the trees beyond a bend in the lane ahead.

"Car coming!" Vince nudged Tom in the ribs. "Wake up, you lazy sod, and get ready to start!"

The three men watched as the intensity of the lights increased and then the unmistakable shape of a Rolls Royce appeared around the bend.

"This'll be him, now get your gear on, keep the chat down and remember don't say any names."

Tom waited inside the car with the lights switched off, his eyes momentarily dazzled by the headlamps of the approaching limousine.

Vince and Frankie slipped out of the car and ran across the road, crouching down below a gnarled old oak tree guarding the mansion's entrance. Both men were dressed in black, with woollen balaclavas pulled over their heads. They peered through slits as the Rolls Royce slowed down and turned into the entrance, stopping in front of the gates. The chauffeur left the car, walked up to the gates and tapped out a series of coded numbers on a brass plate attached to the gate. There was a loud buzz as the gates opened. The chauffeur returned to the car and drove it past the gates, stopping a few yards into the drive. At that moment, Vince and Frankie slid unseen into the bushes that lined the drive. Tom left his car on the grass verge and approached the entrance meeting the chauffeur returning to lock the gates.

"You can't come in here – this is private property."

"You want to bet," growled Tom.

"If you don't go away, I'll have to call the police."

Vince crept out of the bushes behind the chauffeur, grasped him around the neck and spoke into his ear, "Just do what you're told and you won't get hurt – close the gates and drive up to the house."

Then Vince climbed into the back of the car where an astonished fat man was seated. Frankie entered the car from the other side, produced a knife and stuck the point under the fat man's chin. Vince grasped the fat man's ear and twisted it violently, "You be quiet and do what you're told."

Lord Crantock found his voice and spluttered, "This is absolutely outrageous. Who are you men and what are you doing here?"

"Didn't I tell you to be quiet. You'll find out why we're here soon enough," Vince replied, nodding to Frankie who scratched the knifepoint under the fat man's flabby throat.

His Lordship clutched at his throat as a trickle of blood dripped on to the front of his dress shirt. He stared wild-eyed at the spreading stain and groaned, "This is absolutely outrageous."

"So you said before. Now we don't want to mess up your nice Roller with bloodstains, do we, your bleeding Lordship."

"How do you know who I am?"

"We saw your fat face on the telly and my friend thought he'd like to get your autograph in the little book his mum gave him for Christmas," Vince replied.

The sarcasm was lost on Lord Crantock, who had found a handkerchief and was mopping the blood dripping underneath his wobbling chins.

Back at the gates, the chauffeur with an unaccustomed act of bravado, threw a punch at Tom, missed, and ran off up the lane. He was no athlete and Tom soon caught up with him.

"Please, no violence – don't hit me," the chauffeur said in a pleading lisp, backing away with both hands in front of his face.

"Oh! I wouldn't dream of hurting a nice boy like you," Tom replied.

"Oh, thank you," answered the chauffeur, dropping his hands.

Tom hit him hard into the pit of his stomach and then repeated the punch, sending the man sprawling into the ditch.

"On your feet and don't give me any more trouble."

The chauffeur had got the message, "Alright! Please, no more violence."

Lord Crantock's seventeenth-century manor house was constructed in a combination of red brick and Cotswold stone and had two wings around a central courtyard where the Rolls Royce glided to a halt.

"Everyone inside," Vince said, beckoning to the chauffeur. "Get that door open and the lights on."

The building was almost in complete darkness except for a single light glowing somewhere inside the house.

"Is there anyone else inside the house?"

The frightened chauffeur stammered, "No, no, not tonight, the housekeeper has the weekend off."

Lord Crantock emerged from the car, mopping his chin with a large stained handkerchief, howling, "This is preposterous! I'll see you get ten years for this."

Vince rammed his fist hard into the ample stomach, sending his Lordship sprawling and retching on to the gravel path.

"How many more times do I have to tell you to shut your mouth."

The chauffeur, a young man in his mid-twenties, was slightly built with long brown wavy hair and a pouting mouth. Tom noticed he had outlined his large brown eyes with a hint of eye shadow.

He switched on all the lights in the hall, which led into a large expensively furnished living room. His Lordship, gasping and holding his stomach in some pain, slumped on to a gold upholstered settee. For the first time Tom was able to see the famous man properly. He was in his mid-sixties with the florid complexion of a heavy drinker, emphasised by a head of thick silver hair. Although he was well over six feet in height, he was not broad shouldered and his paunch made his body look out of proportion. His pale, blue eyes were damp with fear, sweat was running down his face and his breath smelled strongly of drink.

Tom had never been in such an ornate and exquisitely furnished room before and felt rather overawed by his surroundings. Solemn faces of long forgotten gentry stared blankly from their canvasses on the walls and the green, pink and gold ceiling matched the furnishings below. A huge tapestry above the fireplace had faded with age, but seemed to depict a hunting scene.

Vince was sweating beneath his balaclava and was becoming irritable. "Right, let's get down to business." He pointed at the shaking chauffeur. "You, where's the safe?"

Vince already knew the safe was in the library, but he didn't want to give away the identity of his informant.

The chauffeur stammered, "I'm sorry, I don't know – I just drive the car."

Vince walked over to the fireplace and picked up an ornate cast iron poker from the set of fireside dogs. The chauffeur watched with terrified eyes as Vince walked towards him and then cracked him across the face. He screamed, clutched his face and collapsed scattering rugs over the parquet floor. Vince turned his attention to his Lordship, shoving the poker into his face and screwing the point into a nostril, "Where's the fucking safe?"

"What safe? There's no safe," his Lordship stammered, looking myopically down the handle of the poker.

"I know there's a safe and if you don't tell me where it is right now, I shall pick your fucking brains out with this poker."

Vince applied more pressure, forcing the point into his victim's nostril.

"Take it away, I'll tell you," he gasped, holding his nose as Vince withdrew the poker. A small trickle of blood ran down his top lip.

"I'm waiting."

His lordship gestured to the left side of the room, "In the library – through that door."

Vince nodded to Frankie, who crossed the room and disappeared into the adjoining room. He soon returned saying, "I can't see a safe in there."

Vince was losing his patience. "I won't ask you again – where's the fucking safe?"

He grasped Lord Crantock by his hair, pulled him to his feet, then threw him across the room, sending him sliding on the polished wooden surface, where he ended up in a crumpled, miserable heap by the wall.

The panelled library had bookshelves on three walls, the fourth supporting a window flanked by floor to ceiling tapestries. A small table held a solitary Etruscan vase.

Vince picked up the vase, examined it and said, "A very nice piece of work – looks like an antique. I bet its valuable – we must take great care with a work of art like this."

He then hurled it at a bookshelf. His lordship watched horrified as the vase shattered into a hundred pieces. "That was an antique vase – this is sheer wanton vandalism."

"I repeat, where's the safe?"

Frankie, feeling around the walls, said, "I think I've found it."

He put pressure on one side of a cavity to reveal a safe concealed behind a panel of false books.

"It's an Argent Disque and we'll need the combination to get into it."

"OK. Then we'll force it out of the bastard," Vince said.

Back in the drawing room, the chauffeur, his face cut and bleeding had made another bid for freedom. Tom chased him into a kitchen and caught him fumbling with the bolts on an outside door.

"Where do you think you're going?"

"I've got to get out of here – look what he's done to my face."

Tom unlocked a pantry door and threw the chauffeur inside. There was a loud crash as he collided with a vacuum cleaner and assorted buckets.

"There you are, mate, you can read the meter while you're in there."

Back in the library, Vince was stripping the protesting peer down to his underwear, while Frankie held a knife at his throat.

Vince turned to Tom, "Find some rope as quick as you can."

Tom returned to the pantry, unlocked the door to find the swollen-faced chauffeur sobbing on the floor. Tom kicked him in the ribs, "Where do I find rope?"

The chauffeur howled in pain and gestured into the corner where a length of rope lay coiled.

Vince and Frankie tied his Lordship to one of his antique chairs.

"The combination," Vince demanded, "I want it now."

The apprehensive peer shook his head defiantly. "I can't remember it."

Vince picked up the poker and hit him across his nose. "You're a lying bastard."

There was a loud crack as the nasal bone splintered and blood poured down both nostrils. Lord Crantock screamed with pain and struggled to loosen the bonds.

His Lordship was not a pretty sight with his hairless, corpulent body spilling over his stomach in rolls of bloodstained flesh.

"You're trying my patience – once again, the combination."

Frankie produced a knife and scraped his thumb along the blade in a threatening gesture.

"Go to hell!" replied his lordship, with a sudden unconvincing touch of defiance.

Vince picked up a table lamp and removed the shade. All eyes in the room watched intently as he unscrewed the bulb and the lamp fitting. Using Frankie's knife, he began to pare away the outer covering of the flex revealing two bare wires.

Sweat poured down his lordship's face and he licked the blood still trickling down from his nose.

Frankie slit the peer's underpants with the knife leaving him naked and squirming in humiliation, fear and embarrassment. "This is an outrage."

"So you keep saying," Vince replied, wrapping the bare electrical wiring around his lordship's drooping genitals.

Vince slowly walked over to the wall and inserted the electric plug into the socket.

"When I touch this switch, you're gonna get the sexual experience of your lifetime."

"No, no, not that."

Vince grinned underneath his hood, "Thank you Lord Crantock, my colleague will now write down the combination."

****

"If you have no evidence, you can't hold me, so I'm going," Vince stated, with the confidence of a man who knows his rights.

Sergeant Milner leaned across the interview room table and shoved Vince back into the chair. "You stay where you are, Rothwell. I know it was you that pulled that caper."

"I read about that caper as you call it – very unpleasant for the poor old geezer." Vince took out a packet of cigarettes, selected one and tapped it on his thumbnail. He noted with satisfaction that his hands were steady and hoped Frankie and Tom held in adjacent interview rooms were being just as calm.

Vince took his time lighting the cigarette and then said, "I'm sorry sergeant, I'm forgetting my manners – would you like a fag?" He blew smoke directly into Milner's face.

Milner ignored the offer, coughed and continued, "The victim said in his statement that the gang leader was a man with a London accent and the man who opened the safe was – and here I quote – of diminutive stature. That seems to fit a couple of villains of my acquaintance and I'll lay money that number three was Tom Raggett."

Milner leaned back in his seat, crossed his arms and continued. "I take it you have an alibi for that night?"

"Why should an innocent member of the public need an alibi?" Vince asked.

"Don't play the innocent with me, Rothwell, you know what I mean. Where were you that night?"

"Well, sergeant, I did read about it in the papers, but you'll have to jog my memory. What day was it?"

"Stop playing silly buggers, Rothwell, it was a Friday or rather early Saturday morning to be exact."

"I always play cards on a Friday evening – it's relaxing after a hard week at work."

"Where do you play and with whom?" Milner emphasised the last word.

"At my place with the usual bunch of lads." Vince blew a stream of smoke into Milner's face and added, "We usually play through the night and I give the lads breakfast before they go home."

"And the lads would be Bowers and Raggett?"

"Yeah, with Harry Mindon and Pete Clooney."

"Alias Harry the Dip and Pete the Punter." Milner's voice was filled with sarcasm, "All honest upright citizens."

"Two of the best."

Milner stood up. "I'll be back in a minute."

"Don't be too long 'cos if I'm in here much longer, I'm calling my brief and he'll soon have me out."

Milner left Vince with a bored young constable and went next door to compare Frankie and Tom's statements. It came as no surprise that the stories were identical – they had spent the night playing cards at Vince Rothwell's house. Milner told the interrogators to release them and went back to the interview room.

"One thing puzzles me," Milner resumed, wafting away cigarette smoke with his hand. "The only thing stolen from that house was five thousand pounds from the safe. Nothing else was taken, although there were valuables lying around in just about every room. It seems a lot of trouble and risk to go through for five grand."

"Why ask me sergeant? As I told you in my statement, I was at home playing poker with the lads." Vince grinned, "Of course Lord Whatisname might be telling porkies."

"Why should he do that?"

"Ill-gotten gains, Sergeant, even peers of the realm must have the odd skeleton rattling about in their cupboard."

Vince stubbed out his cigarette. He was remembering his delight when the safe yielded twenty-eight thousand pounds. Lord Crantock certainly had a few skeletons and he didn't want the income tax people poking about in his cupboard.

"By the way, Sergeant," Vince said, pushing back his chair, "How's your wife these days, I hope she's well?"

Milner clipped his pen firmly into his jacket pocket. "You can go – but watch it, Rothwell. One day, I'm going to nail you to the floor."

****

"Where do want your tea?" Ray said, peering out of the cabin.

"I'll drink it out here, thank you, lad," replied Percy Randall. "Come and sit down for five minutes."

Raymond sat on the cabin roof with his mug of tea and grinned at the old man, who was staring at the canal from a seat on the towpath.

"It's been a long day," Ray said.

"Aye, and they don't get any easier."

"We should unload by Friday morning, all being well."

"Aye lad, and I think it'll be me last load. I've decided to pack it in and retire."

Raymond wasn't too surprised by this statement, for he had seen it coming for some time.

Percy sighed and continued, "I really made up me mind after old Wilf died. I don't know whether there's any future in boating for you, but I know there's none left for the likes of me."

"There's still some trade left if you're prepared to put the hours into it."

"Aye, mebbe so, if you have enough puff left in you. What will you do if I sign off on Friday?"

"Ocker wants me to come back. He's hiring an old butty boat called *Quercus* from Farden's yard."

"I know that boat – I didn't realise it was still afloat."

"Ocker seems to think its OK, so he's going to pair it up with *Ferntree*."

"Well, good luck to both of you. Why don't you try to take over these two?" he said, gesturing towards the boats.

"I think Ocker wants to run his own pair. *Ferntree* is still a family boat, even more so now they're married."

"Aye, a man takes on more responsibilities once he's wed. Ocker will be needing the money when the babbies start coming."

They unloaded at the mill and returned empty to the boatyard. Percy went into the office and said, "That's it, I've done me last load, it's time to pack it in."

The company clerk was unmoved. "Are you sure Mister Randall?"

"Aye, lad, I'm sure. I've made my decision."

"Will Raymond Hill be taking over your boats?"

"No, lad, he's going back to work with his brother."

"I wish you'd told us earlier. We could have had another crew waiting," the clerk said with a loud sigh.

"I'm sorry lad, but I've made my decision."

"Oh, very well, I'll work out your wages."

The clerk totted up the amount and wrote out a receipt with the company name at the top.

"I'll read it out to you, Mister Randall."

"Aye, lad, if you will."

"Forty-six tons to Croxley – that'll be thirteen pounds four and nine pence, plus four pounds seven and tuppence for back empty."

The clerk counted out the cash; "There you are, Mister Randall, seventeen pounds eleven and eleven pence."

Percy Randall had retired after sixty years of boating, but there was no gold watch presentation, no gathering of old friends and colleagues, no reminiscing speeches or pats on the back. The company clerk said a brusque, "Good-day," and returned to his bookkeeping.

****

A crimson sunset set the western sky ablaze, silhouetting the trees on a nearby hillside. A chill in the air sent the water birds scurrying to their roosting shelters and a solitary robin chirped its plaintive song. Ocker's hands were numb with cold after tying up the mooring ropes, and his stomach let out an audible rumble.

"Ray, I'm starving, I'll go and get the fish and chips."

"OK, I'll put the kettle on and get a brew going," Raymond replied.

Ocker walked along the towpath, passing several moored boats with smoking chimneys, and crossed the bridge. The lights from the fish and chip shop burned as bright as a beacon and a welcoming smell of fried fish wafted tantalisingly all the way down the street to the canal. Ocker's stomach let out an appreciative rumble as he hurried along the pavement. A figure appeared in the shop doorway, stopping to sample the contents of a bag of chips dripping with vinegar. He looked up at the approaching Ocker, his eyes squinting in recognition through the gathering dusk.

"Hi, Ocker, fancy seeing you here."

"Bloody hell, its Corky. Kitty said you were supposed to be in court this week."

"Yeah, we should have gone to court on Monday."

"We, meaning you and Ronnie Raggett?"

"Yeah, Ronnie's on the boat – we've gone AWOL."

"What do you mean AWOL?"

"It's an old army term, it means Absent Without Leave."

"But you've never been in the army have you?"

"C'mon, Ocker, don't be thick. We didn't turn up at the court."

"Doesn't that mean you're in trouble?"

"Yeah, we're on the run."

"What are you doing with a boat, you're not carrying again, are you?"

"Carrying, do me a favour, Ocker, I told you we're on the run."

"What happened to your lorry?"

"The coppers impounded it after they nabbed Alf at the docks."

"Kitty said you were arrested and let out on bail."

"Yeah, Tom Raggett bailed us out – he's got plenty of money. You should see the sports car he's driving."

"Why are you boating if you're on the run from the coppers?"

"We're going down to London. The last place the coppers will look for us is on a boat and when we get down there, we'll live on board until we get fixed up somewhere."

"Where did you get the boat?" Ocker asked.

"We nicked it from Farden's yard. Old Johnny Farden's in the hospital and the yard was locked up. The boat's been standing there for months, it took us half a day to get it started."

"Kitty was upset when you didn't turn up for the wedding."

"I was going to, but then I had Alf breathing down my neck. He's a vicious bastard if you get on the wrong side of him."

"I don't need reminding – it was Alf that shoved my Dad into the lock."

"Oh yeah, I was forgetting."

"Your Mum was upset as well when you didn't show up."

"Tell her I'm sorry when you see her. I don't know when I'll be back now I've got the coppers after me."

Ocker's stomach reminded him of his immediate duty with a series of loud squeaks and rumbles.

Corky grinned and punched Ocker's stomach, "Some things never change – like your guts screaming for grub."

"I'd better go and get the dinner," Ocker said. "Ray's working with me again."

"That's good," Corky said. "Any other news?"

Ocker's sun-tanned face creased into a broad smile, "Yeah! There is one bit of news – Kitty's pregnant!"

March 1962

"*TONIGHT!*" The singers reached the climax of their song, held the note and then turned to face their audience, who greeted them with rapturous applause.

The *West Side Story* evening at the Locarno was a great success. Everyone who attended was asked to dress as Jets or Sharks and most people had complied. Lucy had studied the still photographs in a magazine about the film of *West Side Story* that had opened that week in London. Her friends compared her likeness to the actress that played Maria in the movie, so Lucy had bought a white dress with blue facings and let her long dark hair rest on her shoulders. She wasn't the only Maria at the Locarno that evening, but she was quite the best looking. Her seventeen-year-old sister Brenda, who wore far too much make-up, had not been quite so successful as Anita.

A tall, spotty-faced youth wearing a leather jacket had taken centre stage under a fierce single spotlight that did little to flatter his complexion. He clicked his fingers in a menacing way and sang one of the songs from the show. Some of the young men on the dance floor ignored their partners and were prancing around, snapping their fingers in rhythm with the song.

Lucy was crazy about *West Side Story*. She constantly played the music on her record player and pinned magazine photographs on her bedroom wall. There was no regular boyfriend in her life, which was surprising, because at nineteen, Lucy was a very pretty, young woman. She worked at the same store as Kitty and shared a bedroom with her sister Brenda, who boasted a series of boyfriends and had lost her virginity before she left school.

Lucy on the other hand tended to be shy when it came to relationships with the opposite sex, but it was her temper that occasionally landed her in trouble.

She watched several boys cavorting around the dance floor, snapping their fingers and then leaping high in the air yelling, "Cool". The spotty-faced singer approached the end of his song. His face was greasy with sweat and he clapped his hands in time with the music. The band attempted an ambitious crescendo that was lost in the applause, as the saxophonist and trumpet player ended the song.

Among the crowd at the opposite end of the floor was a man, who had been observing Lucy for the past few minutes. Older and better dressed than most of the young men in the hall, his swarthy, good-looking face was topped by a fine head of black, curly hair.

He stared intently at the pretty girl in the white dress with the long dark hair who now became aware of his gaze. The band played a hectic dance number and couples were jiving. He threaded his way slowly across the dance floor towards the girl in the white dress, extended his hand, and asked, "Would you like to dance?"

Lucy noticed the man was wearing an expensive dark blue mohair suit and had gold rings on his fingers. He had the cheeky, confident smile of a man who knew his request would be accepted.

"Thank you for asking, yes, I would like to dance."

He twirled her around the floor, catching her hand with a powerful grip and spinning her around, the white dress flying up to reveal her pale shapely legs. At the end of the dance, he pulled her towards him and she had a momentary waft of his expensive after-shave lotion.

"What's your name?"

"Lucy."

"You look hot, Lucy, would you like a drink?"

"Yes, please."

He took her hand, paused and said, "By the way, my name's Tom."

"You're wearing a suit, but you're supposed to look like a Jet or a Shark," observed Lucy.

Tom Raggett pondered for a moment, then said, "Oh! I've come as a film producer."

She noticed his a positive manner when buying the drinks and how he pushed to the front of the queue, snapping his fingers to get the barman's attention. Holding the drinks in one hand, he led her to a table where two youths were sitting gloating over a pin-up magazine.

"Hoppit! This is my table, go find somewhere else," Tom ordered.

One of the youths was about to contest the claim, then saw Tom's expression and visibly withered. Meekly they stood up and surrendered the table.

Tom resumed the conversation, "So you're a *West Side Story* fan."

"Yes, I think it's wonderful. I've got the record and I just love the music."

"Do you live nearby?"

"Yes, with my Mum and my sister. She's come as Anita – I think she's dancing with some of the boys."

"Is she an older sister?"

"No, she two years younger than me."

"But she's dancing with the boys and not you."

"Oh well, she's a lot bolder than me."

"Do you have a boyfriend?"

"No, nobody special."

"I'm surprised."

"Why."

"You're very pretty."

"Thank you."

"Maybe you prefer older men rather than boys?" he asked, hopefully.

Lucy sipped her drink without replying. They sat on a balcony overlooking the dance floor, where scores of people milled around while the band took a break. Tom couldn't take his eyes off her face – he'd pulled the best-looking girl in the hall.

"Where do you work?"

"I'm at Girvans on the beauty counter."

"You seem well qualified for the job."

"Thank you, I enjoy it."

A couple standing behind Lucy seemed enraptured with each other and the man was running his index finger up and down the girl's thigh. Tom felt a quiver in his stomach muscles as he turned his gaze back to Lucy.

"What about your sister, what does she do?"

"Oh! Brenda works in a café as a waitress."

"What does your father do?"

"My Dad's dead, he was killed in an accident when I was little. My Mum had three of us to bring up."

"Oh! I'm sorry, was it a road accident?"

"No, he was crushed to death in a canal lock – he was a boatman."

Tom felt another quiver in his stomach muscles, but this time the origins were not sexual. He tried to appear casual in spite of the tension stiffening his body.

"By the way, what's your second name?"

"Hill, Lucy Hill."

She looked up and thought she caught a fleeting expression of recognition in his dark brown eyes. Tom held the gaze for a second and then picked up his glass and finished the drink, "Drink up and I'll get a refill."

He walked to the bar with the empty glasses, feeling his temples pounding. He grunted to himself, "Bloody hell! This girl must be Ocker's sister and Reg Hill's daughter and I was involved with his death at the lock all those years ago."

At this point, Tom realised he could make an excuse, go back to car and drive out of her life. She would be none the wiser about identity, but then again – he turned and looked back at her sitting the balcony, her dark hair outlined by one of the hall's spotlights, an he thought, "She is a right little darling."

Lucy was flattered by the attention she was getting from this man who conducted himself with such confidence and aplomb, and wanted to know more about him.

"Tell me, what do you do?" she asked him, when he returned with the drinks.

Tom paused for a moment, "I'm the personal assistant to a business man in Birmingham – he makes big decisions and I make sure they're carried out."

"What sort of business is it?"

Tom hesitated, "Oh – er, we're in property."

"Is business good at the moment?"

"Booming," Tom boasted, "Never better. I've just bought a new sports car."

"Is it one of those with an open top?"

"Yeah, I'll give you a lift home. We can have the top down, if it isn't raining."

The band returned to the stage and began to wrestle with the opening chords and complex rhythms of the next song from the show. Lucy, who knew every note of the music, watched and listened attentively. Tom pretended to participate, but like a chess player, was carefully plotting his next move.

The final song was a slow number, which Brenda had described as smoochy. Tom held Lucy very tight in a dance that approximated to a waltz. He could smell the perfume she had dabbed behind her ear and her hair had a vague scent of shampoo.

"I'd like to see you again, maybe take you out for dinner."

"All right, I think I'd like that," said Lucy and then pulled away and looked at him, saying, "I hope you're not married?"

Tom laughed, "No, no, I'm not married."

Afterwards they walked hand in hand to the car park where Tom's gleaming sports car was waiting. He was revelling in his role as a wealthy man about town and swung the car out of the car park into the main road, scattering the pedestrians. He had carefully thought out his next move.

"Did you know the *West Side Story* film has just opened in London?"

"Yes, I can't wait for it to come up to Birmingham."

"You don't have to," replied Tom. "I'll get tickets and take you to see it in London. We can go in the car."

****

When Lucy was young, she went to London with the working boats. She saw Brentford and Little Venice, Limehouse and Kings Cross. Her father would point to the place where the burning *Quebec* sank in the Blitz. At Limehouse, her father had forbidden Dolly and the two young girls to leave the boat because of all the bad people there. He told lurid tales of pigtailed Chinamen, who had opium dens behind their laundries, and of Lascar seamen, who would lure young girls away to a life of slavery in Far Eastern brothels. Lucy would peer out from the cabin hatch and watch the giant cranes lifting timber or bags of flour or sugar. The bags would be deposited into the holds of sea-going coasters, river barges and narrowboats. Sometimes a bag would split, cascading its contents over the dockers below. She would hear a volley of curses, which she pretended not to understand, but would giggle and repeat what she had heard to her sister. On one occasion, the bindings on a load of timber broke and three stevedores were trapped and crushed in the hold. She saw the ambulances arrive on the quayside and the injured men were removed and taken to hospital. Lucy's father returned to the boats saying that the angry dockers had come out on strike and the boats wouldn't be unloaded that day.

She remembered seeing the fine mansions by the canal at Regent's Park and the animals in London Zoo. Raymond said he once saw an elephant drinking from the canal and would point to an elegant bridge that spanned the cutting, known as Blow-up-Bridge. He told a story about a boat full of gunpowder that exploded under the bridge, blowing the crew into pieces.

Raymond also told stories of the murderers incarcerated in the prison at Wormwood Scrubs that they could see beyond the railway marshalling yards. Standing on top of the boats, they glimpsed the gleaming Great Western steam engines, resting before their next journey to Bristol, South Wales and the West Country.

Lucy had never seen London's West End and for years had believed it to be place solely inhabited by toffs wearing top hats and monocles, with elegant ladies in expensive gowns bedecked with jewels.

Now she was riding down Piccadilly in an open sports car towards the bright lights at Piccadilly Circus, and the people on the pavements looked just like her. Tom Raggett expertly manoeuvred the car between black taxi-cabs and tall red buses, occasionally receiving an admonishing toot as he cut across the front of a vehicle, forcing it to brake sharply.

He drove three times around Piccadilly Circus so that Lucy could enjoy the kaleidoscope of coloured lights, before turning the car into a dark side street and parking behind a theatre, where a group of people waited outside the stage door.

"They're probably waiting to get autographs," Tom said, as a limousine drew up and a blonde-haired man emerged to screams from several of the girls, who were waving books and pens.

Lucy immediately recognised the man as a singer currently topping the popular music charts. He waved his hand and blew kisses to the group of young girls, who screamed in appreciation. The young man signed a few books and then, with a cheery grin, he gave a final wave and disappeared into the theatre.

"Let's walk and find somewhere to eat," said Tom.

They walked hand in hand along dingy streets into a wider thoroughfare where there were several restaurants. After some hesitation, Tom chose a restaurant and secured a table by the window.

"What are you going to have?" Tom enquired, peering over his menu. The list was in French, but had an English translation underneath in small print.

"Could I have lamb, please?" Lucy replied with some relief, as most of the items on the menu were completely unknown to her. She looked at the people sitting at the next table to see which knife and fork she should use. Then she recalled reading a feature in one of her magazines that gave hints for girls on a dinner date and remembered her hair had been blowing about in an open-top sports car. She checked her bag and found her comb.

"Do places like this have a toilet?" she asked.

Tom laughed. "Of course, it'll be at the back, over there."

Tom ordered the meal with some aplomb. He had learned a bit about social niceties over the past year. This is what he had been dreaming about – sitting in a London restaurant with a good-looking bird and a new sports car parked outside. He picked up the wine list and decided that discretion would be wise. He was not yet a connoisseur of fine wines and couldn't distinguish an appellation côntrolée from a bottle of cheap plonk. He studied the contents and chose a German white wine that had a familiar name, then handed the list back to the waiter with a flourish. The waiter smiled and said, with just the faintest hint of sarcasm, "That should go very well with the lamb, sir."

After the meal, they walked to the cinema, joining a queue of people waiting outside on the pavement. Tom bought a souvenir programme and eventually they found their seats in the centre stalls. The cinema was far bigger and grander than Lucy's local picture house that everyone called the fleapit. She gazed around in awe at the glittering chandeliers, the gold-leafed balconies and the red plush carpets.

The film opened with aerial views of New York and then the camera paused over a playground where youths were playing a game of basketball. There was the haunting whistle that had become so familiar to her over the past few weeks as the camera zoomed down on to the playground, where a boy loses his ball to the leader of the Jets. His face suddenly filled the screen in sharp close-up and exclaimed, "Beat it!"

Lucy was already under the magical spell of her favourite musical.

Tom would rather have seen a western or a gangster movie, but admitted at the end that he'd enjoyed himself.

As they left the cinema, Tom said, "My brother's working in a club near here. I haven't seen him for a while, so I'd like to say hello and have a drink."

They walked into Soho along sleazy narrow streets lined with strip clubs and dirty stairways. A drunk was vomiting into the doorway of a bespoke tailor's shop and in another doorway, two more drunks waved bottles and shouted obscenities.

"Is it always like this?" Lucy said, wrinkling her nose.

"Pretty average night, I expect," Tom replied. "I don't get into Soho all that often"

They turned into a street where the gutter brimmed with discarded vegetables and broken pallets piled against the wall suggested the recent presence of a daytime market. At the end of the street was an alley brightly lit with garish neon signs, where Tom stopped outside a club bearing the legend 'See Nipples and Die!'

"Is this where we're going?" Lucy yelled above the noise of amplified music from the interior of the club.

"Yeah, this is where he works," replied Tom.

They stepped inside and Tom spoke to a large shaven-headed black man who nodded and told them to wait. Lucy stretched on to her toes to peer into the smoke-filled interior of the club, where the crowd of men encouraged a young girl, who was stripping to rock and roll music. The doorman disappeared behind a curtain, then reappeared accompanied by a young man who resembled Tom.

Tom squeezed Lucy's hand and said, "Just wait there for a minute." He pushed his way through the crowd of people, who were noisily clapping their hands to the rhythm of the music.

"Heyup, Ronnie, what are you doing in a place like this?" he said, shaking his hand.

"I know it's not much, but it's the best I can do now I've got the coppers after me."

"That was a bloody silly stunt you tried to pull with Alf."

"Yeah, I'm sorry about losing your bail money."

"Well, at least I can afford it." Tom nodded towards the curtain. "Are these blokes paying you?"

"Yeah, it's not a lot, but sometimes we chuck out a drunk who's loaded with cash and then Corky and me gives him a seeing to."

"Where the hell is Corky?"

"At the moment he's looking after the bookshop next door. It's all part of the same set-up."

The brothers paused a while to watch the stripper conclude her performance. After the applause subsided, Tom pointed towards the entrance, "You see that good-looking bird with the dark hair by the door. The one looking a bit anxious. She's with me and guess what – she's Ocker's sister and she's crazy about me. Sit her down in a quiet corner, get her a drink and, for Christ's sake, don't leave her on her own in this place or some randy bastard'll have her away for the white slave trade. I wanna speak to Corky. Oh! and whatever you do, don't tell her you're a Raggett."

"Bloody hell, you're not knocking off Ocker's sister are you?"

"Not yet, but I will be later, all being well."

"You're bloody mad. If Ocker finds out, he'll kill you."

"Let me worry about that. In the meantime, I'm going to see Corky."

Tom left Lucy with his brother and went into the bookshop next door. The unwashed windows were adorned with flyblown posters. He pushed aside a beaded curtain and saw shelves lined with magazines and sex-aid books. At the far end of the shop, Corky McCann sat on a high stool in a haze of cigarette smoke, looking bored as he watched for shoplifters.

Tom crept up behind him, slapped him on the collar and cried, "Gotcha!"

Corky let out a howl of protest, spun around, then recognised Tom. "Christ! I thought you were a copper. What the hell are you doing here?"

Tom grinned, "I've got Lucy Hill next door – Ronnie's looking after her."

"You mean Ocker's sister?"

"Yeah, I brought her down to London to see a film in the West End."

"Does Ocker know?"

"No, it's the first date – I met her at a dance hall."

"He'll go potty – he'll probably kill you!"

"Yeah, and that makes it all the more exciting."

Corky looked around furtively. "Come into the back room for a minute, I've got a hot punter in there."

Tom followed Corky through another curtain into a smaller room to a counter covered in pornographic photographs. In place of wallpaper, the walls were lined with erotic posters and various implements masquerading as sex-aids. A middle-aged man with thinning hair and prominent ears examined a set of explicit photographs with one hand, while the other hand vigorously worked away inside his trouser pocket.

Corky spoke to the man politely, "Good evening, sir, can I find something to interest you?"

"Oh! I'm just browsing," said the man.

"Is that what you call it?" Corky replied.

"Just browsing," the man repeated.

"In here you're buying, otherwise get out and play with yourself in the alley outside."

The man picked up a set of photographs, paid Corky a large amount of cash, and quickly left clutching his prize.

Corky put five pounds into his back pocket and shoved the rest into the till behind the counter.

"Thanks for bailing us out, Tom. I'm sorry we lost your money."

"You seem to be doing OK here, maybe some day you'll pay me back." He looked around the room again and sighed, "Be seeing you, Corky."

Lucy and Tom crossed Piccadilly Circus and stood on the steps underneath the statue of Eros, looking at the maelstrom of flashing coloured lights. A combination of the incessant noise of traffic and people, coupled with strong alcoholic drinks, plied to her by Ronnie at the club, had Lucy's head spinning.

Tom drove through heavy traffic back to Hyde Park Corner and along Knightsbridge to Kensington. He stopped outside a large hotel and wiped his brow with a handkerchief.

"I've had too much to drink to drive all the way back to the Midlands tonight – let's book in to this hotel."

Lucy guessed that the double room booking had been made earlier, but she didn't care. She had fallen in love with this good-looking, extrovert young man and was quite prepared to spend the night with him.

Half an hour later, she was lying in a double bed in her underwear, wondering what her mother would say, while watching Tom Raggett's muscular body emerging from underneath his shirt.

****

Frankie Bowers had become a slave to routine and he was bored. Every day was the same, starting with a morning session at the gymnasium, followed by an afternoon in the betting shop.

He left the gymnasium and crossed the road into a small municipal park, where a group of elderly people chatted in the spring sunshine underneath flowering cherry trees. Frankie chose an empty seat by a flowerbed aglow with daffodils. He sat down and opened his daily paper to the racing page.

An old lady on a nearby bench crumbled a loaf of bread and scattered crumbs for the birds. Very soon the area around Frankie was seething with cooing pigeons and twittering sparrows, squabbling and fighting for the bread. A young couple pretending to be amused by the antics of the birds occupied another bench.

Frankie peered over the top of the racing page and with some fascination watched the progress of the young man's right hand, which crept around the girl's shoulder and slowly descended to her right breast, where it came to rest with the index finger caressing the nipple. The girl laughed and glanced towards the old lady, who was still busy feeding the birds, and then looked sharply across the flower border at Frankie, who quickly raised his newspaper and continued studying the racing column.

After a few moments, curiosity forced his gaze above the paper and back to the couple, who were now passionately kissing, oblivious to any spectators. He noticed the man's hand had now found its way inside the girl's blouse and her hand was enthusiastically pressing his thigh.

Suddenly the man stopped his fondling, stood up and shouted at Frankie, "Hey you! You're a bleeding Peeping Tom?"

Frankie ignored him and resumed reading his paper.

The young man disengaged himself from the girl and walked across to confront Frankie. He stood with feet astride and said belligerently, "Listen, pervert, I'm talking to you."

Frankie carefully folded his newspaper, sighed and said, "Do yourself a favour sonny and go back and play with your lady friend."

The young man leaned forward sneering, "I reckon you've got a serious problem."

Frankie replied, "No son, it's you that has the problem."

He braced himself against the seat and fiercely kicked the young man between the legs. The man's eyes popped, his mouth expelled a loud gasp of air and his hands groped at his groin. The girl wrapped her arms around the man's shoulders and led him away, screaming, "Look what you've done you bastard, you've ruined him."

Frankie grinned, "It's ruined him for today that's for sure."

He watched the couple leave the park and disappear from sight before returning to his newspaper.

Endless rows of runners and riders in the newspaper and the warm spring sunshine made him drowsy. His chin dropped on to his chest and the newspaper had fallen limp on to his lap, when someone tripping over his feet disturbed his slumbers.

"Oh! I'm terribly sorry, I'm getting clumsy in my old age," said the old lady, who was feeding the birds. She had dropped her bag on the ground, tipping various items around Frankie's feet. One of the articles was an expensive gold cigarette case that had a small inlaid insignia, and the engraved initials J.C. Frankie picked it up and examined it.

"You should look after this, it looks expensive," Frankie observed.

"Oh yes, it belonged to my husband, a retirement present. They had his initials put on it."

He noticed as she took the case from him that she carefully handled it with a handkerchief, and then dropped it into her bag, "Thank you again, I'm sorry to disturb you."

Frankie sighed, picked up his newspaper, and resumed his examination of the runners and riders.

****

Frankie Bowers was still bored. He lay on his bed watching the sky darken through grimy windows and wondering whether to liven up his life by doing a job that didn't involve Vince Rothwell. Underneath the mattress he was lying on was about five hundred pounds left from the Crantock robbery, so there was no immediate financial pressure, but he felt the need for a little bit of excitement.

Tom Raggett had bought a flash new sports car and was having a marvellous time with his girlfriend. Vince had his large house in the suburbs, big car and nice clothes. All Frankie ever did was go to the pub, the betting shop and the gymnasium.

Vince was under constant harassment from Sergeant Milner and his colleagues and because of that, he had not planned any fresh escapades.

The overgrown tree in the street outside his window had a sheen of new leaves and an appreciative blackbird was in full springtime song. Frankie eased himself into his pillow, took a swig from his bottle of beer and closed his eyes.

The room was in complete darkness when the doorbell rang. He rubbed his eyes, yawned and went downstairs to answer the door. Sergeant Milner stood on the step, backed up by two uniformed police constables.

"Hello, Frankie, this is not a social call, so don't put the kettle on."

"Sergeant Milner, what the hell do you want?"

Milner produced a warrant card and wafted it under Frankie's nose.

"I have reason to believe you are in possession of stolen property and I have a warrant to search your premises."

"Do me a favour, sergeant, there's nothing here."

"I'm hoping to do you for more than a favour, sunshine," Milner replied, and then turning to the two burly constables, "OK lads, upstairs front room, turn it over."

The constables turned out all the drawers, tipping their contents on to the floor. Milner sifted through a pile of socks, underwear and betting slips. Inside the rickety wardrobe were Frankie's one and only jacket and a battered old suitcase. Milner opened up the suitcase, which contained nothing but a few old newspapers.

It took them another minute to find the money under the mattress.

"Look Sarge, it must be pay day," the constable said, waving a brown envelope filled with notes.

Milner riffled through the notes and whistled, "So where did this lot come from?"

"I won it on the horses."

"He won it on the horses," Milner repeated in a voice laced with sarcasm.

"I spend my day studying form. I don't have anything else to do since I can't work."

"You mean since you can't go out thieving."

"No, I'm medically unfit. The doctor said I've got fluid on my lungs."

"Do you expect me to believe that? What rubbish you talk!"

One of the constables, who was feeling through the pockets of Frankie's jacket, said, "Hey Sarge, look at this!"

"Just a minute, let me see that."

Milner picked out a gold cigarette case, which he held up between two fingers.

"Well, well Frankie, what do we have here?"

Frankie's gaze was riveted on the cigarette case. He opened his mouth and then decided to say nothing.

Milner examined the case. "Oh look, it's engraved J.C. – but your initials are F.B. Don't tell me it belongs to your Uncle Joe!"

"I've never seen it before."

Milner continued. "There seems to be a sort of coat of arms as well as the initials." He pretended to look thoughtful. "Well now, J.C. could stand for James Crantock and I reckon that's his family crest."

"Fuck you, Milner, you've planted that, this is a bloody frame-up."

"Ill-gotten gains, Frankie. I'll bet this is on the list of stolen property from the Crantock robbery."

Frankie opened his mouth and once again declined to say anything. He knew that only cash was taken in the robbery and this plant must be with the collusion of Lord Crantock.

Then he recollected the incident in the park earlier that day. He remembered helping the nice old lady pick up that same cigarette case.

His fingerprints were all over it!

Milner was enjoying himself. "Do you know, I think we've caught you red-handed this time, Frankie boy."

****

Tom Raggett was smitten. He hadn't intended it this way, but it had happened. His previous conquests ended with a casual promise to meet again soon – a promise he usually had no intention of honouring. His seduction of Lucy Hill had gone exactly to plan, but the execution had proved a memorable experience that left him both exhilarated and guilty. He wanted to see her again and again, although he knew a liaison with Ocker's sister would prove difficult and dangerous. He realised it was time to admit his identity.

He stopped the car at a lay-by and said, "Would you like to go for a walk?" She pulled down the vanity mirror and combed her long, dark hair, while Tom closed the open top of the sports car.

"There's a canal bridge over there, we can walk along the towpath."

They crossed the road and Tom squeezed through a narrow gap between the bridge parapet and the hedge. He held out a hand to help Lucy, who wasn't wearing suitable shoes for scrambling down steep slopes.

Once she was through the gap, Tom lifted her by her waist down to the towpath, held her level to his face and kissed her.

"Where are we, I don't recognise this stretch of the cut?" Lucy said.

"This is the 'Ampton Pound, your family probably didn't work this far north."

Lucy furrowed her brow, "Only a boatman would know that term 'Ampton Pound – you said it like a boatman."

Tom paused, then plucked up courage to say, "That's because I once was a boatman."

"You – you were a boatman!" she said, staring at him in amazement.

"Lucy, I have a confession to make."

Lucy smiled and then frowned, as his expression became serious.

"Alright, go ahead and confess."

"I haven't told you my name."

"You have, it's Tom. Do I need to know more?"

"My second name is Raggett."

Lucy looked at him full in the face, her brow furrowed, as she took in this information. She heard her dead father's voice echoing in her head, "Raggetts always mean trouble." Resentment between the two families, kindled by old vendettas, had etched deep hatred into her consciousness.

"You are Tom Raggett."

She emphasised the word 'you' and then repeated with some venom, "You are Tom Raggett – I've just spent the night with Tom Raggett!"

She swung her fist at his face, but he caught her by the wrist. "Lucy, these canal family feuds are ridiculous. Most folk are fighting each other over something that happened in their grandad's time."

"You killed my dad, that wasn't in my grandad's time. I was there with Mum and Brenda down in that cabin, while you and your brothers pushed him into the lock."

"No, Lucy, I was steering the boat. It was Alf who pushed your dad."

Lucy burst into tears and ran down the towpath with Tom in pursuit, scattering a flock of ducks that dived into the water, quacking their displeasure. Eventually, she slipped on a patch of mud and splashed into a puddle, her legs wet and shiny shoes soiled. She sat on a damp grassy mound and snuffled, "I hate you, Tom Raggett."

"Yeah, I know."

"How long have you known who I am?"

"In the dance hall, when you told me how your dad died."

"You think it's OK to admit it, now you've got what you wanted."

"No, Lucy, it's not like that."

"It seems like that to me. Now you can tell your pals how you bedded Ocker's sister."

"I won't be doing that. I fell in love with you the minute I saw you at the dance."

Lucy sat scraping the mud from her shoes and was quiet for a while. Then she looked up and said, "Ocker will kill you when he finds out."

Ocker said, "We're looking for a back-load and we'll take most things within reason."

The clerk turned in his chair and looked at a blackboard on the wall behind him. Details of boats, their steerers, destinations and cargoes were almost indecipherable after many rubbings-out and re-entries.

"Company boats have got all the Midland loads, you'll be lucky to get anything this week."

"Are you sure?" Ocker's voice raised to a tone of desperation. "Look here, mate, my wife's about to have a baby, so I'm missing her wages. I can't afford to go back empty."

"Well, I'm sorry about that, but your best bet is to get back up to the colliery and load again as quick as you can."

Ocker paused at the top of the office steps, pushed his long black hair underneath his cap and looked around the yard for Raymond. Lines of boats were moored in a canal lay-by at the end of the yard, their chimneys smoking as evening meals were being prepared.

On one boat, a man was carefully cleaning the brasswork on his boat's chimney, while his neighbour sat on his cabin roof rolling cigarettes from a tin of tobacco. Several children played with a ball, which eventually bounced into the water.

A woman came out of a boat cabin, leaned over the side of the boat and scooped the ball out of the water in a colander. She threw the ball to the children, telling them in a loud voice to play away from the edge of the canal.

Raymond appeared on the far side of the yard, lighting a cigarette as he limped across the cobbles.

"Any luck with a load?"

"Nothing doing, the company boats grabbed the lot."

"We'd better get moving in the morning."

"I hate going back empty," Ocker said, removing his cap and running his fingers through his hair.

"How long before the baby's due?"

"Kitty said it could be anytime next week."

"Hadn't you better wait at home until it's born. She's not going to like it if you're down here in London when it comes."

"I can't afford to wait around, I've got to get some money on the table."

"Blimey, Ocker, you sounded just like Dad when you said that."

The return journey was made in pouring rain. At one lock, a broken mechanism meant that boats were tailing back in both directions. Ocker had an argument with the skipper of a loaded pair of company boats that came up behind and demanded priority because they had a load and Ocker was empty.

Ocker had been like a bear with a sore head all the way back to the colliery. Before loading up with coal for the paper mills and heading south, he made a telephone call to check on Kitty, who was now living with her mother while he was away. Raymond reluctantly agreed to this rapid turn round. "Christ, Ocker, I could do with a break. It would be nice to have a bath and sit down with a drink. Apart from that, I haven't seen Susie for nearly two weeks."

"Look Ray, I haven't seen Kitty either and she could be having the baby any time."

"So let's take a few hours off."

"We can't afford to stop without back-loads," Ocker replied with some finality. "Come on Ray, untie those ropes and let's get moving."

The rain stopped and a golden dawn was followed by a glorious day with blue skies. They were away from their moorings before the chill had left the air and continued their journey south on the meandering canal.

A heavily built young man with brawny arms poking from a check-patterned shirt slowed his motor down and shouted "'Owdo!" Ocker responded in kind, cutting the speed of *Ferntree* as the two motorboats passed each other. The young man cheerfully passed the time of day until he was out of earshot. He repeated the courtesies again when he passed Raymond, who was steering the butty boat a rope's length behind. Ocker waved his free hand to the wizened elderly man steering the approaching butty and exchanged the time-honoured greeting, "'Owdo, mate!"

Ocker looked at the boats on their journey north from London, heavily loaded with timber. He grimaced and spat into the water, "Bloody company boats, we could have done with a load like that on the way back."

The warm sun began to disappear as a huge build-up of cumulus cloud drifted in from the west, heralding the advance of a storm. As he approached a tight bend in the canal, he glanced over his shoulder to check the rope length on the butty boat. Immediately, he was aware of Ray frantically signalling to pull in.

They were close to a road bridge next to a lock and a pub – a popular stopping place for boatmen. Ocker pulled *Ferntree* into the edge, jumped off the boat and secured the ropes to the mooring bollards. Ray brought *Quercus* behind and not alongside the motorboat as Ocker expected.

"What's to do, Ray?"

"I'm taking on water from somewhere – there's a flood on the cabin floor."

The gunwales of the fully laden butty boat were ominously low in the water.

"Christ! It looks like its going down. When did this happen?"

"I dunno. I noticed it wasn't pulling properly and then I saw the water down there."

Ocker clutched his head in anguish, "There's no way we gonna get this unloaded before it sinks."

The boat creaked ominously as it settled lower into the water. Ocker removed his cap, ran his fingers through his hair, then kicked the boat in frustration.

Ray tugged at Ocker's shirtsleeve, pointing towards the bridge where a man was waving his arm.

"Heyup Ocker, that looks like George to me," Ray observed, shading his eyes against the sun.

"What the hell is he doing here?"

Cousin George appeared on the towpath, picking his way around muddy potholes in brightly polished shoes. "By heck you boogers took some finding." He stopped short of the declining butty boat, looked long and hard and pointed a finger. "Bloody hell, that's a bit low."

"Low be buggered, it's sinking."

"How much you got on?"

"Twenty tons for the mills."

"You're not going to make it with that booger."

"Any more bright remarks, keep 'em to your bloody self," Ocker retorted. "Anyway what are you doing here?"

George tapped his forehead, "Sorry Ocker, I've come to get you. The Jag's parked in the pub car-park."

"Look, George, this is no time for jokes, I've got forty tons to shift and a sinking boat."

"No, no, you don't understand, it's Kitty. She's in the hospital and she's gone into labour. She asked me to find you and get you back for the birth."

Ocker looked helplessly at George, Raymond and the listing butty boat. "What the bloody hell to I do now?"

Raymond intervened. "Ocker, go with George, and see your baby, I'll sort out the trouble here." He turned to George with an aside, "The way he's been slave-driving recently, a sinking boat will be a rest cure."

****

Christmas 1962

It was baby Alan Hill's first Christmas and he was the centre of attraction as he sat in his chair in the front room of Cousin George's new house. George was celebrating Christmas with a house-warming party for family and friends and everything in the house was ostentatiously new or freshly painted. The showpiece, an indoor swimming pool with concealed lights, led to a terrace overlooking a spacious garden. Pool and terrace were separated by a long, electrically-operated, double-glazed patio door, which George proudly demonstrated.

"You see all I have to do is press this button and the door opens and closes."

He pressed the button and the door silently opened, sending a blast of icy wind into the swimming pool area. Several voices howled in protest and George hastily reversed the process.

"What do you think of the new house?"

"Very impressive," observed Kitty. "There's a bit more room than in those cabins on *Proteus* and *Valentine*."

"That's exactly what me Dad said when he came in tonight." George said, swilling the contents of a brandy glass in the manner of a connoisseur. "There's still time to join me in the motor business. There's no brass to be made in boating."

"It's all I know George," Ocker answered. "Anyway I'd be no good in an office job."

George looked around the pool area and beyond into the lounge where Kitty's mother, Gracie, was playing with the baby.

"Nice little kid you've got there. Think of the future, Ocker, not just for you, but for him and Kitty."

Ocker's cheeks began to flush with a combination of annoyance and George's brandy.

"By the way, I invited Lucy and her new bloke, but they haven't turned up," George said, looking around the room at his guests.

Kitty grimaced and tried desperately to change the subject, but Ocker had got the bit between his teeth.

"Do you have any idea who Lucy's bloke is?"

"No, who is he?"

"I'll tell you who he is, it's Tom bloody Raggett. That's who my sister has moved in with."

George blenched and attempted to drink from an empty glass. Inside the expensive suit was an acutely embarrassed man. "I'm sorry mate, I had no idea."

Ocker nodded. "'Scuse me, George, I need another drink."

Kitty looked at George and shook her head. "Let him go, he'll cool off when he's had a drink. I just wish we could have avoided that subject tonight, but I suppose that's expecting too much with all these friends and relatives around."

"I hope she's not expecting – you know what I mean?"

"No, George, not as far as I know, and that situation doesn't bear thinking about. For goodness sake, don't make that sort of joke in front of Ocker or he'll probably hit you."

Ocker headed towards a quilted bar gleaming with gilt and strip lighting, which dominated one side of the lounge. He felt uneasy in all this sumptuous luxury, comparing it to the cramped little rented flat he shared with Kitty and the baby. He wondered whether Kitty was thinking along the same lines.

"What do you think of George's new place?"

Ocker turned and saw the grizzled, lined face of his Uncle Billy smiling up at him.

"Oh, it's very nice, he's done very well."

"It's good to see your own flesh and blood doing so well, but I wish it had been from carrying." Uncle Billy's face assumed a wistful expression, "Not that I've got anything against the motor business, as you well know, and I know there's no future in boating."

Ocker sighed and poured himself another drink. He wasn't used to brandy and two glasses had already gone to his head.

Uncle Billy continued to press his subject. "I'm glad I retired when I did, but I do miss the old days. It was hard work, but they were good times. Do you remember those years when you worked with Rose and me when George was in the army?"

"I remember Auntie Rose's cheese and bacon pies."

"Aye, she always made a good pie."

Auntie Rose sat in a corner clutching a mince pie and staring blankly across the room. A stroke had left her paralysed down one side. It had become more and more difficult for Uncle Billy, who had to do everything for her, so she lived in a council rest home during the week and came home at weekends.

"How is Auntie Rose?"

"Not so good," Uncle Billy answered. "She don't know where she is or what she's doing most of the time."

"Can she talk?"

"Sometimes she says nowt for days and then she'll talk non-stop for half an hour. She thinks we're still on the boat and she wants to know where we're tied up." Uncle Billy changed the subject, "Ray tells me you lost the butty."

"Yeah, the booger sunk with a full load. I had to salvage the boat to cover the costs."

"How are you managing without a butty?"

"Sub-contracting – the company hires me a butty and gets me back-loads. I can't survive on my own anymore without back-loads. I'm still running *Ferntree*, so at least I can get some maintenance on the motor done by the company."

"Are you making enough to keep your wife and babby?"

"As long as I get a back-load on every trip." Ocker rested his elbow on the bar and added, "I don't know how Ray's gonna manage this winter with his knee. Have you noticed his limp these days? It's getting worse. He can hardly straighten his leg out some mornings."

"Aye, the cut's no place for a man who isn't fit. He'll have to be doing summat else before he's much older."

Ocker usually enjoyed meeting his relations, but on this occasion was finding them increasingly depressing. Uncle Billy excused himself to attend to Aunt Rose, who had crumbled her mince pie over George's new carpet. George's wife, Gwen, was taking flash photographs of the children in a group around baby Alan, who smiled broadly at all the attention he was receiving.

Gwen showed off the expensive camera to her friends, telling them it was a Christmas present from George. Now she wanted a picture of everybody and was hustling them to form a large group. Raymond saw Ocker receding into the background and said, "Come on, Ocker, you've got to have your photo done."

"I don't like photos."

"Too bad, Gwen wants you in her group and she's paying for the drinks."

George fussed around, arranging a group that looked like a school photograph, with guests sitting on the floor, some on chairs and the rest standing. Ocker stood partly hidden behind Kitty's bouffant hairdo as Gwen took the photograph.

Afterwards, Raymond limped across the room towards a window and pulled back a corner of the curtain. He motioned towards Ocker, "Hey, look at this, mate."

Ocker went to the window, shielding his eyes to peer out into the dark. George's garden was under an inch of snow and a blizzard was blowing. Ocker clutched his head, "Oh! Bloody hell, that's all I need!"

****

An industrial dispute at the factory prevented the boats from being unloaded. Ocker and Raymond waited for four days behind several other loaded pairs in freezing weather with six inches of snow on the ground and conditions worsening. Finally the boatmen agreed to help each other by unloading the boats in teams, shovelling the coal on to the quayside. It was better than doing nothing and hard work kept them warm. After dark, they sat in the pub discussing the deteriorating situation in both trade and the weather. Sammy, an old retired boatman, came into the pub every night and sat there in his own chair next to the fire, telling tales about working on the canals in his youth. Sammy was partly deaf and almost blind in one eye, but these deficiencies did not diminish his enormous capacity for ale, especially when someone else was buying. On this occasion the inclement weather had spiked his memory.

"I remember the winter of 1894, when all the canals froze over."

"Blimey Sammy – how old are you?" Raymond asked.

"I beg yer pardon, young feller," Sammy replied, cupping his hand behind his ear.

"I said, how old are you?" Raymond shouted.

"I was born on me dad's boat at Braunston in 1873," the old man said proudly, and looked around at the group with large watery blue eyes. "They were none of them newfangled motors then. We only had 'osses in them days."

"Go on about the winter."

The old man paused to confirm he had everyone's attention. "It were so cold, me dad's 'oss froze to death on the towpath, even though he was covered in blankets."

There were murmurs of sympathy from the group and then the old man cackled with laughter, displaying two surviving nicotine-stained teeth. "The canal company did this experiment up on the Old Main Line. The ice breakers couldn't cope wi' the cold, so they brought in a boat wi' this big boiler and pumped boiling water into the cut to melt the ice."

"What happened?"

The old man cackled again and vigorously slapped his knee, "They couldn't keep the fire going and the bloody boiler froze – it was stuck there until the spring!"

The old man coughed, spat accurately into the fire and drained his glass. He rapped it on the table and looked expectantly around the group.

Raymond took the old man's glass and refilled it. Sammy gulped down half the contents and then produced a clay pipe from his waistcoat pocket. He stuffed it with a few strands of an evil-smelling weed from a tin box and then struck a match, ignited the mixture and produced clouds of noxious fumes. The old man sat back happily into his chair, puffing his pipe as his companions gasped for air, wafting the pall away with their hands.

"What have you got in that pipe?" Raymond gasped. "Horse shit?"

"It's me own special mixture," Sammy replied. "I've smoked it all me life and me dad before me."

"And how long did he live?" Raymond asked

"I don't know how old he was and I don't think he knew either, but he must have been over ninety."

The old man removed his pipe, spat into the fire again and continued his reminiscences. "I remember one winter we were stuck fast at the bottom end of the Moira Cut waiting for the ice-breaker. After a few hours, me and some of the lads went off to look for it and we found it outside the Navvy pub. They'd stopped for a quick one and had been in there all afternoon. They were as drunk as lords when we got 'em out onto the boat. Them boogers were swaying already, so we had to go on the boat and help them."

"Did you get back to your boats?" Raymond asked.

"Ah well, they were all singing their heads off like a bloody church choir when one of 'em looks round and said, "Ere we've lost young Hiram'."

"Where was he?"

"The poor little booger had fallen in. We stopped and went back to look for him, but he'd gone under the ice. They found him ten days later blowed-up like a balloon, poor little sod."

"How old was he?"

"He were only sixteen, but he weren't old enough to hold his drink."

At this point Ocker emptied his glass and said to Raymond, "I'm off to phone George and leave a message for Kitty."

The telephone box outside the pub was in darkness and stank of urine. Ocker used a torch to dial George's number, stamping his feet in the intense cold as he listened to the buzz, buzz, over the line and imagined George and Gwen sitting in their centrally heated house, watching television.

"Is that you, George?"

"Yeah, who else would it be. Is that you, Ocker? Where the hell are you?"

"Still in London, we've just unloaded today. Tell Kitty I'm coming back empty with the motor 'cos there's no back-loads."

"What's happened to the butty? You haven't sunk the bugger again have you?"

"Don't be bloody silly. It's Ray's knee, he can't do another trip in this cold. It's taking him half an hour to straighten his leg out in the morning and his limp gets worse every day. I'm leaving the butty at the depot and Ray's off back home on the train."

"Do yourself a favour Ocker and go with him. Have you heard the weather forecast?"

"I've heard it's bad up on the summit level, so I'm hoping it'll be better by the time I get there."

"I think you're bloody mad. There's a message from Kitty, she's got her old job back at the shop."

"Who's looking after the baby?"

"She says her mum's going to have him."

"Last time I spoke to Kitty she said her mum wasn't well." George paused and Ocker could hear Gwen's voice shouting in the background. George had another message, "Listen Ocker, Gwen's just seen the weather forecast on the news. There's another blizzard coming in tonight, they're warning people to keep off the roads unless their journey is necessary."

Ocker ended the conversation with a sigh. "Thanks, George, you've made my day."

Raymond helped Ocker break the ice around the boat before he left for the station. He took extra blankets from the butty boat and stocked the cabin with food.

Raymond was concerned. "Are you sure you want to do this?"

Ocker looked at the lowering grey sky, shivered and pulled his woolly hat over his ears. "I'm not looking forward to it but I..."

Raymond interrupted, "Yeah, I know, you've got to get some money on the table."

The engine started in a cloud of grey smoke and Raymond watched his brother edge *Ferntree* through cracking ice into the centre of the canal. As he approached a bridge, Ocker increased the speed of the engine, sending thickening ice splintering with a metallic 'zing' as the boat's bow ploughed through the water. He turned and waved before disappearing under the bridge, leaving Raymond to limp away in the opposite direction towards the station.

The canal had frozen from bank to bank except for a narrow channel in the middle kept free by the occasional moving boat. At each lock, ice built up behind the gates making it difficult to enter. Ocker used a boatman's pole with a hook at the end and grappled with the ice, pushing and breaking the heavy floes. Steering a boat and working through wide locks is a difficult task for a solo boatman in good weather, but in these conditions it tested Ocker's experience to the full.

It was just after mid-day when he met a pair of boats travelling in the opposite direction. The boats had just passed through a lock and the crew left the gates open as Ocker approached. The skipper, standing in deep snow at the lock-side, wore an expression of deepest pessimism.

"Heyup, young feller, you'm not taking that boat over the summit on your own are you."

"'Fraid so."

"You'll never make it, son. It's taken us all day to get across, and it's getting worse all the time."

"I've gotta try, I can't afford to tie up."

"Well, good luck to you, son. I hope you'm stocked up wi' enough food."

"Yeah, I'm OK and at least the locks should be set in my favour from now on."

The first flakes of the impending blizzard began to fall as Ocker left the lock. The intense cold penetrating his clothing increased the feeling of loneliness as he battled against the elements. Sometimes his thoughts turned with bitterness to his sister, Lucy, who, at that moment, was sunning herself in the Canary Islands with Tom Raggett.

The blizzard intensified as the afternoon wore on, making steering through the narrowing gap in the centre of the canal even more difficult. Glowering, snow-filled clouds squeezed out the little daylight left in the afternoon as darkness began to close in. Despite his thick gloves, Ocker's hands began bleeding as slivers of ice on the frozen ropes tore into his flesh. Each successive lock increased the agony as thickening snow made progress around the lock gates slippery and dangerous. At one point, an off duty lock-keeper took pity on him, abandoned his warm fireplace and helped him work through three locks.

After closing the gates on the third lock, the lock-keeper stuffed his windlass into his belt and said, "C'mon son, tie up and come back to the cottage and we'll have a brew-up. The wife's got a stew in the pot and we can spare a plateful for you. It's bloody daft carrying on in this weather."

Ocker thanked him, but stubbornly continued his journey through the gathering gloom. When he eventually reached the canal's summit level, he managed to moor the boat with some difficulty, before collapsing exhausted on to his bed.

He awoke at dawn, still fully dressed apart from his boots. His feet, protruding from the blanket, were frozen despite his heavy woollen socks. He became aware of a strange silence. The familiar sound of lapping water was missing and there was no birdsong. He stood and pushed back the cabin's hatch, which dispatched a shower of snow down the back of his neck. For a moment, he found it difficult to comprehend the scene in front of him – an immense fall of snow throughout the night had obliterated the landscape.

Mounds of snow indicated the position of the towpath leading to a flatter section, where snow was lying on the ice-covered surface of the canal. Branches of overhanging trees were groaning with accumulated snow.

He pulled on his boots and stepped on to the boat's counter platform, shaking the snow from the tiller, and heard an ominous creaking as his weight moved the boat, grinding it against the packed ice.

The first thing he did was to re-light the stove that had gone out during the night, then put a lamp in the engine-room. He crouched in front of the stove, feeling the warmth gradually raising the temperature in the cabin and thawing out the water, which had frozen inside the kettle. After a few minutes, a mug of tea and some bread and cheese revived his spirits and once again he ventured outside the cabin.

It began to snow again, backed by a penetrating northerly wind that plucked at his overcoat and threatened to blow away his cap. He looked around him trying to discern the distant hills, now almost invisible after the blizzard. Undulating farm country lay between the hills and the canal, with just a few isolated cottages and farmhouses dotted here and there in the bleak landscape. Ocker estimated that the nearest villages were about three miles back along the canal, or five miles in front of him.

He desperately needed his shovel, but it lay with the coal stock in the cratch at the front of the boat. It was seventy feet away underneath a white hump that indicated the position of the boat's fore-end. The depth of the snow on the towpath was impossible to judge, so he jumped and landed in waist-deep snow. His feet lost their grip and falling backwards, he slid on his back on to the frozen canal in a flurry of snow and ice. For a few moments he lay spluttering, kicking out his feet, and then realising that the ice was so thick that it was able to support his weight, he gingerly stood up and edged his way along the boat's gunwales to the cratch.

Ocker spent the next two hours shovelling snow from the boat and its surroundings, until it was possible to reach the towpath without further mishap. He brewed up more tea and settled down, wrapped in a blanket to review his situation.

The boat was frozen solid in the ice and there was no hope of an ice-breaker freeing him from this isolated section of the summit level. He was a mile or so from the nearest road bridge and three miles from a village. The nearest point of any habitation was a farmhouse with a furiously smoking chimney on the opposite side of the canal, just visible half a mile across the fields. A farm accommodation bridge, about three hundred yards away, would have a track leading to the farmhouse.

He had enough food and fuel to keep him going for several days, but would soon need fresh water. He also needed to telephone George to pass on a message to Kitty, warning her of his current plight. Ocker managed to start the engine, which produced clouds of black smoke staining the pristine whiteness, until another blizzard late in the afternoon soon obliterated the discoloration. Before darkness set in, he shut off the engine and drained off the cooling system to avoid the frost splitting the cylinder-block.

Afterwards, he cooked a hot dinner and lay on the bunk huddled in blankets, listening to his battery radio. The news was all about the weather and the equally cold relationship between Kennedy and Khruschev. After the news, he listened to music by a new pop group from Liverpool called the Beatles and wondered if Kitty was doing the same, while she fed the baby in the warmth at home.

Ocker looked out next morning to find the overnight blizzard had deposited several inches of fresh snow. After breakfast, he took his shovel and repeated the previous day's labours. Only then could he turn his attention to the prospect of reaching the distant farmhouse. With a water-can strapped to his back, he began clearing a path towards the bridge. Very soon a wall of snow confronted him, five feet high between him and the bridge. Attacking the drift with the shovel, he found it difficult to ascertain where the towpath ended and the canal began. The whiteness was disorientating and he found himself straying into the bushes and, at other times, towards the edge of the canal. Eventually, he reached the bridge and, still digging, scrambled on to the track. Looking back he was amazed to see the wavering path he had dug, when he was convinced he had followed a straight line.

Ocker continued digging through the drifts along the track towards the farmhouse, feeling the sweat hot on his skin underneath the layers of clothing, in sharp contrast to the icy frost biting his nose and fingers. Presently, he reached a point in the lane where the farmer's tractor had flattened the snow, and he slipped and slid along the patterned tracks made by the tyres. The farmhouse, with its chimney still belching smoke, loomed ahead and Ocker staggered exhausted into the farmyard.

"That's far enough – what's your business?"

Ocker turned and saw a man standing in the shadow of a barn.

"What do you want – what are you doing here?" The man stepped out into the light and Ocker saw he was brandishing a shotgun.

"I've got a boat on the canal. I'm iced in and I need fresh water," he stated, waving the decorated water-can. "I also wondered if I could use your phone to tell my wife I'm OK."

"If you think I'm letting a bloody dirty gypsy in my house you can think again," growled the farmer, releasing the safety catch on the gun.

Ocker, who hadn't washed or shaved for several days, was unaware of how scruffy and dishevelled he looked.

The farmer's attitude became increasingly menacing. "I've had enough of thieving boat gypsies, here today gone tomorrow, bloody rootless itinerants."

Ocker tried to reason, "Look, conditions are bad. I wouldn't ask for a favour if I wasn't desperate."

The farmer gestured with his gun, "There's a tap over there at the back of that barn, fill your can and be on your way – and don't let me see you round here again."

Ocker found the tap and finding it frozen solid, shrugged his shoulders in defeat and trudged through the snow back to the canal.

****

"We'll have a bottle of this – Rio – Rioojar."

The waiter cocked his head and looked puzzled, saying, "Que?"

Tom Raggett jabbed a finger at the wine list, "That one!"

The waiter leant forward peering at the page. "Ah! Rioja," he said triumphantly, and then carefully pronounced the word phonetically, "Reeocker."

Lucy laughed, "Sounds more like my brother's name than a wine."

The waiter squared his shoulders, took a deep breath and after a moment announced, "Eeet is a ver' good vin from Espagne."

"We'll have it now while we're waiting," Tom said, waving his hand in dismissal.

The restaurant had a terrace overlooking the sea and was situated on the east side of the island away from the boisterous breezes of the Atlantic coast. Evenings were warm and a full moon reflected in the calm waters of the bay. Sweet-scented orange trees bordered the terrace where tables were discretely arranged to allow maximum privacy.

"I can't believe we're eating outside in January," said Lucy.

"Stay with me Lucy and we'll be here every January," Tom said, then added confidently, "From now on we'll live in the sun."

"What a wonderful idea!" said Lucy. "No more ice and slush."

"And no more cold hands and feet," added Tom with a lascivious grin.

The waiter returned with the bottle, removed the cork and splashed a taster into Tom's glass. Tom stared at the glass for a moment and then remembered what convention expected of him. He picked up the glass, swilled the wine around his palate and nodded sagely to the waiter.

"The wine is OK, sir?" the waiter questioned, rhetorically.

"Yeah, it's fine," replied Tom.

"You did that like an expert," Lucy laughed, and then added with an edge to her voice, "I bet it was Vince who taught you how to do that."

"OK, but Vince does know about wine, so I've watched what he does."

"I often wonder just what it is that Vince does?"

"How do you mean?" Tom queried.

Lucy said, "I still don't know exactly how you earn your money."

"Don't worry about it."

"But I do worry," Lucy insisted. "Vince Rothwell is so sharp, he'll cut himself one day. Quite frankly I think he's a crook."

"Vince is OK. Alright so he does a bit of dodgy dealing from time to time."

"Like when you finished up in jail."

"Alright, so I got caught with a load of bent gear – it could happen to anybody."

"Rubbish! Honest people don't go to jail."

"A lot of honest people end up starving like Ocker. Where's he at this moment? Probably flogging his guts out somewhere on a frozen canal."

"Cousin George has done well and he's not a crook."

Tom laughed, "Obviously you haven't driven one of his second-hand motors. I've seen 'em, they're known as scrapyard specials."

"That's as maybe, but I still worry. Since I moved in with you, my mum won't talk to me anymore, I've given up my job and Brenda says Ocker will murder me next time he sees me. What happens if you go to jail again?"

The question tailed off into the night as the waiter arrived with the first course.

Lucy examined her plate, "What's this?"

"They're calamari," Tom answered." It's squid – it's one of Vince's favourite meals."

Lucy sighed, "It's always Vince. Sometimes I think he owns you body and soul."

"At the moment he probably does," Tom replied.

****

"The police were here again today looking for Corky. I told them I haven't seen hide nor hair of him for eighteen months, but I don't think they believed me."

"Don't worry about him, mum, he'll turn up one fine day, full of himself as usual." Kitty's attempt at cheerfulness fell flat as she tried to conceal the worries that seemed to mount higher every day.

Gracie McCann caught her daughter's mood and enquired, "Any news about Ocker?"

"Nothing at all, mum. Ray saw him leave the wharf and since then nothing's been seen or heard of him."

"How long is it now?"

"Nearly two weeks, Ray reckons he's snowed up on the summit level. All the roads and villages round there have been cut off since the turn of the year. Ray says he'll probably have to sit it out until the thaw."

"I hope he's alright for food. You know how Ocker likes his grub."

"Ray said he was well stocked up when he left."

"How are you managing? If you're running short I can lend you a few bob, though I've not much as you know."

"Thanks, mum, but I'll manage." She kissed her mother's wrinkled forehead, "As long as you can look after the baby, so I can go to work."

"I hope I can go on looking after the babby, but, to be honest, Kitty, there could be a problem." Gracie continued, "I've been to the hospital to get the results of the x-ray."

Kitty saw the expression in her mother's thin face and feared the worst. "Go on, mum, what did they say?"

Gracie took a deep breath. "There's something on my lung."

Kitty took her mother's hand. "They can't always be sure about these things. Can you get a second opinion?"

"I think that was a second opinion."

They sat in silence for a while, Gracie staring into the fire, while Kitty, stifling the tears welling up in her eyes, studied a row of icicles hanging from the gutter on the adjoining property. Little droplets of water hung at the bottom of each one and then fell with a plop to be replaced by the next in line. Kitty vaguely wondered whether this indicated the start of the thaw. She felt lonely and vulnerable, desperately wishing Ocker would suddenly return.

"Kitty, I've got to get something off me chest and now seems to be a good time as any."

Kitty's attention returned to her mother sitting by the fire, looking old and haggard. Her father's clock relentlessly ticked away on the wall, sharing the faded wallpaper with yellowing photographs of smiling holiday-making relatives in forgotten bygone days. A fragment of an old Christmas decoration hung by a nail high in one corner of the room and Kitty wondered why she had never noticed it before.

"Yer dad was a good man, he worked hard and was a good provider. It was a hard life on the boats, but we never went hungry and he thought the world of you and Corky."

"What are you trying to say, mum?"

"I'm not sure how to put this," Gracie paused and rubbed her wrinkled cheek. "There was one thing yer dad couldn't do."

"Go on."

"He couldn't make babies."

"What! But how..." Kitty's voice tailed off.

"Wilf never knew, he really thought you and Corky were his own."

"Mum! I came here this afternoon to collect the baby and have a cup of tea. First you tell me you're ill and now this. What next?"

"I'm sorry, Kitty, but it seemed like the right time to tell you, things being as they are."

Gracie looked at Kitty with an expression of deep sadness as she waited for the inevitable response.

"If Dad wasn't my real Dad, then who the hell was my real father?"

Gracie took a deep breath and confided, "Joe Raggett's your real father, yer blood father – but Wilf was yer father in every other respect."

"Joe Raggett!" Kitty blurted. "Joe Raggett was my father?"

At first Kitty felt she couldn't breathe. Then she burst into tears, running into the next room where the baby was peacefully slumbering in Gracie's bed. She lay down next to the baby, wiped her eyes on the pillowcase and slumped back with the pillow over her face. Her arms and legs began to shake uncontrollably as anger, fear and sadness swept over her, all at the same time. After a few minutes the baby began to stir, making little whispering moans, and Kitty sat up and secured the baby's blanket.

She took a few deep breaths, composed herself and returned to the sitting room, where her mother sat miserably staring into the fire.

"What about Corky?"

Gracie snuffled, "Yes, him too. Joe Raggett is his father as well."

"You made the same mistake again?" It was a rhetorical question and Gracie nodded dumbly.

They sat in silence for some time, Kitty desperately trying to make some sense of the bombshells delivered by her mother.

"I suppose it's the Raggett blood that's made Corky go off the rails. That would explain a lot, he's got the Raggett character and I've inherited Raggett looks. I don't know what Ocker's going to do when he hears about this. His son has Joe Raggett for a grandad, and his wife..." her voice tailed off.

Kitty sat glaring at the remnant Christmas decorations in the corner while Gracie continued. "Joe Raggett was a good-looking man, a bit of a rogue but I suppose that was part of his attraction. There was never any real love between him and me, and I know he's fathered loads of kids all along the cut from Lunnun to Birningum."

The inexorable ticking of the clock broke the silence that followed.

Kitty said, "I'm taking the baby home."

"Will you be back tomorrow?"

Kitty choked, "Yes," picked up the sleeping baby, put him into his pushchair and stepped out into the darkness. The frost seemed to freeze the tears on her cheek as she stumbled and slipped on the frozen pavement.

She turned into a main road where council workmen had shovelled piles of snow into the gutter. The snow had turned into slush by the traffic and then frozen again. Access points had been cut every fifty yards to allow pedestrians to cross the road and into one of these Kitty stepped, anxiously looking for a gap in the traffic flow. A group of boys were throwing snowballs at passing cars, yelling in triumph whenever they scored a hit.

The snowballing youths, pushing and shoving each other into the slush piles, elbowed Kitty out of their way and one of them aimed a snowball at an oncoming double-decker bus. The snowball smacked against the windscreen right in front of the driver, who instinctively braked and showered slush over Kitty and the pushchair. The driver angrily sounded his horn and passed safely on his journey.

Kitty was soaked and the baby began to cry. She looked up at the sky and shouted, "Oh! bloody hell!" at which point it began to snow again.

****

Ocker had lost all count of time since his radio's battery expired. Until then, he had voices to listen to and could keep in touch with the news. Now the silence was broken only by his own raucous cough. For several days he had felt unwell, probably due to drinking melted snow before it had properly boiled. Food supplies were becoming ominously low, although he still had plenty of fuel for the stove and the lamps. He relieved the boredom by shovelling snow from the towpath after each new covering and reading books in the cabin.

Sometimes there was a bright day when the sun appeared, but the promise of a thaw ended later in the afternoon with winter's cruel renewal.

A scuffling and rattling of tins woke Ocker in the middle of the night. The culprit had vanished by the time he had raised the cabin hatch, but he saw his sack of rubbish had been knocked over. In the cold light of dawn, he could see the tracks of a fox in the snow. Apart from the occasional bird, this was the first encounter with any form of life since his ill-fated meeting with the farmer almost two weeks ago.

The fox returned later that day. It approached the boat from the canal, sniffing the air. Ocker could see the poor animal was emaciated, the ribs clearly sticking out of its fur. He kept very still as the animal advanced across the frozen surface to about ten feet from the boat and stopped. It then paced sideways, afraid to come nearer, but hunger was overcoming its fear.

Ocker, eating corned beef from a tin, felt obliged to share his meal with the unfortunate animal, despite his own shortage of food.

"Here you are, boy! C'mon, take it!" He held out a slice of beef towards the fox, which whined and slavered in frustration. Finally he threw the beef on to the ice. The fox snapped it up and returned to the centre of the canal to devour it.

Ocker shared the rest of the tin with the fox, which squatted on the ice and ate every scrap. When lunch was over, the fox trotted away along the canal, leaving behind a set of tracks, the memory of a meal gratefully shared and the answer to solving Ocker's present predicament. At first he had quite enjoyed the thrill of isolation, but now he had become desperately bored and hated feeling cold and unwell. He was determined to try and reach the road and the fox's departure pointed the way. He decided to chance walking along the frozen surface of the canal where the snow hadn't drifted.

Early next morning, he locked the boat and began his icy odyssey towards the bridge a mile distant. Occasionally, he would prod the canal's surface with his shovel, but it held his weight and after a cautious half-hour, he rounded a bend and with relief saw the bridge. Very soon, he was standing in a lane covered in snow compacted by the passage of vehicles. The welcome sound of an engine drew his attention to a tractor that eventually turned out to be driven by the farmer, who had sent him away two weeks ago. The farmer glanced once at the wild, bearded man on the bridge brandishing a shovel, hesitated, then accelerated on along the lane. Ocker yelled expletives that cast doubts on the farmer's parentage and started to walk towards the hillside village and civilisation.

Spring 1963

Vince Rothwell handed his ticket to the collector and greeted the man who was to be his host for the day. "Hello Lenny, how's business?"

"Can't complain, Vince" he replied with a grin. "I'm making a living."

"I'll bet you are, you old bugger," Vince said, looking around the station concourse. Shops, bars and cafés were dotted around its grimy perimeter and groups of people stood or sat on their luggage, anxiously studying the departure board. Flocks of pigeons swooped from the station rafters on to the concourse and squabbled over scraps of food. Occasionally, a railway official bustled by, trying hard to appear busy.

"It doesn't change much does it?" Vince observed.

"Well, the diesels are cleaner than the old steam engines."

Vince punched the arm of his companion, "Nice to see you again, you old bugger."

Lenny Delancy was a short, heavily-built man in his mid-forties, with thinning dark hair, a swarthy complexion and an accent which betrayed his South London origins. He wore expensive clothes with the casual manner of a well-to-do man who could afford anything Saville Row had to offer without denting his bank account. Lenny owned a gambling club in Covent Garden, a couple of strip clubs and four pornographic bookshops in Soho. There was an office at the back of his gambling club that served as the base for his multifarious activities. Apart from a few brushes with the police in his teens, Lenny had managed to keep ahead of the law and had no serious convictions.

They took a taxi from outside the station and the two men within earshot of the driver talked about football and the political scandal that was making news. The taxi went into Mayfair, crossed over Berkeley Square, turned into Curzon Street and then down a maze of narrow streets, stopping outside a fashionable restaurant.

"I'm lost – where the hell are we, Lenny?"

"We're in Shepherd Market, where the whores wear furs and get shagged by cabinet ministers."

"So I've been reading in the papers," Vince said, and added sarcastically, "I think it's bloody disgusting. If I paid any tax, I'd be really offended."

It was an excellent meal. Vince leaned back in his chair, lit a cigarette and said, "That was nice Lenny, but I reckon there's more to me being here today than just admiring the décor."

Lenny grinned, lit a cigar and said, "Why don't you smoke one of these – fags are dead working class?"

"No thanks, mate, they make me cough." Vince was getting impatient, "Come on, mate, I'm busting a gut."

Lenny leaned forward over the table, speaking quietly in a conspiratorial manner. "That job you did on Crantock got a lot of attention in certain places."

"Go on."

"I hear some of the heavy mob down the East End were a bit upset."

"Do I have a problem?"

"I should stay this side of Petticoat Lane. No nostalgic visits to your old stomping grounds."

"OK, fair comment."

"I'm not prying, but I reckon you earned more than was reported in the papers."

"A lot more."

"You only took cash. That was a clever move."

"There was plenty, we didn't need anything else. Anyway, it's difficult to shift stuff when the owner is so well known."

"The lads down South London didn't think a Brummie mob had the bottle to pull a job like that, so I told them you were an East End lad on the run and you was as sound as a bell."

"Nice to know I'm appreciated."

"What about the help, are they clean?"

"Yeah, I used two of my best lads, but one of them has just had a pull that was a complete stitch-up. The other one does the driving and helps around the shop, so to speak."

"Is he a good driver?"

"One of the best."

"Does he gamble, booze, do drugs?"

"No. He's had one pull for receiving, apart from that he's clean. He's even settled down with a bird."

"Sounds OK." Lenny leaned so far across the table that Vince choked on the cigar fumes. "I'm putting a team together for a big job. This could be one of the biggest ever."

"Are we talking cash?"

"We're talking cash alright – in millions."

"Millions!" Vince pursed his lips and softly whistled, "You have my full attention, mate."

"I take it you're interested."

"Yeah, but why me?"

Lenny pulled on his cigar and continued, "The job will have to be done quickly. I'm going to need guys with muscle and plenty of bottle."

Lenny tapped his cigar on the edge of the ashtray and looked around, checking to see whether any of the other lunchtime diners were within earshot.

"Most of the team are my lads from South London, but we've added a few more from a firm on the South Coast, who have had experience in this sort of job. I want you 'cos you're an old mate and I know you'll not shit your pants in the middle of the job. I can also use your lad as a back-up driver and a bit of extra muscle if things get a bit dodgy."

"How big is the team?"

"About sixteen."

Vince pursed his lips and blew a perfect smoke-ring.

"It can't be a bank, unless you're turning over the Bank of England."

Lenny stubbed out his cigar, leaned back in his chair and blew a plume of smoke towards the ceiling. He grinned and said, "We're gonna rob a train."

"Bloody hell, Lenny, that's Wild West stuff! How you gonna do that and where?"

"Dunno yet, some of the lads are working on it this week and we're having a meeting on Saturday."

"What sort of cut are we talking about?"

"Even split all round, minimum about a hundred grand each in used notes, but could be more if everything works out OK."

Vince opened a silver cigarette case, chose a cigarette, tapped the filter on his thumbnail and grinned, "Lenny, you can count me in and that applies to Tom, my driver, as well. He'll follow me, especially for that sort of money."

"I'll give you a bell when we've got more details. In the meantime, we'll have a drink at my club and then I'll get one of my lads to give you a lift back to the station."

Lenny talked endlessly about his clubs and shops in the cab on the way to his office, but never mentioned the subject that was dominating Vince's thoughts.

"A hundred grand minimum – a hundred fucking grand. This is it, Vince boy. The big one you've been waiting for."

He made affirmative grunts, pretending to concentrate on Lenny's conversation while staring out of the cab's window as the blur of streets flashed by. "You haven't heard a bleeding word I've said, have you?"

"Sorry, Lenny, no offence, mate."

The club was located in a narrow street near Covent Garden station. Lenny paid the cab, while Vince stood on the pavement in a daze, preoccupied with his thoughts.

"A hundred fucking grand!"

Lenny laughed, "By God Vince, you look like you could use a drink."

"I've got to admit, you've taken the wind out of me sails."

"Come on, mate, it's only money." Lenny pushed open the door to the club, turned to Vince and winked, "Except this time it's a lot of fucking money."

Although it was a midweek afternoon, the tables were busy with punters playing roulette, blackjack and chemin de fer. They crossed the floor, Lenny acknowledging greetings from members of his staff, and went into a well-furnished office at the rear of the club. A small, balding man wearing thick horn-rimmed glasses was sitting at a desk, totting up rows of figures in a ledger. Lenny spoke to the man, who closed his books, shook hands with Vince and went across to a well-stocked bar in the corner of the room. He poured a large brandy for Lenny and turned to Vince.

"What can I get for you, Mister Rothwell?"

"Whisky will do for me, thanks."

He handed Vince a generous glassful, made his excuses and left the room.

"It always pays to get yourself a good accountant. This guy's got a eye for detail and understands money."

"He understands how to fill up a glass as well."

Lenny laughed, "He says he was once a barman in a synagogue – he doesn't believe in short measures."

Vince was eager to return to the main subject. "Will you be on this raid?"

"I dunno yet, probably not, but let's see how things work out."

Lenny changed the subject, made himself comfortable in a leather chair behind his desk and returned to anecdotes about his youthful exploits around the Elephant and Castle.

"We had a midget called Benny, who we used to hide in offices and factories before locking-up time. Me and the lads would roll up with the vans about two in the morning and wait for Benny to open up the gates. We'd be in, sort out the watchman if there was one and clean out the place. This worked out fine until one night we turned over this factory down New Cross. Benny had been waiting in this old shit house in the corner of the yard and had been taken short. Of course there was no water laid on and no paper, so the silly bastard wiped his arse on an envelope from inside his coat pocket. Trouble was it had his address on it and he ended up getting five years. It ruined a bloody good scam, but you couldn't help laughing. Anyway he never grassed on his mates and we saw his old lady OK for readies while he was inside. She was a midget as well, but what a boozer! She used to sit in this pub down the Old Kent Road, downing pints of Guinness like they were going out of style."

Lenny's reminiscences were interrupted by the telephone ringing. He sat back in his chair with his feet on the desk next to several framed photographs. Vince noticed that most of the photographs were portraits of children and realised that he had no knowledge about Lenny's private life and wondered if these kids were his. Vince looked around the office, noting the quality of the fixtures and fittings. Although he and Lenny came from similar backgrounds, it was obvious that Lenny had acquired an extra touch of class along the way. Vince was aware that his own club back in Birmingham looked garish and flashy in comparison to what he was looking at now. After an hour or so, in which Lenny took several telephone calls, he pressed a button, saying, "Get Ronnie to bring the car round and take Mr Rothwell to Euston Station."

He escorted Vince out of the club, where a car was waiting.

"We'll be in touch soon. In the meantime, make sure your lad is primed. There's one or two real hard cases on this job, so warn him to keep shtum – not a word to anyone and that includes his bird. If he's not reliable, then leave him out."

"Don't worry Lenny, Tom will be OK."

Vince sat in the front seat next to the driver who enquired where he was going to from Euston. "I'm going back to Birmingham."

"You're not a Brummie are you?"

"No, I'm a Londoner. I moved up there a few years ago."

The driver grinned and said, "I was born in Brum and moved down here."

Vince studied the young man's profile and thought he detected something familiar in both his features and his accent.

"What's your name, son?"

"Ronnie – Ronnie Raggett."

Vince watched the young man expertly manoeuvre the large car through the traffic and thought he recognised the same confident manner of Tom Raggett.

"Do you have any family, Ronnie?"

"Yeah, I've got family in the Midlands."

"Any brothers and sisters?"

"Yeah, I've got two brothers."

"Oh yeah, what do they do?"

"Tom works for a guy in Brum – sort of driver and personal assistant."

"And the other brother?"

Ronnie laughed, "Oh, he's in the nick!"

"And your dad?"

"Oh, he works on the canals in the Midlands. He used to be a boatman, but now he's a maintenance man. He's getting on now, so he'll be retiring soon."

"Does Tom ever talk about his employer?"

"No, he doesn't talk much but, I think his boss is a bit of a fly boy."

Vince grinned, "Well, it's nice to meet you, Ronnie. I'll say hello to Brum for you."

****

In 1891, fifteen thousand boatmen and women worked on Britain's inland waterways. By the end of the disastrous winter of 1962-63 just a handful was left.

The company clerk shook his head, "Sorry, mate, but we're shutting down and selling up."

Ocker frowned and said, "What do you mean?"

"I've got a job in the council office. I start next Monday, so I'm just clearing up the paperwork and paying off the remaining bills, then I'm off. That winter killed off the trade, it's all gone elsewhere off the water. You can't blame the customers, they were desperate for coal and we couldn't deliver. It's nobody's fault but that's it, they're using road transport, so they've gone for good."

The clerk placed his elbows on the desk and tapped his teeth with a pencil. Some of the office fittings had already been removed, leaving dusty outlines as a reminder of where they had been. On the notice board a new white sheet explaining the company's decision to go out of business was pinned on top of outdated papers already yellowing with age.

Ocker slumped into a chair, removed his cap and scratched his head, "What the bloody hell do I do now?"

The clerk, busy folding papers and fitting them into envelopes, didn't reply.

Ocker had returned to *Ferntree* the day before the ice-breaker arrived. The thaw had already started to melt the ice, but there were too many frozen layers to move the boat independently. He could hear the ice-breaker when it was over a mile away, splintering the canal's surface into icy shards. A group of men stood on the boat's flat deck, rocking the vessel from side to side as the motor drove it forward. They stamped their feet against the cold, smoked endless cigarettes and shouted ribald encouragement to each other. A ragged procession of boats, all recently released from winter's grip, followed resolutely behind the ice-breaker. Ocker had prepared the engine that coughed, spluttered and started, staining the melting snow with a cloud of black smoke. Presently, he took his place behind the cavalcade and returned very slowly back to the Midlands.

The clerk finished his envelope packing and went into the back room. He returned holding two mugs of tea. Ocker looked up to see the clerk offering him a mug of tea. "You look like you could do with a cuppa."

Ocker warmed his hands around the mug, "Thanks, mate."

"How long were you iced in?"

"Dunno exactly. Too bloody long, by the look of it."

Ocker removed his cap, scratched his head and sipped his tea. He looked around the scruffy office with its peeling paintwork and dirty windows. This inevitable feeling of decay was eating into his life, especially as Raymond had announced his intention to accept Cousin George's offer of a job in the motor trade. Now relations with Kitty were becoming strained and Ocker was under even more pressure to pack up boating and take a land-based job.

"You haven't earned a penny since before Christmas," Kitty said.

"I'm sorry, but how can I work when the boat's snowed in."

"Ray says the companies are closing down and most of the families are packing in. George has made him a good offer, so he's leaving the boats."

"Oh, he'll be back when things improve and the sun starts to shine again."

"His knee is never going to improve while he's working on the canal, and he knows the only way he's going to avoid being a cripple for the rest of his life is to take an inside job."

"Then I'll have to manage on my own."

"With only one boat, you'll be working seven days a week to make a living. I'll never see you nor will the baby. As it is with my mum looking after him all day, the poor little bugger soon won't know who his real mum and dad are."

Kitty paused, glared at Ocker, then continued, "I don't know how much longer my mum can cope with the baby, so what do we do then? I certainly can't afford to give up my job."

There was a long silence before Ocker cleared his throat and said, "The boat is the only thing I know. I'll stick with it until the summer."

"Then what? You know it's not going to get any better."

"I suppose I'll have to get a job in a factory or work for George."

Kitty sighed. "You seem to have made up your mind, so I suppose we'll have to leave it at that. By the way, I need to see George very soon because my mum is desperate to find Corky. She's asked me to help and George is the only person I can think of who could find him."

"The last time I saw him he was with Ronnie Raggett on their way to London in a boat they'd nicked from Farden's yard."

"I hate to say it, but I think Lucy might know where he is."

"Then George can sort it out 'cos if I see her with Tom Raggett, I'll probably throttle the pair of 'em."

"Thanks, Ocker, you're a great help," Kitty said, and left to attend to the baby, who had begun to exercise his lungs in the next room.

****

It was the end of a wet day and most of the stallholders in the street market were beginning to pack up their wares. Some of the locals were buying perishable produce at reduced prices.

Raymond and George picked their way between the stalls, trying to avoid puddles and jostling customers. One stallholder shook a sodden tarpaulin over George as he passed by. The man grunted an unconvincing apology in reply to George's outcry.

The market ended at a squalid alley, where sleazy strip clubs and seedy bookshops plied their dubious trade. A blind beggar seated against a wall played a monotonous tune on a harmonica. He shook a few coins in his cap and George dropped him a shilling, which was accepted without comment.

They stopped outside a club where red and blue flashing neon signs repeated 'Girls! Girls! Girls! Now showing Boobs in the Wood!'

"This could be like the place Lucy described," said Raymond.

George turned back the collar of his raincoat, straightened his tie and pushed back his dripping hair, "OK. Let's go in."

A large black man with a shaven head stood inside the doorway and directed them towards the paybox.

"We're not here for the show – we'd like to see the manager," George said, apprehensively.

"I haven't seen you here before. What do you want?"

"We're looking for a relative and we think he might work here."

"Oh yeah! What's his name?"

"His name's McCann, known as Corky. He'll be with a mate called Ronnie Raggett," George answered.

"Never heard of 'em. Now look 'ere, man, don't waste my time. Get lost."

Raymond retreated into the alley. "Have we come all this way for nothing?"

George moved along the alley and pointed to a bookshop next door to the club. "Didn't Lucy say Tom Raggett went into a bookshop? Let's go in and ask some questions."

A pale-faced young man with long greasy hair sat on a high stool at the back of the shop, picking his teeth with a spent matchstick. In front of him, magazines showing girls in various stages of undress were displayed all around the walls, beneath racks of well-fingered books. Behind the youth hung a beaded curtain, beyond which was where the hard pornographic material sought out by most of the shop's clients was to be found.

George and Raymond went into the shop, stared at the shelves for a moment and then turned towards the shopkeeper. "Excuse me, I wonder if you know a guy called Corky McCann or his mate Ronnie Raggett?"

The long-haired youth eyed George with suspicion, removed his toothpick and asked, "Who wants to know?"

"We're his relatives. His mother's very ill and wants to see him."

The youth, unmoved by this information, returned to his dental probing. George produced a five-pound note from his top pocket and waved it in front of the young man's face. The young man looked up and said, "He used to work here."

George withheld the note. "I need to know where he is now."

The youth's gaze was fixed on the five pound note. "I think he's working for the Guvnor."

"OK! And who's the Guvnor?"

The young man frowned, "You're the Old Bill, ain't you?"

"No, we're not. I told you we're Corky's relatives."

"OK, it's Mister Delancy. He owns this shop and the club next door. Corky and Ronnie work at his gambling club."

"Where is it?"

"It's called the Mirabelle. Don't know the address."

The youth snatched the five-pound note, stuffed it into his trouser pocket and resumed the attack on his dental tartar.

****

The diesel train slowly rumbled and wheezed towards the end of the platform. Some people in haste to avoid the crush, flung doors open and jumped to the platform while the train was still moving. The train screeched to a halt a few feet short of the buffers and a stampede of passengers headed for the ticket barrier.

Corky standing on the station concourse just to the left of the barrier had a perfect view of the departing crowd. He had performed this recruiting exercise several times and there was usually at least one potential victim on the Manchester train. Corky moved a few paces forward as he spotted his quarry. A girl carrying a battered old suitcase had the familiar bewildered expression of someone arriving at a large crowded London terminal for the first time, not knowing what to do or where to go. Corky could see she had good legs and probably a neat figure hidden under her coat. She handed her ticket to the collector and Corky noted with satisfaction that it was for a single journey only.

He pushed through the crowd and placed a hand on her shoulder, "Excuse me, miss, are you Sally Jones from Manchester?"

The girl turned to see a smartly dressed, good-looking young man smiling at her.

"No, I'm sorry, my name's Pauline. I come from Blackburn."

When the girl shook her head, Corky could see dark roots at the base of the blonde hair.

"I'm sorry, too, but I've never met her and you fit her description."

"I'll be on me way then."

"Do you know where you're going?"

"No, I've never been to London before." The girl began to walk away.

"Hold on a minute. Is there someone meeting you?"

"No, I don't know anybody in London," the girl replied, a little uncertain of what she may be getting into. She had read stories about London in magazines and what could happen to unwary girls, but this young man seemed very nice.

"I've got a car outside, I can give you a lift. Finding your way around in the underground during rush hour can be difficult if you've never done it before. I came down from Birmingham last year for the first time, so I know what it's like."

"What about your friend – Sally whatsername?"

"Oh! She doesn't seem to be coming. You're the only pretty young blonde carrying a suitcase on the train."

The girl blushed and smiled as Corky picked up her case. "Come on I'll buy you a cuppa at the buffet."

The dispersing crowd scurried like mice towards the underground and taxi ranks. Corky steered the girl across the station concourse into the cafeteria and found seats at an empty table. He bought tea and chocolate cake, sat down and opened a new packet of cigarettes. "Do you smoke?"

"Thanks, I'm gasping for a fag."

He lit their cigarettes with an expensive lighter stolen from a wealthy drunk he and Ronnie had escorted to his car outside the Mirabelle.

"Look, I can help you if you haven't got anywhere to stay. I could even find you a job, to get you started."

The girl was hungry and between puffs of her cigarette, she wolfed down the chocolate cake, leaving chocolate stains around her mouth. Corky had a sudden urge to lick it off for her, but first he had to play his trump card.

"I'm going into the gents, so if you feel nervous and don't want anything to do with me, then this is the time to scarper. London's a big place and you'll not see me again. I won't try to follow you, so it's up to you, but I hope you'll still be here 'cos I think we could be friends."

Corky left the cafeteria without a backward glance. He knew the girl would watch every move he made and then make her decision. Corky made this approach with all the girls he accosted on the station and only once had he returned to find the girl had gone. If she was still there, he would take her for a drive around the West End, show her the sights, buy her a meal, then take her back to his flat. Tomorrow he would take her down to the photo studio to meet Andy and Clive, where she would be persuaded to do some artistic posing and start to earn her living in the big city. Corky would keep her on at the flat for a while, until he got fed up with her or she walked out. He couldn't care less one way or another, it had happened a dozen times before and there was always another girl with a suitcase, walking along the railway platform.

He washed his hands in the basin, admired himself in the cracked mirror and combed his long, dark hair. He strolled back to the cafeteria and saw the girl was still there, finishing her cigarette. He took her hand, stubbed out her cigarette and smiled. "Come on, Pauline – let's show you round London."

****

Raymond limped into the pub opposite the Mirabelle and saw George sitting at a corner table, sipping a pint of bitter. "I've just seen Ronnie Raggett, he's sitting in a car parked behind the club."

George was feeling tired. All this trekking around London's sleazier nether regions was getting him down and they still hadn't found Corky. They had been politely but firmly shown the door at the Mirabelle by a heavily built man dressed in a tuxedo, who sported a spectacular broken nose. He denied any knowledge of anyone called Corky or Ronnie and requested them to be about their business.

"Are you sure it's him?"

"Well, he's wearing a suit and he seems to have had his hair cut, but I'm pretty sure it's Ronnie."

"Did he see you?"

"No, he's sitting in a car reading a paper."

George picked up his glass and swilled down its contents, "OK. Ray, let's talk to him before he drives off."

Ronnie Raggett sat in the driving seat of a large black saloon, deeply engrossed in the sports page of a national daily. The window was wound down to disperse clouds of a foul-smelling French cigarette.

George approached from the rear of the car, pushed his face into the car and said, "You should give those bloody things up, they'll shorten your life."

Ronnie, startled from his sporting reverie, growled, "Who the hell are you?"

Raymond made his entrance," Hi Ronnie, remember me?"

"Bloody hell, it's Ray Hill. What are you doing here?"

"We're looking for Corky. His mum's really sick and she wants to see him. By the way, this is my cousin George. I work for him in the motor trade."

"Have you finished working with the boats?" Ronnie asked, ignoring George.

"Yeah, there's no trade left and anyway I've got a bad knee."

"What's Ocker doing?"

"Still working the boats, as far as I know."

"Have you seen Lucy since she shacked up with Tom?"

"A couple of times, but Ocker won't have anything to do with her."

George interrupted, "What about Corky. Do you know where he is?"

"At the moment he's at the stations looking for fresh talent. He's a dab hand at that. I stick to driving the Guvnor and rolling a few drunks at kicking out time."

"What sort of talent is he looking for – music hall or crumpet?" asked George.

"He picks up girls at the stations and takes them to the photo studio." He winked at Ray, "You know, lots of pictures of girls with no clothes on."

"Is this how the Guvnor makes a living?" Ray asked.

Ronnie shook his head. "Don't ask those sort of questions or you'll end up getting your face rearranged. He's a big wheel in the West End and down in South London. I'll tell you where you should find Corky, but go easy. The Guvnor doesn't like people poking around in his business so don't stir up any shit or it might stick on me."

****

They walked through a maze of grubby back streets behind Kings Cross Station, where a long line of arches supported a railway viaduct. The arches contained numerous businesses displaying garish signs, ranging from motor repairers to scrap merchants. One arch remained anonymous to the outside world, except for a discreet number and a bell.

George pressed the bell and sighed, "Oh well! Here goes."

There was no immediate response as all sounds were drowned by a train passing overhead into the station. Eventually, it became quiet again and Ray put his ear to the door. "There's someone in there. I can hear music playing."

It was only after George pressed the bell for a second time that a tall thin man with a pale, bony face that hadn't seen a razor for several days opened the door.

"What do you want?"

"We've come to see Corky."

"Never heard of him."

"Ronnie said he was here."

"What's your names?"

"George and Ray Hill, from Birmingham."

The man slammed the door without uttering another word. After a few minutes the door reopened and Corky McCann, almost unrecognisable in a mohair suit, stood there, grinning.

"Hello, lads, what are you two doing here?"

"Hey, Corky, you took some finding!"

"I should hope so, don't forget the Old Bill's still after me." Corky looked nervously along the street as if expecting the long arm of the law to descend onto his shoulder. "You better come inside."

An express train passed overhead and the whole building seemed to shake and vibrate.

"The studio's sound-proofed, so you can hardly hear the trains from in there," Corky explained, locking the outside door. He led them down a dark corridor into a brightly-lit room where a Beatles record was playing at full volume.

There was a pervading musty smell of stale sweat in a room that hadn't experienced fresh air for a long time. Several spotlights were trained on to a double bed where a naked couple were locked in a simulated embrace. The man kneeling astride a young girl had an erection and was just avoiding sexual penetration. A bearded cameraman made encouraging and occasional salacious remarks and the tall man who originally opened the door adjusted the lighting. George and Ray stared transfixed, but Corky yawned with the attitude of someone who has seen it all many times before. Standing in the darkness at the back of the room was a girl wrapped in a dressing gown. She appeared to be shivering, despite the heat in the studio.

"I'd like you to meet Pauline. She comes from Blackburn." Corky fondled and stroked her long blonde hair.

The girl looked distinctly unhappy.

"Honest, Corky luv, I don't think I should be doing this."

"Nonsense, just lie back and think of all that money you're gonna get." Corky kissed her on the lips.

"I'd like you to meet some friends of mine from Brum."

The girl shook hands and George noticed how cold and clammy they were.

She looked terrified and George felt sorry for her, but remembering Ronnie's warning said, "It's nice to meet you. I'm sure you're going to find London interesting."

"So what are you doing in the sinful city and why are you looking for me?" Corky said, diverting George's attention from the sordid scene in the centre of the studio.

"Kitty asked us to find you. Your mum's very ill. She's got cancer and she wants to see you. Kitty says there's something else you should know, but it's private and she wouldn't tell us."

"How do I know the Old Bill isn't sitting outside mum's house?"

"Oh! Come on Corky, they've got better things to do than wait for you to turn up."

The photographer finished his close-up shots and told the couple to take a break. Shielding his eyes against the spotlights, he shouted, "Who are these geezers?"

"Friends from Birmingham," Corky replied.

"You know I don't like people nosing around in here."

"There's no problem."

The photographer turned his attention to the girl. "Is this the latest skirt?"

Corky replied, "Yeah, her name's Pauline."

"Let's have a look at her."

Corky gave Pauline a shove and she walked forward into the glare of the spotlights. The photographer prowled around her, sniffing like a dog about to urinate on a street corner.

"Did she have a bath before coming here?"

"She's a bit nervous," Corky explained. "You know how it is."

The photographer examined her from top to toe then said, "OK, Pauline, take the gown off and lets have a look at your tits."

The girl cast a terrified glance around the room and stayed immobile. The photographer stepped forward, pulled the dressing gown cord and slipped the garment over her shoulders to lie in a heap around her ankles. She stood shivering in a tiny pair of knickers, her arms flapping wildly like a stranded bird.

"Not bad, eh!" Corky said, with much enthusiasm.

"She's OK – I've seen better," the photographer replied. " OK, Pauline, take your pants off and sit on the bed. We'll see how you look through the camera."

Pauline looked helplessly at Corky. "I can't do this, I want to go."

Corky's voice took on a sharper tone. "You're gonna get paid, so do what Andy tells you."

There were loud guffaws of laughter from the couple, who had hitherto been posing on the bed and now stood drinking coffee on a settee in the corner of the set. Pauline burst into tears, snatched up the dressing gown and ran blindly away from the lights straight into George's arms.

"Go and get dressed and I'll sort this out," said George, holding the girl's arm.

Ray grabbed his shoulder, "Come on George, don't get involved in this, remember what Ronnie said."

The photographer screamed at Corky, "For fuck's sake, get her out of 'ere, she's wasting my bleeding time."

"I'm sorry, Andy, but she seemed like a goer," Corky blurted and then, turning on Pauline, shouted, "You said you'd pose and you wanted to earn some money."

Pauline sobbed, "I didn't realise what I had to do."

"Which fucking planet have you been living on for Chrissake?"

"I'm sorry, Corky, you didn't tell me I had to take all me clothes off."

"What the fuck do you think this is, Country Life?"

"I'm sorry, Corky."

"You're sorry. It's me that's fucking sorry – now get out of here."

She dressed quickly, collected her possessions in a plastic bag and headed for the door. George followed her, leaving Ray to remind Corky not to forget Kitty's message. At that moment, Corky seemed more preoccupied in a heated argument with the photographer.

George caught up with Pauline outside in the street. "Do you have anywhere to go?"

"Nowhere, I only arrived two days ago."

"Did you know Corky before you came down to London."

"No, he picked me up at the station. He seemed very nice, so I stayed with him for two nights."

"I see," George sighed, "Did you bring a suitcase with you?"

"Yeah! It's at Corky's place, but there's nothing in it but a few old clothes, so he can keep them."

"Why don't you go home – Blackburn wasn't it?"

"I'm not going back there."

Ray closed the studio door, shouting, "I'll see you Corky." He limped towards George, who stood by his car deep in thought.

George made his decision. Turning to Pauline, he said, "Ray and me are off back to Birmingham. Why don't you come with us? I'll find you somewhere to stay. There'll be no strings attached and mebbe I can get you a respectable job."

"That's what Corky said. How I do I know I can trust you?"

"Ray and me are respectable people, but it's your decision."

Pauline dabbed her eyes with the sleeve of her cardigan, "Is it nice in Birmingham?"

George held the car door open. "Pauline love, it's the finest place on God's earth. Come on home with us to Brum."

****

Ocker, totally exhausted, slumped into an armchair, and promptly fell asleep. He awoke two hours later when Kitty came in and placed the baby on his lap.

"Hi stranger! Let me introduce you to your son. Ocker this is Alan, Alan this smelly lump is your Daddy, also called Greasy Ocker. This is how he used to smell when I first met him."

"Leave off, I'm tired, how about a cuppa?"

"You've been away for over a week. Did you find any work?"

"Yeah, I got a one-off load down to Banbury, but the levels were down and I got stuck in half of the bridge holes. I didn't see another moving boat in three days. It's really bad down that cut."

Kitty sat down in the other armchair, "Mum's gone into hospital. I had to call the doctor because she was in so much pain."

"So who's looking after the baby?"

Kitty smiled, "I saw this problem coming so I organised a crèche at work."

"You organised a what?"

"A crèche – it's a nursery for babies and young children. The shop said they would provide a room and pay half the wages for a nurse, if we could pay the other half. I had a meeting in the canteen and the women were queuing up to join afterwards. We found a young girl who's qualified as a nanny and she started on Monday. Alan seems to like her and so do all the other kids."

Ocker bounced the baby on his knee, while Kitty made tea.

"What happened about Corky?"

"George and Ray had to stay on in London to look for him."

"Did they find him?"

"It took them ages, but they found him."

"Is he boating down there?"

"Boating! As far as I know, him and Ronnie probably sold the boat they stole from Farden's yard."

"If he isn't boating, what's he doing?"

"Oh! I tell you Ocker, Corky's turned really bad."

"What's he done?"

"He's getting young girls into pornography. They found him at a studio with a girl he'd picked up at a station. They were taking dirty photos. George brought her back home."

"Blimey, what's George doing with prostitutes. Gwen's not gonna like it."

"Don't be so thick, she's not a prostitute and hasn't done anything. George rescued her from a fate worse than Corky. He says she's a nice girl but not very bright, so he's trying to find her a job in Brum."

"Has Corky come home?"

"No sign of him yet. I think I'll hit him when I see him. It's the Raggett blood coming out in him." Kitty bit her lip as she spoke but it was too late. Although he was tired and slow-witted, Ocker had still registered Kitty's comment.

"What've the Raggetts got to do with this?"

Kitty tried to cover up, "Oh! George and Ray found Ronnie Raggett first, so he told them where to find Corky."

"Is Ronnie up to the same tricks as Corky?"

"I suppose so – you'll have to ask Ray."

They sat in silence, Ocker drinking tea and playing with the baby, while Kitty wrestled with her conscience. After several minutes she finally made her decision.

"Ocker, if I told you something really awful, would you promise me not to get mad?"

Ocker shrugged his shoulders and looked bemused. Kitty continued, "I want to tell Corky that he went down to London with his half-brother."

"He hasn't got a brother, he went down to London with Ronnie."

Kitty took a deep breath, "Ronnie is his half-brother and so are Tom and Alf."

Ocker suddenly felt very tired, "I don't understand. Is this some sort of a game?"

"I only wish it was."

"Well, hang on a minute. Where do Gracie and Wilf fit into this puzzle?"

Kitty sighed and wished she hadn't started these confessions. Perhaps this was the wrong time, and maybe she should stop and explain at a better time. Ocker stared at her with his large brown eyes and those ridiculously long eyelashes. Kitty saw he needed a shave, a haircut and a bath. A deep frown appeared on his sun-tanned forehead, "Well, woman, don't stop now."

"Gracie is his mum, but Wilf wasn't his real dad. Gracie said that Wilf couldn't make babies."

"Where do the Raggetts fit into this?"

"Joe Raggett is Corky's father. He'd been having an affair with Gracie for years."

"Joe Raggett had affairs with dozens of women up and down the cut. He was famous for it," Ocker stated.

"I suppose Gracie was one of his regulars," Kitty said limply.

Ocker finished his tea, stood up and gave the baby to Kitty. He prowled across the room to the window and stared blankly into the street. He scratched the stubble on his chin and produced a roll-up cigarette, which he placed unlit into his mouth. He returned to his chair, looked at Kitty, opened his mouth and then said nothing. Silence descended in the room, oppressive and menacing like an approaching storm. Ocker paced backwards and forwards across the room, rubbing the back of his neck. Kitty watched apprehensively, feeling like a turkey on Christmas Eve.

"If Wilf couldn't make babies, how did he make you?"

Kitty's mouth had become as dry as a birdcage floor. "He didn't. I'm the same as Corky. Joe Raggett was my father as well."

Ocker's eyes blazed with an intensity Kitty had never seen before. His jaw muscles bulged and his nostrils flared. Kitty watched petrified as a sliver of spittle ran down the side of Ocker's chin. The unlit cigarette flew out of his mouth as he screamed, "Are you telling me I'm married to a bloody Raggett and my son's a bloody Raggett as well?"

"Ocker, I didn't know until mum realised she was ill. She didn't want to go to her grave without confessing. I'm as upset about it as you are."

"You can't be as upset as I am, that's for sure," Ocker growled. He clenched his fist and smashed it into the side of a wall cabinet, sending its contents spilling out on to the floor. Then he picked up a chair, held it over his head and paused staring wild-eyed at Kitty, who screamed, "No, Ocker, don't do it!"

"Bloody, rotten, stinking Raggetts!" he yelled, hurling the chair at the window. "I'll kill the bloody lot of 'em."

There was a loud crash of splintering glass and the chair hung, caught in the net curtain, half in and half out of the shattered window. Ocker stormed out of the door, down the stairs and then began kicking down a wooden fence that formed a boundary between the houses. He uprooted a stake and hit out at the rest of the fence, sending splintered wood flying through the air in all directions. He staggered past a small group of bystanders, before falling in front of a braking police car. One of the policemen picked Ocker up from the gutter, took away the stake and said with the merest hint of sarcasm, "Now then sir, feeling a little bit upset, are we?"

****

Summer 1963

Summer in suburbia was resplendent with floral displays of roses in front gardens fronted by shady avenues of chestnuts and flowering cherries. These were the affluent homes of the rich with a car in the garage, and two more parked out in the drive. Weekend suburbia was alive with growling lawn mowers and the snip, snip of secateurs dead-heading the rose bushes. Weekday executives wearing green wellingtons washed their executive cars before the call for Sunday lunch. Suburban man following the age-old traditions of a summer Sunday morning was repeated in row after row of respectable residences. These homes would be described by local estate agents as being in a much sought-after area.

Tom Raggett swung his red sports car into the drive of one of the respectable residences, with its respectable front garden belonging to a not-so-respectable owner.

Vince Rothwell, on this warm summer morning, dressed in a blue shirt and matching shorts, opened the door and greeted Tom.

"Hello, you bastard, how are you?"

Tom looked at him and said, "Blimey, Vince, did you have a hair transplant on those legs?"

"Come in, you cheeky sod, and get a drink. We'll sit out in the garden and have our talk before lunch."

A balustraded terrace led into the garden. There were two large urns overflowing with pelargoniums at each side of a flight of steps. Below the steps was a well-kept lawn, flanked with rhododendrons and other flowering shrubs, ending at a row of Leylandii evergreens that made a high, impenetrable boundary with the neighbour. The two men sat at a white terrace table, shaded by a colourful umbrella, and opened their bottles of beer.

"It's just like the South of France," said Vince, flicking the top off a bottle.

"Who looks after the garden?" asked Tom.

"I've got an old geezer who comes in twice a week."

Tom filled up his glass, took a drink, wiped his mouth with the back of his hand and said, "It's nice to come here for Sunday lunch, but we normally meet at the Maple Leaf, so what's the special occasion?"

"You're right, my son," Vince replied affably. "This is a special occasion and what I've got to say is strictly between the two of us. I want no interruptions and nobody earwigging from the next table."

He selected a cigarette from a box on the table, lit it with a gold lighter and watched Tom's face through the cloud of smoke.

"No doubt you are aware that Sergeant Milner has been giving me a hard time since the Crantock job. I swear that I'll find him in bed with me one of these mornings. It's difficult to do a bit of villainy when you're looking over your shoulder all the time."

"We've all had to be more careful after what happened to Frankie."

"Well, at least I've managed to get Frankie a few home comforts while he's doing his bird."

A squirrel appeared on the terrace wall, sat up on its hind legs and looked hopefully at the two men at the table. Vince blew a plume of smoke in its direction, then shouted, "Push off, I've got nothing for you." He turned to Tom, "However, I do have something for you, mate."

Tom helped himself to a cigarette, tapped the filtered end on the table, lit it with Vince's lighter and waited for him to continue.

"I've been down to London to see an old mate – no names, no packdrill. Most people call him the Guvnor. He's got a big job lined up – and I mean a big job."

June, wearing a flowery apron, appeared at the end of the terrace "Hi Tom, how are you? Are you two ready to eat?"

"Give us ten minutes please, love?" Vince replied. He wondered whether he should tell Tom about his chance meeting with brother Ronnie, but after a moment's thought decided to keep it to himself.

"The Guvnor has asked me to join his team and he wants you as a back-up driver. There's gonna be about sixteen geezers on the job."

"Sixteen! How much is the job gonna be worth?"

"They reckon we'll pull over a hundred grand each – maybe a lot more, if we're lucky."

Tom inhaled and choked on the smoke. Vince laughed at his reaction, then said, "This is the one I've been waiting for. We're gonna be rich and Milner will be none the wiser 'cos it's off his patch."

"Did you say a hundred grand? What are we doing to make that sort of money?"

"We're gonna rob a train."

"A train? What do you mean a train? What train and where?"

"It comes down from Glasgow with a compartment stuffed with bags of used notes that are completely untraceable. Beautiful isn't it"

Tom suddenly felt light-headed, as though one bottle of beer had made him drunk. "How heavy is a hundred grand?"

"That's a very good question, my son. I was coming round to that later. The guys who are organising this have done their homework. They've even had a rehearsal on a railway down in Surrey. What they're planning is bloody cheeky, but it'll work."

"Who are these guys?"

"Most of 'em are from South London with another team from the South Coast. I'm told most of them have got some form and they've done some tasty jobs in the past."

"Why have they picked us?"

"The Guvnor wanted me 'cos I'm an old mate and he likes the way we turned over the Crantock job."

"Blimey! Do they know about that down in London?"

"It's common knowledge. Don't you realise we upset one or two faces in East London over that job?"

"When do we do it?"

"Soon, probably after the Bank Holiday. They reckon there'll be more cash on the train after a holiday weekend."

Tom paused, letting the enormity of this bizarre situation sink in as the mundanity of suburban Sunday morning continued unabashed all around them. Children shrieked with pleasure as they splashed in a neighbouring swimming-pool and the ubiquitous mowers growled and whirred over immaculately kept lawns.

"Why do they want me? Any idea what I'm supposed to do?" Tom asked.

"We haven't finalised things as yet, but I think your job will be to drive, look after the vehicles and see off any nosy parkers, while the rest of us are up on the track doing the heist. You'll be one of the geezers loading the bags into the trucks."

"Am I gonna be tooled up?"

"There's no shooters on this one. You might have a cosh, but you'll only use it in an emergency. This job's gonna be in the middle of the night and we're all dressed up as soldiers on manoeuvres. The place we're stopping the train is miles from anywhere, so we shouldn't get any interference from the law while we're doing the job."

"How do you stop a train?"

"To be honest mate, that's not your concern, but I'll tell you anyway. They've got a brilliant idea of fixing the signal so it shows red."

"Is the train driver in on this?"

"Not as far as I know – that's why we have to stop the train on a red signal."

"Where's the money gonna be?"

"As I said before, it's in a separate compartment. They'll be blokes inside sorting and counting. The idea is to detach it from the rest of the train."

"Where do we meet these blokes?"

Vince held up his hand to stop further questions. "Let's eat now and carry on this discussion later."

Tom had been hungry when he arrived but now his gastric juices seemed to have turned to acid and his appetite had waned. He picked over his food and grunted replies to June's lively conversation. The implications of what he had just learned had brought on an unprecedented bout of flatulence.

After an hour or so, they resumed their positions on the terrace, where Vince had provided Tom with a large whisky to settle his stomach. "They've bought a farm out in the sticks as a hide-out before the heist and for a stow afterwards," Vince told him.

"What's a stow?" Tom queried.

"A stow is a place to hide up and sort out the cash, and this is the point where I'm not happy about the job." Vince lit a cigarette, inhaled deeply and continued. "The law's gonna go potty when they find we've nicked all that loot. They'll block the roads, the railways and the airports and when they don't find us, they'll start searching all the buildings, including farms, for miles around. Now these geezers intend to go back to this farm for the share out and I for one don't go along with this idea."

Tom eased himself into his chair, "Yeah, go on."

Vince produced a sheet of blank paper and a pencil. "Now I'll show you what I've got in mind. I went down there last weekend and had a look around."

He drew a rough map, showing the railway and nearby lanes. Over to the west, he drew a large cross. "That's the farm where they want us all to go afterwards, dressed up as soldiers."

Vince drew another cross by the railway. "Here's where we do the heist." He drew another line to the east of the railway and tapped it several times with the pencil. "And here, mate, is a canal less than a mile away, with road access."

"I don't understand, how does the canal figure in this?"

"It's the slowest form of transport – you should know, you were a boatman once. It's the last place the coppers will expect any villain to use as a getaway."

"You must be mad – sixteen blokes with all those mailbags! You'll need a fleet of boats to carry that lot."

Vince grinned. "There won't be sixteen blokes – just me and you, Tom, and a load of money."

"Where's the rest of the blokes?"

"They're on their way to the farm. Hang on a minute, I'll explain."

He paused to refill the glasses with whisky, then continued. "There's going to be an army truck and three Land Rovers. The third Land Rover is back-up and that's the one you're driving. Most of the mailbags are going in the first three vehicles, but as you'll be doing a lot of the stashing, you'll make sure quite a few of those bags go into the last one. Now the tricky bit is to stop anyone else but us riding in our vehicle. You leave that to me. If we get a passenger, then I'll have to get rid of the bleeder somewhere along the road. We follow the others at first, then we'll turn off down a lane – I'll show you where on the map. This is where you'll get your foot down before the others realise we're not with 'em anymore. We drive to the canal, where you will have arranged to have boats waiting, and unload the bags. I'll have a couple of geezers there who'll take the Land-Rover and sink it into a lake somewhere."

Vince finished his drink and placed the glass on the table. "Now, do you know a bloke who has a couple of boats and who we can rely on to wait for us?"

Tom thought for a while and then said, "The only one who might do this is Lucy's brother, Ocker. The trouble is he hates my guts, but I know he's broke. There's been no business on the canals since last winter."

"Tell him there's a 'monkey' in it for him."

"I wonder if that will tempt him."

"It'll tempt him, especially if he's broke. Approach him in the right way – it's called diplomacy. Give the bleeder some sweet talk and remember every man has his price."

"It won't be easy, but I'll try him."

"Once we're aboard, we'll sort out the money while your boatman mate quietly takes us north. What I will want from you is the length of time it will take to get to this bridge at the far side of Leighton. I'll have a car waiting for me to take me to a private airfield. Then I'm gonna disappear until the heat is off."

"Where are you going?"

"That's my little secret, mate"

"I take it I'm not going with you"

"No, you have to make your own plans. If you get nicked, you keep quiet and do your bird. You're gonna end up with a lot of money, so don't go mad with it or you'll draw attention to yourself, and not a word to your girlfriend or anybody else before the heist. I'll be in touch later and then you and your girlfriend can join me for a holiday in the sun."

Tom shook his head and grinned. "Bloody hell, Vince, you are a devious bastard."

****

The past few weeks had been among the worst in Ocker's life. Kitty was not speaking to him since the incident that had led to his appearance in court and a fine for wilful damage to public property. He had returned to living on the boat and was desperately trying, without success, to find some sort of work.

It was Friday lunchtime and he was sitting in the Navigation Inn, reading a discarded newspaper and making a pint of beer last as long as possible. Banner headlines proclaimed salacious details of a juicy scandal involving a cabinet minister, a call girl and a Russian spy. Ocker had read the story with interest, tracing the lines with his finger. Finally he looked up at the clock behind the bar and pushed the newspaper aside.

Mysterious messages had been left for him at the boatyards he frequented with an offer of well-paid work that had lured him to a lunchtime assignment at the pub. Ocker had no idea as to the identity of his potential benefactor, but curiosity and his parlous financial situation had led him to keep the appointment.

Three men sat at the bar counter, listening to the landlord predicting that soon all pubs would have to serve food at lunchtime and in the evening. He looked around the almost empty bar and waved his arm to underline the point to his three companions.

"It's not worth opening the pub at this time of day. Six customers hardly covers the cost of electricity – and he (pointing to Ocker) has been supping one pint for over an hour."

The older man in the group swilled his beer round the glass, saying, "Pubs are for supping ale, not eating your dinner. Next thing, you'll be filling the place with kids." He placed his glass on the bar. "Fill it up again, Bert. Oh look, you've another customer."

The door opened and a well-dressed, dark-haired young man entered, looked around the bar and walked towards Ocker, who had returned to the newspaper.

"There you are. Hello, Ocker, long time no see."

Ocker looked up from the newspaper. "I think you've got the wrong bloke."

"Don't you recognise me – I'm Tom Raggett?"

The last time Ocker saw Tom, he was a working boatman. Now he was transformed into a smart, well-dressed young man, wearing a suit and tie.

Tom flinched as Ocker's expression changed from surprise to aggression.

"You've got a bloody cheek."

"Hang on a minute mate, I've got some business for you."

"You can stick your business up your backside."

"Listen, I'm talking about earning money."

"Oh yeah!"

"Yeah, a lot of money."

"Stuff your bloody money!"

Ocker's raised voice caught the attention of the landlord and the three men at the bar turned round and were watching with interest. Tom stepped back, holding both hands with flattened palms in front of him.

"I'm offering you a job."

"I don't want your bloody job."

Tom pulled out a chair and sat down, observing Ocker, who loomed ominously above him.

"Sit down, mate, and listen to what I'm offering."

Ocker grunted and sat down and the men at the bar resumed their conversation.

Tom leaned forward, acutely aware of the proximity of his face to Ocker's clenched fists.

"I've got a very well paid boating job for you and from what I hear there's not much work around. I don't reckon you're in a position to turn down the sort of money I'm offering."

"Go on, I'm listening."

"I'm talking about a hundred quid right now, in your hot sticky hand, and five hundred more when the job's done."

Ocker sat back in his seat, picked up his glass and finished off the dregs. Tom picked up the glass, "Let me get you another. Are you drinking bitter?"

Ocker didn't answer. Despite his hatred for Tom Raggett, he was aware that six hundred pounds for one job was unheard-of money and he was broke. Tom returned with two full pints of bitter.

"What have I got to do for that sort of money?"

"Not a lot," Tom replied, and added, "It won't be too much hard work."

"It can't be legal for that amount, if you're involved with it."

Tom grinned, "There's no risk for you. All you have to do is be in the right place with a pair of boats and keep your mouth shut afterwards."

"I dunno."

"Come on, Ocker. Can you really afford to turn it down?"

Ocker took a long drink and carefully replaced the glass on a beer-mat. He stared down at his left knee poking out of a hole in his trousers, sighed and said, "No, I don't suppose I can."

"All you have to do is be at the place I tell you with a pair of boats and wait until I get there in the early hours of the morning."

"Is Lucy involved in this?"

"No, it's nothing to do with her and she mustn't know anything about it."

"And if the police turn up?"

"I promise you, there'll be no police."

"I don't like the sound of it."

Tom looked around the bar and saw the customers were engrossed in their conversations. He took an envelope from his pocket and placed it in front of Ocker.

"Here you are – open it!"

Ocker looked inside and saw it was full of banknotes.

"There's a hundred smackers in there"

Ocker felt like throwing the envelope in Tom's face, but instead he picked it up and pushed it into his pocket.

"OK, I'll do it. Where do you want me to be?"

****

They left just before midnight. There was one army truck and three Land Rovers in convoy through empty lanes, their radios tuned into the police frequency. Tom, driving the back-up vehicle, was alone and had little to do but follow the tail-lights of the car in front. Eventually they arrived at the railway, where Tom reversed his vehicle to face the end of a lane that ran underneath the railway, and parked it last in line on the grass verge.

Some of the gang changed their army uniforms into railwaymen's blue overalls before scrambling up on to the railway track, their boots showering stones and rubble behind them. Tom could see some of the men silhouetted against the night sky and heard splashing as one of the gang relieved himself down the slope. Very soon they disappeared along the track and Tom could hear the crunch of their boots on the ballast as they receded into the distance, then all was quiet.

Two other members of the gang, one dressed as a major, drove off in the leading Land Rover to cut telephone wires.

Now he was alone, peering along the little lane for signs of anything that might jeopardise the job. Even at two thirty in the morning, an occasional train passed by and, at one point, one actually stopped on the track above him. For a moment, Tom thought that the meticulous planning and timing had gone wrong. After a few minutes, it moved on, leaving only the rustling of small nocturnal animals in the undergrowth to disturb the eerie silence.

The rough cloth of the army uniform was making his back itch and he rubbed himself on the outside of the Land Rover. He stood alone in the harsh moonlight by his vehicle, clutching the walkie-talkie radio handset, and wished he had brought something to drink. Tom now had time to reflect on the extraordinary events that had led to him being in this country lane in the middle of the night.

The raid had been postponed for one day and Tom fervently hoped that Ocker was still waiting with the boats at the wharf. Tom's stay at the farm had not been convivial for although the rest of the gang had readily accepted Vince, Tom's contribution to the heist was regarded with suspicion. Some even suggested that Tom's participation didn't merit even shares of the spoils. He spent his waiting hours lying on a bed reading or watching the birds flitting past the window, while the rest of the gang played cards.

The two men in the Land Rover returned and the one dressed in the major's uniform spoke urgently into the hand radio.

He really looked like a military man as he walked quickly towards Tom, saying, "Any problems?"

"No, not a thing," Tom replied.

"Right then, you're on your own for a while so don't start having a kip. Keep your eyes peeled and use the radio, if anything goes wrong."

He went back to the Land Rover and the two men drove off down the lane to stop a train and to start a chain of events that would change all their lives.

****

Lucy had finally made a decision. For hours she'd tossed and turned alone in the large double bed, wondering where Tom was for the seventh consecutive night.

His recent strange behaviour followed the Sunday lunch meeting at Vince's house. She didn't mind not being invited as she didn't like

June and couldn't stand Vince's Cockney 'Jack the Lad' mannerism. Tom had become nervous, secretive and uncommunicative. Her questions were received with irritable grunts and, if she persisted, he would get up and leave the flat without uttering a word, returning hours later the worse for drink. On one occasion, she returned from work to find him still asleep in bed, unwashed, unshaved and uncaring. He was only interested in the telephone calls from Vince that he took on the bedroom extension, conducting his conversation in low, inaudible, muttered tones. Finally, after receiving a telephone call, he packed a bag with a few clothes and announced he had to go away for a few days on a job. That was a week ago and Lucy had not seen or heard from him since then.

She lay alone in the dark remembering the wonderful holidays, walking hand in hand on deserted beaches, eating sumptuous dinners in waterside restaurants and making love in expensive hotel rooms. Sitting next to Tom in his open-top sports car with her dark hair streaming behind her as he drove through France to the Mediterranean.

They drove along the coast, visiting exotic places Lucy had hitherto only read about in magazines – Nice, Monte Carlo and Monaco. They stayed in the mountains above Cannes and went into the town, where a film festival was in progress. Lucy saw several famous film stars besieged by autograph hunters and scantily dressed starlets surrounded by press photographers on the beach. Later, they drove to Paris and stayed at a hotel overlooking the River Seine with a view of the Eiffel Tower. Tom had promised to take her to Venice, but he seemed to have lost enthusiasm for that trip since his meeting with Vince.

That was a different Tom from the recent surly man, hiding behind a newspaper in the morning before she left for work. This was the man for whom she had abandoned her family, who had pledged his undying love and who had now disappeared out of her life without a word. She realised that something important was happening in Tom's life and she wasn't playing a part in it. She also knew that if Vince was involved, it was probably illegal.

Lucy had made her decision. In the morning she would pack her bags and, as tradition would have it, go home to mother.

****

Ocker anticipated Tom's arrival each time a vehicle passed on the nearby road, but so far nothing had happened. This was the third night waiting at the wharf and his patience was wearing thin.

Tom had said it would probably be around dawn before they came, so the cabins had been cleared, the engine was warm and the boats were pointing north and ready to go. He'd gone for a walk during the day to try to clear his head of the confusion that was invading his brain like a paralysing disease. First, Kitty had dropped her bombshell regarding her unfortunate parentage and then Tom Raggett of all people turns up to make him a financial offer he couldn't refuse.

He knew Tom Raggett was up to no good and it could all end in more trouble with the police, but he had been promised five hundred pounds and, despite his hatred of the Raggetts, he was desperate for money. But could he really trust Tom Raggett to pay him the money and where was it all coming from? He had no idea what Tom did these days, but he had seen the way he dressed and the flashy red sports car he drove. He knew he had an expensive flat and was living the fast life with his sister, Lucy.

Tom's brother, Alf, was back in prison after his escape and his other brother, Ronnie, was on the run from the police, so it was a fair bet that Tom was up to something crooked as well. A shiver of anger surged through his body whenever he remembered that his son, Alan, had Raggett blood flowing through his veins. His son's grandfather was that foul-mouthed, randy old bastard, Joe Raggett, who for years had fought and fornicated along every inch of the canal from London to Birmingham. On top of all that, his sister Lucy was living with Tom Raggett.

For hours he sat on top of the cabin, ruminating and watching the moon, bright as a new shilling, glinting on the water. Now he looked to the east where, on the horizon, an indigo sky was turning pink and grey, heralding the start of a new day.

****

Vince parted the branches of the bush where he was hiding to get a better view of the train that slowly approached. It stopped with a hiss in front of the gantry where the signal was glowing red and a light appeared in the driver's cab. A man climbed down from the train and walked across to the telephone attached to the gantry to call the distant signal box. The gang, hidden on both sides of the track, collectively held their breath. The only sound was the crunch of the driver's feet on the ballast and the diesel motor ticking over. The driver picked up the telephone and, finding the line dead, replaced the handset. He turned around to see a shadowy figure dressed in railwayman's uniform.

"There's summat wrong with the line."

"Yeah, I know," came the reply.

"We don't usually have to stop here in the middle of the night. Is there an emergency?"

"You could say that."

The driver shrugged his shoulders and said, "I better get back to the train."

As he turned away, Vince slid up behind him and grasped him around the throat in a vice-like grip, at the same time twisting the driver's arm into the small of his back.

Vince shoved his mouth close to the driver's ear and snarled, "Now listen carefully, do what you're told and you won't get hurt."

The driver gasped something unintelligible.

Vince released the pressure on his throat and prodded him with his fist saying, "Back to the train. You've still got some driving to do."

The driver stumbled on the ballast and Vince dragged him on to his feet.

"What's going on?" stammered the driver.

"Don't ask any more questions. Get back into that cab and do what you're told."

There was a clanking noise from behind the cab, as members of the gang uncoupled the locomotive and the coach containing the money from the rest of the train. Vince pushed the driver up the ladder into the cab, where other gang members joined them. Someone on the track shouted to start the train.

"Right. Get this thing moving!" Vince ordered the driver.

The driver stared at the controls, "The brake pressure's too low. We have to wait for it to build up."

"Fuck the brake-pressure, just get it moving."

"Regulations state..." the driver never completed the sentence as Vince smacked him hard across the mouth.

Further down the track, Tom was glancing at his watch for the hundredth time in half an hour as he paced up and down the lane, nervously kicking the tyres of the stationery vehicles. The tension was getting unbearable and he could picture the gang up on the track, faces blackened, waiting for the train. Tom lit another cigarette from the butt of the previous one, inhaled and coughed. He desperately wanted a drink and anything would do, even a bottle of kid's lemonade would taste like nectar at that moment.

A distant metallic, clanking sound stopped his pacing. He listened intently, "Yes! There it goes again," and then shouted aloud, "By God! It's the bloody train, they've nicked it!"

The creaking and clanking got louder and then Tom saw the lights of the diesel engine. The locomotive, silhouetted against the night sky, hissed to a halt directly above him. He heard excited voices and saw shadowy figures emerge from the cab, jumping down on to the track.

There was a loud crash of breaking glass as one of the robbers used an axe to smash the window of the coach containing the money. Several members of the gang squeezed into the interior of the coach through the window and presently the doors were flung open. Mailbags cascaded on to the track and men were sliding down the embankment to form a chain. Now the heavy bags were descending down the slope at a tremendous rate and Tom began stacking them into the leading vehicles. Suddenly, he felt a hand on his shoulder and he turned to see Vince, his face blackened like an end-of-the-pier minstrel, grinning back at him.

"Right, let's start getting a few of those into our wagon."

Vince dragged mailbags along the lane behind the parked vehicles that masked him from the others, who were too preoccupied to notice. The leading robber shouted from the track, "That's it. Time's up. Let's get the show on the road."

The line of grunting and sweating men broke to load the last of the bags and then, abandoning their railway uniforms, returned to their vehicles dressed as soldiers again.

Tom dragged two more mailbags to Vince, who was cramming a pile of bags into the back of the Land Rover.

"Shove those two in the back while I make sure we don't have any company," Vince shouted as he disappeared around the front of the vehicle. The sound of starting engines blended with triumphant cries as the exuberant convoy moved out of the lane.

Vince jumped into the passenger seat and lit two cigarettes. He leant across and placed one in Tom's mouth. "We're on our way, mate, now do what I say. Follow them into the road, then start to drop behind. Do it slowly so that driver in front doesn't get suspicious."

Tom nervously missed a gear change with a loud grinding noise. Vince slapped him on his knee, "It's OK, mate, calm down, we're almost there."

After a short while the convoy approached a sharp bend in the road. Vince gripped Tom's shoulder. "There's a little lane after the bend on the left. Put your lights out just before it. Make a turn and don't rush it."

Tom did what he was bid, braked a little too hard as he turned into the lane, corrected the skid and flicked the headlight switch in one deft movement.

"Now get your foot down. It's about a mile to the canal and God help your mate if he's not there."

The headlights picked up the familiar outline of a canal bridge and Tom swept the Land Rover on to the wharf, scattering gravel as he braked. He saw the moored pair of narrowboats and sighed with relief as he saw Ocker's head appear from the cabin of the butty boat.

"Good to see you, Ocker. Come and help me get these bags on to the boat."

Ocker grunted a reply and complied with the request, while Vince ran across the bridge to a telephone box to contact the colleague whose job was to get rid of the Land Rover and then meet him further up the canal for the getaway.

Tom began emptying the Land Rover that was stuffed to the roof with bags, pulling them out and throwing them on to the ground.

"What's all this?" Ocker demanded.

"Don't ask bloody silly questions – just get them into the cabins as quick as you can."

"What's in these bags?"

"What do you think is in them – Christmas presents?"

"Well, I dunno."

"Yeah, that's right, they're all presents and I'm bloody Santa Claus."

Tom and Ocker had removed all the mailbags into the cabins by the time Vince returned. He peered inside the butty cabin, now stacked to the ceiling.

"Bloody hell, there's not much room in here. Is this where you all lived in the old days?"

"And brought up large families," replied Tom, panting like a bloodhound.

"OK, let's get moving. What's your name, son?"

Ocker grunted his name. He already disliked Tom's anonymous Cockney friend. In his experience, all Londoners were loud-mouthed and bumptious – and Vince was no exception.

"What's in the bags?" Ocker ventured once again.

"Don't worry about it. Get these boats moving, keep your trap shut and you'll get a bonus on top of whatever Tom promised you."

Ocker started the engine and moved the boats out into the middle of the canal.

With the butty boat cabin stuffed with mailbags, Vince and Tom sat in the motorboat cabin and began opening the first bag of money. Vince tipped the contents on to the table and bundles of five-pound notes showered from the table to the floor.

Vince whistled, "Just look at that – isn't that the most beautiful sight you've ever seen?"

Tom, open-mouthed, stared at the gleaming pile of money. "Bloody hell, Vince, how much do you reckon we've got?"

"Enough to keep us both in the manner to which we have become accustomed for the rest of our natural."

"How can we split this? There's not enough room to count out all this lot."

"Yeah, I take your point. There's a lot less space in these cabins than I thought. We'll count out this bag and divvy it up between us. That'll give us an idea how much there is altogether. Then we'll just take an even split of the rest without opening them – it'll be easier for me."

Vince produced a bottle of whisky. "In the meantime, let's celebrate while we work, so get your laughing gear around this."

Ocker's mind was in a whirl as he steered the boats northwards. At the first lock, he looked into the cabin and saw his passengers counting out a huge pile of banknotes. Just beyond the lock a police car, blue lights flashing and siren screaming, speeded over a road bridge, oblivious of the boats below. He opened the butty boat cabin and kicked one of the mailbags.

"Blimey! What have they done?"

The enormity of the haul was becoming apparent to Tom, now emptying the contents of a whisky bottle with alacrity. His brain, already befuddled with drink and tension, couldn't cope with arithmetic. "How much do you reckon, Vince?"

"Must be well over a hundred and fifty grand each – mebbe even two hundred."

Tom rested his head against the wooden cabin wall. He averted his gaze from the pile of money and drunkenly surveyed a display of lace-plates on the opposite wall. One of them said 'A present from Blackpool' and featured the tower and a crowded beach.

"I went there when I was a kid"

"You went where?"

"Blackpool, for a week and the sun shone every day."

"What the fuck are you talking about?"

"Blackpool – I made sand-castles and rode on a donkey."

"Who the fuck cares about the bleeding donkey."

"I remember it's name. After all these years, I still remember its name."

"You remember whose name?"

"The donkey – it was called Ethel."

Vince shook his head vigorously, "We've just pulled the biggest heist in history and all you talk about is a fucking donkey called Ethel."

"I loved that donkey. I rode her every day and I was in tears on the last day when we had to go back to the station."

"Alright, go back to Blackpool and buy the fucking donkey – you can afford it."

"It was over twenty years ago."

"Well, buy another fucking donkey – buy a hundred fucking donkeys, if that's what you want."

Vince eased himself on to the cabin steps looking up at Ocker, who was silhouetted against the early morning sun as he steered the boats.

"How much longer before we reach that bridge where I'm meeting my mate?"

"Half an hour, maybe quicker if Tom will help with the next lock."

"You must be joking, he's pissed out of his mind. All he does is talk a load of bollocks about donkeys."

Vince sat down on the step, "Hey, Ocker, do you have a radio on this boat?"

"There's an old one attached to a battery in the butty."

"Is that this one or the boat next door?"

Ocker jerked his thumb. "The one next door."

Vince climbed out of the motorboat and crossed into the breasted-up butty. He found the radio crushed and useless underneath the pile of mailbags. Suddenly, he felt very weary and lay down on the mound of bags, putting his hands behind his head and stretching out his feet.

He saw an out of date calendar pinned on the cabin wall that had drawings of wildflowers and a motto that said: 'I'm tired of Love: I'm still more tired of rhyme, but money gives me pleasure all the time.'

"Too bloody true!" grinned Vince.

Vince's friend was waiting by the bridge with a large white van already backed up to the canal. Ocker pulled the boats into the bank and moored up, while Vince hurled mailbags out of the cabin and on to the towpath. His friend quickly threw them into the back of the van and covered them with a tarpaulin.

Vince patted Ocker on the back and shoved a wad of five-pound notes down the front of his shirt, saying, "There you are, old son – you can take your missus for a nice fish supper. Look after Tom, I don't think he's feeling too well at the moment." Vince jumped into the passenger seat and the van roared off at high speed.

Ocker pulled out the money and looked cautiously around him. He slowly counted the notes that added up to one hundred and ten pounds. He ran his fingers through his long, greasy hair, pursed his lips and said, "What the hell is going on?"

Tom Raggett, wild-eyed and unshaven, slumped on the counter of the motorboat clutching an almost empty bottle of whisky.

"Come on, Ocker, let's get going."

"Where to?"

"Up to Buckby. I left my car at the wharf."

"I hope you'll help with the locks when you sober up."

"Yeah! But I need some sleep, so I'll see you later."

Tom gripped the tiller for support, turned and fell down the steps into the cabin. He crawled over the floor, pulled himself up into the bed and immediately fell asleep. When Ocker started the engine, he could see money scattered all over the cabin floor. Before casting off, he looked into the butty boat cabin, noting that Tom's share of the money was still stacked against the walls in unopened mailbags.

Ocker slowly travelled northwards through the morning, unaware that he was carrying some of the proceeds of a two and a half million pound robbery. At lunchtime, he stopped at a waterside cottage where they sold groceries.

He entered the shop and banged his fist on the counter, "Is anyone at home?"

An elderly, white-haired lady appeared from the back room. "Oh hello! It's Ocker, isn't it?"

"Yes, missus, can I buy some bread and cheese?"

"You certainly can, my dear. I don't get many boatman calling in these days."

"Aye, well there's not many of us left."

The old lady busied herself with the cheese, while Ocker looked around the shop. The dusty shelves were covered with dead flies and the windows hadn't been cleaned for months. A large faded poster festooned with cobwebs advertised a bottle of dandelion and burdock. Ocker wondered how much longer the shop would stay open.

The old lady placed the bread and cheese on the counter and said, "Have you heard about the robbery last night?"

Ocker felt like his heart had skipped a beat. "Robbery, what robbery?"

"My word, haven't you heard? They robbed a train not far from here.

The police are searching for them all over the place."

"My radio's packed in. I didn't know."

"It was a mail train from Glasgow, full of used banknotes. Could be millions they say."

Ocker suddenly felt weak in the stomach, as he realised he was probably carrying a drunken train robber with his share of the loot.

"Thanks, missus," Ocker grunted, "How much do I owe you?"

He put his hand in his pocket and pulled out the wad of five-pound notes given to him by Vince. Fortunately, the old lady didn't notice as Ocker hastily shoved the notes back into his pocket and paid with a few coins.

He returned to the boats, started up, cast-off and, after a mile, moored up before a lock. He filled the kettle, made a cup of tea and sat in the sun, eating the bread and cheese. He ate slowly, calming himself as he realised the implication of his position. Tom Raggett, now lying in a drunken stupor, was certainly one of the train robbers. There was money lying all over the motor's cabin floor and a huge amount in mailbags in the butty boat.

He entered the motorboat cabin and began to pick up the money from the floor. Very soon he was holding hundreds of pounds and felt reluctant to let them go. Tom Raggett, slumped in the corner, snored loudly and had a dribble of spittle running from the corner of his mouth down his chin. The cabin reeked of stale sweat and whisky.

Ocker sat down with both hands crammed with five-pound notes, remembering that day long ago when his father was killed in a lock, not all that far from where he was now. He was sure it was Alf Raggett who had pushed him over the edge, but it was Tom who had steered the boats that crushed him, screaming with pain against the lock chamber. It took hours to get medical attention in the middle of the night and he could remember all the excuses made by the Raggetts at the inquest. He still couldn't escape the Raggetts, even when they had stopped working the boats. There had been all that trouble with Lucy and Tom, making him look a fool, when everyone seemed to know what was going on but him.

He remained sitting on the cabin steps with a pile of notes in his lap, looking at the sleeping figure in the corner for over an hour until Tom began to stir. Ocker watched him as he straightened himself up, opened his bleary eyes and said, "Hi Ocker, have you got the kettle on – I'm dying for a cuppa tea?"

"I'll make you tea to sober you up. Then you'll do your share of the work."

"What do you mean – work. What work?"

"You said you'd help work the locks. There's plenty to get through between here and Buckby and I'm not doing them all on my own."

"Stuff the bloody locks. That's what I'm paying you for."

"Oh, I know you can pay, you've got all this money from that train robbery last night."

"What do you know about a train robbery? I thought your radio was broken."

"The woman in the shop told me. Everybody's talking about it. It's in the newspapers."

Tom stared blearily at the notes in Ocker's lap. "Hey, what are you doing with my money?"

Ocker screwed up the notes and threw them into Tom's face. "Here, take your bloody money and now get outside and sober up."

"Stuff you!" Tom growled, picking up notes from the floor. As he bent forward, Ocker grabbed him by his collar and dragged him across the cabin, up the steps and hauled him off the boat on to the towpath. Ocker threw a windlass after him, yelling, "If you want your tea, then earn it. There's a lock up there and it needs setting."

Tom tried to pick up the windlass, failed, and rose unsteadily to his feet, "You've got a right old temper haven't you, Ocker. Your sister can be a bit feisty sometimes – it must run in the family."

"Leave Lucy out of this," Ocker replied.

"Oh yeah! Lucy – the lovely Lucy, who's sitting around waiting for me to come home. She's a very sexy lady, but of course you wouldn't know that, would you, Ocker? You'd be surprised at some of the things she's learned since she's been with me. She can be a wild thing once she's got all her clothes off. I could tell you things that would make your hair even curlier than it is."

"You shut your filthy mouth!" said Ocker, stepping off the boat.

Tom continued with a lascivious smile, "I bet Kitty could do a fair turn under the sheets. Shame she's wasted on you mate. I've always fancied getting my hands around Kitty's tits. Never mind, Lucy's got nice ones as well."

Ocker leapt forward, shouting, "You dirty foul-mouthed bastard!" He punched Tom on the nose and Tom fell backwards into a patch of nettles. He tried to stand up and then slipped again, blood streaming from one nostril.

"Get up on your feet!" Ocker said, menacingly, and Tom now saw the iron-mooring pin clenched in Ocker's fist. He also saw the windlass lying on the towpath between himself and Ocker and made a grab for it.

Tom's grasping fingers missed the windlass, but the impetus of the forward lunge sent him crashing headfirst into Ocker's stomach and the two men fell on top of each other at the edge of the canal. Ocker was holding the mooring pin like a lance and as they fell, the point of the iron pin pierced Tom's eye, lodging itself in the socket. Tom screamed, pulled the pin from his eye, then rose to his feet with blood streaming down his face. He made a ghastly pirouette, then lost his balance and plunged face down into the water. Ocker jumped into the canal after him and when Tom's head broke the surface, Ocker pushed him back under the water and held him there until the thrashing limbs became still and the air bubbles stopped rising.

****

A group of leather-jacketed young men were standing by their motor bikes, their faces illuminated a pallid yellow from the lights of a fish and chip shop. George, in his parked Jaguar, noted with some amusement that the noisy clique were using their chips as ammunition to catch the attention of girls, who were trying to leave the shop under a fusillade of fried potatoes. He remembered doing the same thing himself not all that long ago, in those days when he was a carefree young boatman. Now he sold second-hand cars, drove a Jag and lived in an up-market, green-belt suburb, where his neighbours regarded him as a nouveau riche upstart. Gwen was making an effort to socialise with the neighbours, but George kept telling her she would never be accepted as an equal until she got rid of her accent.

A bus pulled into the stop just beyond the motor cyclists and George saw Raymond hop off the platform and limp along the pavement towards him. The bikers spotted Raymond's limp and made unkind comparisons with the lame Chester Goode in the popular TV series *Gunsmoke*. Raymond ignored the taunts and got into the car. "I got the message. Where's the fire?"

"No fire as far as I know," George replied. "I got a phone call from Ocker – he sounded in a hell of a state."

"He's improving – it's not all that long ago he didn't know how to use the phone."

"He said he couldn't talk, but asked if could I find you and meet him as soon as possible. It sounded really urgent."

"Where's he been for the last few weeks?"

"He didn't say."

"There's hardly any carrying work left on the cut and Kitty's going crazy worrying about him. The last she saw of him was at the magistrate's court."

"I know, she spoke to Gwen the other day and said she was worried."

"I still don't know why he went berserk and smashed up that fencing."

"Gwen tried to get it out of her, but all Kitty would say was that it was bad news and something to do with the Raggetts."

"Isn't it marvellous!" Raymond said. "If it's bad news you can be sure the Raggetts are involved somewhere."

George turned the ignition key and started the engine. "Anyway, Ocker's down by Stoke bottom lock with a pair of boats. Let's go and see what the problem is."

It took an hour to reach the locks, by which time it was dark. George slowed down on the main road and turned down a dirt track, towards a group of cottages. The white-painted lock-beams gleamed bright in the moonlight and George's headlights picked out a pair of boats moored below the bottom lock. He parked near the cottages and the two men walked down the slope to the boats where Ocker, smoking a cigarette, was pacing up and down the towpath.

Raymond greeted his brother, "Hey up, Ocker, what's to do?"

"Thanks for coming so soon. I don't know what I'm gonna do."

They went into the motorboat cabin and sat down. George noticed that Ocker's hand was shaking as he smoked the cigarette.

"I thought you'd given up on the ciggies."

"I had, but I've started smoking again."

"Is this something to do with Kitty, 'cos if it is, that's your business and I don't think we should interfere?"

"No, it's nowt to do with Kitty."

"Is it to do with the Raggetts?"

"You could say that," Ocker said, stubbing out the cigarette. "Come and look inside the butty."

He unlocked the cabin door, struck a match and lit the lamp. George and Raymond peered inside at the pile of mailbags that almost filled the interior of the cabin.

George poked a finger at the nearest bag, "What are these?"

Ocker gulped, "Mailbags – full of money."

Raymond squeezed into the cabin and ran his hands down the mailbag. "Is all this money?"

George turned to Ocker standing at the top of the cabin steps, his face illuminated by the lamp.

"Blimey, Ocker, what have you done?"

"It's from the train robbery."

The light from the lamp emphasised the hollows around Ocker's eyes and his long, uncombed greasy hair blew about in the breeze. The effect was almost theatrical and George suddenly thought of the pantomime villains that he had seen, when he was a boy.

"The train robbery!" George repeated, lamely.

Raymond intervened, "Blimey, Ocker, you weren't in on the train robbery, were you?"

"Not me, but Tom Raggett was one of them."

"Tom Raggett? I might have guessed. Where's Tom now?"

Ocker sat down on the cabin step and took a deep breath. "He's dead."

"Tom Raggett's dead?" Raymond said in amazement.

"Yeah," Ocker grunted, and quietly added, "I killed him. We had a fight and he finished up in the cut. He was drunk and hurt and I drowned him."

"But why – why did you fight? Was it over the money?"

"No, it wasn't the money, it was what he said about Lucy and Kitty. I just saw red and went for him."

George slumped on to the bed, "Oh, bloody hell, Ocker, what are you going to do now?"

"That's why I called you – you always know what to do."

"Mebbe, but this is murder on top of all this money from the train robbery. It's hardly the sort of problem I have to solve every day."

Raymond and George stared at each other and a long silence followed as the implications of Ocker's story sank in.

Eventually George said, "Right, let's put the kettle on. This needs some thinking out." In George's experience, the universal panacea in the face of any crisis was to sit down and have a cup of tea. To him this was a logical overture to solving any problem.

"OK. Ocker, I think you'd better start at the beginning," George said, spooning sugar into his tea.

"Tom left messages at the boatyard to meet him at the Navvy Inn. I didn't know who it was until he walked through the door. I thought he was a customer wanting a bit of carrying. When I saw who it was I nearly thumped him, but he said he had a job worth over six hundred quid so I decided to do it."

Raymond was about to make a point but George interrupted holding up his hand, "Let him go on."

"I had to be at the wharf near Maffers with a pair of boats. He gave me a date and said I had to stay there until he turned up. I waited for three days and nights, then he arrived in a big hurry with his mate in the middle of the night and started loading up the boats with those mailbags. I didn't hear about the train robbery until the next day, by which time his mate had gone off in a van with his share."

"Who was his mate?" Raymond asked.

"I dunno, he never introduced himself. He was a Cockney – older than Tom and real flash and loud-mouthed."

"So what happened after his mate left?"

"Well, Tom finished most of a bottle of whisky. I carried on moving the boats while he drank himself senseless down in the cabin with the money. Then I stopped for a bite to eat and a cup of tea."

"Then what happened?"

"When he woke up, I told him to sober up and do his share of the work. We had an argument, I threw him off the boat, and then we had a fight."

"Was there anybody around when this happened?"

"Nobody."

"Are you sure nobody saw you?"

"No, I looked all round."

After a few moments silence, George asked, "What did you do with him?"

"I buried him in a wood next to the canal on the Jackdaw Pound."

"Bloody hell, Ocker, I hope there was nobody around."

"No, I tied up there and got rid of him when it got dark."

"What's going to happen when the foxes dig him up?"

"It shouldn't happen. I dug him deep, it took me most of the night."

There was a long silence with all three men occupied with their thoughts.

Eventually, George rubbed his mouth with the back of his hand and then glanced at his watch. "After what I've just heard, I need a drink. Let's get to the pub before it closes."

The pub was crowded and very smoky, but George saw an empty table in the corner and motioned his companions to sit down. Almost immediately a voice boomed out, "Goodness gracious, if it isn't me old pal Ocker – and his brother too!"

Ben Barnwell, his face russet with sunburn and beard moist from his drink, strode towards them, clutching a pint glass in his huge fist. He clasped them both by the hand and sat down, almost tipping the table with his knee.

"What are you lads doing here tonight? Are you still boating?"

"Trying to scrape a living. You know how it is these days," replied Raymond.

"I heard you'd finished with the boats on account of your knee."

"I have, but Ocker's still on the cut," said Raymond, as George returned with the drinks. "Do you know our cousin George?"

"Yes, I remember George when he was boating," boomed Ben. "I can remember his mother's pies. By God, you never taste anything like them these days."

"What are you doing this far south?" asked George, easing himself past Ben into an empty seat.

"Business lad, business," replied Ben, stroking his beard. "I want to get back on the cut with a marina. Pleasure boating, that's where the money's going to be. The problem is capital to get started. I've got the ideas, but no blasted money." Ben emptied his glass and thumped it on to the table.

"It looks like I'll have to rob a train. That's where the money is these days." He roared with laughter, without noticing the uneasy shuffling of his companions, who glanced at each other nervously.

Ocker stood up and, without a word headed for the gents. Ben watched him depart, commenting, "Ocker's quiet tonight. He normally doesn't have a lot to say, but he's said nowt at all."

"He's having a bit of trouble at home," George confided.

"Ah! Yes, the delectable Kitty. If I'd been a few years younger, Ocker wouldn't have had a look in. Don't tell me Ocker's got a bit on the side – or mebbe she has, eh?"

"No, nothing like that. It's all about money. She wants him to leave the cut and get a job."

"Ah, yes!" Ben sighed, "It always comes down to money. The love of money is the root of all evil. It says that in the good book you know."

George drained his glass and motioned to Raymond to do the same, "It's been nice talking to you again, Ben, but we only popped in for a quickie before closing time and we got to get back to Brum tonight."

They pushed their way through the crowded bar and diverted Ocker to the exit. Ben picked up Ocker's untouched pint and shouted after him, but Ocker had already gone. He scratched his beard, shrugged his shoulders and proceeded to empty the glass, "Ah, well! Waste not, want not. Now who was it that said that?"

****

The three men returned to the boats, picked up the one opened mailbag and took it into the motorboat cabin.

"Tip it on to the floor, I want to see just how much there is in one of these bags," said George.

Ocker and Raymond lifted the bag, shook its contents and stood open-mouthed as bundles of money cascaded over the floor.

"Blimey, have you ever seen so much money?" George gasped.

"It's a fortune. I never thought I'd ever see so much," said Raymond.

George sat down on the bunk, "Look let's get a few things straight. We can't return it because we don't want any involvement with the law, especially after what Ocker's done. I assume we all agree that we're not going to dump all this lot in the cut."

"You've gotta be joking," said Raymond.

"According to the news reports, all these notes are used and therefore untraceable. Nobody knows we've got it now that Tom has – er – departed. It's your money, Ocker, do you want me and Raymond to be – how can I put it – partners?"

"Yeah! That's why I called you here, I can't handle this on my own."

"OK. Now the first thing to do is to get these bags off the boat to somewhere we can count it without being disturbed. We'll take it to my office. That'll give us till eight o clock, when the cleaning lady comes in."

"What we gonna do once it's counted?" asked Raymond.

"Well, lads, it looks like we're going be rich men after tonight, which means being very careful, especially for Ocker's sake after what he's done. We've got to make the money legitimate without anyone finding out where it came from. There are ways and means of doing this if you're happy to trust me and my accountant, who has had some previous experience in these matters."

"Do we have to include your accountant in this?" Raymond asked.

"As I said, he knows how to handle a situation like this so we'll have to cut him in as a partner."

Ocker nodded in agreement, and then said, "How do I explain to Kitty? I can't tell her what really happened."

"I think a big win on the football pools is called for."

"But she knows I never do the football pools."

"Alright, so we'll say I won the pools and you and Raymond were members of my syndicate. We will have to wait a few weeks until the football season is under way, but that'll give us time for me and the accountant to figure ways of converting the money so we can get it into bank accounts without anyone getting suspicious."

"That sounds OK to me," Raymond said.

George leaned back in the bunk, shoved a shoe into the pile of banknotes and flicked a bundle at Ocker. "Cheer up mate, your money worries are over. And do you know, I think old Ben Barnwell's given me an idea."

****

"Come in gentlemen and take a seat."

Ronnie Raggett and Corky McCann sat down and shuffled uneasily on the leather chairs. Lenny Delancy surveyed the two young men through the smoke haze from his cigar and leaned forward with his elbows resting on his desk.

"No doubt you're wondering why you're here."

"Would it be OK if I had a fag," asked Corky, nervously.

"Certainly, lad. Help yourself to one of my Turkish specials."

Lenny pushed a walnut box across the desk. Corky opened the lid and took a cigarette. His hand shook slightly as he lit the cigarette with the expensive lighter he had stolen from a customer.

"Is this anything to do with the geezer we helped to his car last night?"

"You mean the old fart you robbed and gave a beating to after he left the club."

"Well, we did think we might have gone a bit over the top."

"As it happens, I have had a complaint from the Old Bill about that, but it's all been squared as usual."

Lenny looked carefully at the young men. Corky, confident, good-looking and loud-mouthed, and Ronnie, great driver, reliable but quietly menacing. Neither of them were the brightest apples in the barrel, but good lads to have on the team.

"Ronnie, do you remember driving a friend of mine to the station a few weeks back? A big guy with thinning black hair and a moustache. He probably didn't say his name."

"Yeah, I remember him."

"Did you talk to him on the way back?"

"Yeah, he recognised my Brummie accent and we had a chat about the old place."

"Did he ask after your name?"

"Yeah, as a matter of fact he did."

"And, did he tell you he knew your brother?"

"No, he didn't. Which brother – I've got two?"

"Your brother, Tom."

"No. Why didn't he say he knew Tom?"

"I think you'll find he had his reasons."

Lenny leaned back in his chair and puffed at his cigar. He stared at the ceiling for a minute and then turned back to the two young men. "What I'm about to tell you is between us in strict confidence. You mention one word of this outside and you are cat's meat, you follow?"

Corky and Ronnie nodded apprehensively.

"I have a – well, let's call it a financial interest in that little bit of private enterprise that took place on the railway out in Buckinghamshire a few days ago. That friend of mine that Ronnie drove to the station and your brother Tom were part of the team that redistributed a lot of money."

Ronnie gasped in surprise. "Are you saying Tom was one of the train robbers?"

"Exactly, it comes as some relief to see you didn't know."

"I'd no idea, honestly Guv."

"OK. Well, what you don't seem to know – and I hope that's true – is that your brother and my friend Vince split off from the main party at some point after the job, and made off with a lot more loot than they were entitled to. Some of the lads are very angry indeed, although they've got plenty of other things to worry about at the moment, as you've probably seen in the papers. I'll tell you straight, son, I'm also angry because some of that money your brother and his mate made off with is mine."

Ronnie squirmed in his seat and blurted, "I'm sorry, Guv, but what can I do?"

Lenny slammed his fist on the desk. "I'll tell you what you can do. You can bloody well find him."

Ronnie stammered in reply, "I haven't seen Tom for weeks and I've no idea where he might be. Do you know how they got away?"

"Ah yes, you'll appreciate this. Your brother had a canal boat waiting nearby and they filled it up with my bloody money and chugged off to God knows where, while the coppers were checking the airports, the railway and blocking the roads. We know Vince left the boat somewhere and was taken to a private airfield. He landed somewhere near Agen in southern France and then made his way into Spain, where he is now. There was only room for him and the pilot, once the plane was filled up with mailbags, so that leaves your brother with the boat and his share. Now, my enquiries have informed me that once upon a time you were all boatmen. You find your brother and mebbe we can come to some sort of agreement, otherwise he's gonna wind up wearing a concrete overcoat under one of those new motorways they're building."

There was a long silence.

"So do you want me to help Ronnie find him?" Corky asked.

"No, I've got another job for you. You're going to Spain to find Vince."

"Spain!" Corky blurted, "I've never been abroad."

"Now's your chance to widen your horizons."

"There's a problem. I've got a passport that I never used, but it's no good 'cos I've still got the law after me."

"So, we'll get you a new name and a new passport. I'll get it sorted right away. Now a reliable source tells me that Vince has been seen in Marbella, which is down in the south. There are a lot of villains hiding out in that neck of the woods, so it's a likely place. Don't get into a confrontation with him because he can be a vicious bastard. Find out where he's hanging out and let me know. I'll probably go down there myself with some muscle and sort things out."

Lenny stubbed out the remains of his cigar and added, "I expect you to get results, so I don't want you back here sporting a suntan with a dolly bird on each arm, telling me you couldn't find him"

Lenny brought the interview to a close. "Right then, gentlemen, you know what I want, so go do it."

****

"You look terrible – where on earth have you been?"

Ocker, standing in the doorway, shuffling his feet and fumbling with his cap, didn't reply.

"You have a key – why didn't you use it?"

"I dunno where it is."

"You dunno where it is!" Kitty repeated. "Well, I dunno where you've been for the last few weeks, I'd just about given you up."

"I got some work carrying ingots from Coventry down to Oxford – regular run, but no time to stop."

This was the story Raymond had concocted for him when, in fact, he had been holed up on the canal at a quiet spot between Farden's boatyard and the Anchor Inn.

"Well, don't stand in the doorway. Come in and close the door. You do live here – or have you forgotten?"

Ocker muttered something unintelligible, entered the room and glanced at the window, "I see you've had it repaired."

"I'm hardly going to sit around with a gale blowing through my living room. Do you have any idea how long ago it is since you smashed that window?"

"I've been busy. I lose all track of time."

Little Alan Hill, sitting in his high chair, earnestly watched the proceedings, while the spoonful of rice pudding originally destined for his mouth dripped down the front of his cardigan.

"Oh, by the way, that's your son over there – getting a big boy, isn't he?"

Ocker fumbled in his pocket and produced a handful of banknotes, "Here, buy him a present and get something for yourself."

Kitty whistled when she saw the money. "Wow, this new carrying job must be paying you well – or perhaps you've been robbing a bank or doing the train robbery?"

Ocker's face flushed, "No, I haven't had time to spend much and they've paid me well."

He remembered George's warning not to throw money around and attract attention and bit his lip.

"Did Raymond say anything about Corky?"

"No, like what?"

"Like him going to see his mum in the hospital."

"Hasn't he been?"

"No sign of him."

"Didn't Ray and George see him down in London?"

"Yes, but it hasn't done any good. He's disappeared – and so has Tom."

Ocker gulped, "Tom? Which Tom is that?"

"Tom Raggett – how many more Toms do we know?"

"Where's Tom Raggett gone?"

"That's what your sister Lucy would like to know. He walked out on her at the beginning of August and she hasn't seen him since. No letter, no phone call – nothing. What is it with all the men around here – you and Corky and Tom Raggett – just coming and going as you please, with no sense of loyalty or responsibility?"

"Where's Lucy now?"

"Well, she was here for a week. Dolly had a row with her and chucked her out when she went home. I managed to get her her old job back at the store and she's moved in to share a flat with that Pauline girl that's working for George."

"George didn't tell me that."

"Oh, you've managed to see George then?"

"Yeah, I ran into him at the pub."

"Did he tell you that your brother Ray is going out with Pauline?"

"No, and Ray didn't say anything either.

"So, you've seen Ray as well as George."

"Yeah! He was in the pub with George."

"Oh, I see! Obviously you've had quite a regular meeting."

"No, no!" Ocker stammered, "It was just the one time when I was passing by."

"So which pub was this where your meeting took place?"

"The Anchor."

"Did you see Ben Barnwell there?"

"Er – no, I haven't seen Ben for ages."

"That's funny, because I saw Ben the other day shopping in the market and he said that he'd seen you with Ray and George in a pub at Stoke, and you left without drinking your beer."

"Oh yeah, I forgot that."

"It's not like you to leave your beer, even if George was paying for it."

"I wasn't feeling too well that night."

"What a shame! So how come you were in a pub at Stoke?"

"It's on the run south with the load."

"You were loaded then?"

"Yeah, the usual – about twenty odd tons."

"What was the load? Oh yes, you said it was ingots."

"That's right – ingots."

"But didn't you say the load was for Oxford? If so, what were you doing on the London road."

Ocker cleared his throat loudly and said, "That load wasn't ingots, it was a coal run down to the paper mill at Ricky – a one-off job."

"I see. So Ray and George just happened to be there in the pub when you called in for a drink you didn't finish because you were not feeling well."

"Yeah, that's about it."

"Well, if you don't mind I'll carry on feeding the baby – he makes a lot more sense than you do."

****

Corky mopped the sweat from his forehead and sat down on a chair outside a cafe. He ordered a Coke and was relieved to get a tall glass, brimming with ice cubes. He cooled his forehead on the glass before sipping the drink, and looked around him. The street was lined with palms and orange trees laden with fruit. Traffic was heavy in both directions and impatient drivers sounded their horns. At first, he forgot that cars drove on the opposite side of the road to England and was almost run down by a taxi, when he looked the wrong way crossing the street. After two days, he was beginning to acclimatise to his surroundings, although the heat was getting to him and he realised he should be wearing a thinner shirt and trousers.

Lenny gave him an address that turned out to be in a scruffy back street that smelled of urine and rotten fruit. Corky found the house and banged a rusty doorknocker. Presently, a man wearing a grimy vest and several days' growth of beard, opened the door. He spoke in English with a strong accent.

"What do you want?"

"How do you know I'm English?" Corky demanded.

"Don't tell me my business."

"I was told to contact you for some names and addresses."

The man refused to let him enter his house and took him to a nearby park, where he wrote down several addresses on a sheet of paper.

"Here – you take, and no mention my name, OK?"

"Who are these people and where do I find these addresses?" Corky asked.

"They might know where Englishman is, OK?" said the Spaniard, staring shiftily around the park as if he expected an unseen assailant to spring out from the bushes. "You go find – you not tell them my name, OK? You not know me, OK? You no come back to my house, OK?"

With that the Spaniard leapt to his feet and walked swiftly out of the park, leaving a bemused Corky holding the piece of paper.

It transpired that all the addresses were cafés or bars tucked away in narrow Andalucian streets, behind the sea front and harbour, where forests of cranes marked a plethora of new building developments. So far his enquiries had drawn blanks when he realised the very café he was sitting outside was on the list.

He beckoned to the waiter, who came across to his table, wiping his hands, saying, "Another drink, sir?"

"No thanks. Tell me, do you know an Englishman called Vince Rothwell?" Corky asked, adding without too much conviction, "He's an old friend of mine."

"What name again?"

"Vince Rothwell. Here I'll write it down for you."

Corky took the waiter's pencil and wrote the name on a paper napkin. The waiter glanced at it and said, "You wait here and I'll go ask."

The waiter paused at the door, took a long, hard look at Corky and went into the back of the restaurant, where he picked up a telephone, checked a number and dialled.

"Meester Gibson, I 'ave a customer 'ere asking do I know a Meester Rothwell."

The voice at the other end said, "Who is he, and what's he like?"

"He's an Englishman, he says Meester Rothwell is his friend and he likes Coke."

"That's not what I meant. Tell him to come back at eleven tonight and tell him I'll make enquiries about his friend."

The waiter returned and presented Corky with another cold Coke, "With compliments of Meester Gibson. He'll ask about your friend and come and speak to you here at eleven tonight."

Corky returned to the café at the appointed time and sat at the same table. A dark-haired, bearded man sitting at a table was almost invisible, hidden from the lights of the cafe. He sipped coffee and regarded Corky with interest. Eventually, he stood up and spoke to Corky, "Are you the young man making enquiries about Mister Rothwell?"

"Yeah, that's right."

"I'm Ricky Gibson. I own this place. And you are?"

"My name's McCann, everyone calls me Corky. Do you know Vince Rothwell?"

"Yeah, I know of him. He keeps himself to himself, if you know what I mean. You don't look like a policeman, so who are you?"

"Well, to be honest, it's my boss who wants to speak to him."

"And who might that be?"

"His name's Lenny Delancy. Do you know him?"

"I know of him. I think I met him once at a charity do in London. Why does Mister Delancy want to speak to Mister Rothwell?"

"I'm sorry, but that's their private business. I'm just here to make the contact."

"You're just the messenger boy."

"Yeah, I suppose so."

"Well, I spoke to Mister Rothwell earlier this evening and he seems quite happy to see you for a few minutes."

"Does he live near here?"

"Not quite. You see, he lives on a boat just outside of town. A discreet location, no questions asked, you know the score. My car's parked over there, so let's go now."

The car was Italian, open-topped and sporty. It was also very new and Corky was impressed.

"This is the way to live, a posh car, warm weather, lots of money and plenty of birds."

"You fancy this lifestyle, do you Corky?"

"Yeah, I've only been here two days but I like it."

"Is this the first time you've been to Spain?"

"It's the first time I've been abroad anywhere."

They were driving along the coast road and leaving Marbella. Ricky Gibson flicked on the headlights and changed down the gears to negotiate a steep hill. Corky heard a throaty roar from the twin exhausts as the car purred up the hill and he looked back to see the town's lights reflected in the water.

"You have a familiar accent, Corky, where's your home?"

"I live in London now, but I was born in the Black Country."

"I thought I recognised it. Tell me what does your father do?"

"He's dead now, but he was a canal boatman."

Ricky Gibson said no more as he left the main road and turned on to an unmade track. Clouds of dust flew up behind the speeding car and the headlights picked out darkened buildings with piles of empty wooden pallets and fishing nets. Eventually, Ricky stopped the car by a curved wall which looked like part of a harbour. Apart from moonlight, there was no illumination and Corky's eyes strained to take in his surroundings. They were parked at the end of a jetty that gently sloped down towards the sea.

"His boat should be at the end of the jetty," said Ricky, as they walked down the slope. "Of course, you know all about boats being in the business. Did you ever meet a boatman called Tom Raggett?"

Corky stopped and turned to see Ricky Gibson standing a few feet behind him, his bearded face sharply illuminated by the moonlight.

"Yeah, I know Tom Raggett. In fact, his brother Ronnie is my best mate."

"It's a small world, is it not?"

"Hang on a minute, how come you know Tom Raggett?"

"You're not very bright, are you Corky?"

Corky rushed to the end of the jetty and looked over the side. No boat was moored there, just a rickety flight of slippery wooden steps leading into the water. He turned to face Ricky Gibson, who stood pointing a revolver that glinted in the moonlight.

"You're not Ricky Gibson – you're Vince Rothwell!"

"At last the penny has dropped."

"Oh shit!"

"Oh shit, indeed. Goodbye Corky."

The first bullet hit him just above the navel and the second in the throat, blasting away a large section of his neck. The impact of the bullets threw Corky backward over the edge of the jetty, and he hit the water with a loud splash.

Vince Rothwell wiped his prints from the revolver and then hurled it far into the sea. "Oh well, such is life," he mused, and returned to his car.

****

"I told you Ben Barnwell had a good idea. So, we are going to open up a marina."

Ocker and Raymond put down their pints at the same time.

"Say that again, George," said Raymond.

"A marina. Hills Marina – with moorings, boat building and chandlery for leisure boaters. That way the money's not going to sit around until some people get suspicious. It's going to be absorbed into a legitimate business, with us three as partners and my accountant as a sort of sleeping partner. He's the guy with the know-how who's straightening out all that lovely money."

"Can we really get away with it?" Ocker queried, as a worried frown creased his forehead.

"Sure we can. It's all being taken care of. Now we need to find a suitable location, get planning permission and we are in business."

"OK, me and Ray can handle the boating side, but who's gonna do all the business?"

"I've decided to sell the motor business, so I'll run the marina with the accountant."

"Can Pauline come in as a secretary?" Raymond asked.

"Well, we'll see. At the moment she's OK working for me. We'll give her a job at the marina when I sell up."

"I don't know what Kitty will say. She's getting very suspicious about how I'm making a living with the boats."

"You'll have to keep pretending you're a boatman for a bit longer."

" Its getting boring sitting around in that boat doing nowt, day after day."

"Better doing nowt on the boat than doing time in the nick," George said.

"Too bloody true," Ocker replied.

"Have we really got away with it?" Raymond asked.

"I reckon we have," replied George, swilling his beer. "Come on, Ocker, you're a rich man, so you can buy the next round."

****

Spring 1981

Inevitably, a group of protesters arrived each time Doug Bartram and his crew began work on a new patch of virgin woodland. Doug had seen the same old faces for over ten years, standing there with their headscarves and green wellingtons, waving banners and shouting the same old slogans. He had been called everything from a vandal to a despoiler of England's green and pleasant land, but the expanding new town had provided him with a lucrative living for a decade. He was aware that his job on the big digger wasn't exactly creative, unless creating space for new houses fell into that category.

The section of undulating woodland that bordered the canal was very pleasant. Primroses and wood anemones flourished in the glades and Doug noted a large old oak tree by the water, which officialdom had deemed to be spared. That old oak would be shading the garden of someone's elegant townhouse in a couple of years from now. He wondered how much the farmer had received for the land he had recently sold off to the developers. His next job would be to pull down some of the farm buildings, leaving the farmhouse and barns to be converted into flats.

Doug paused on the lip of a small depression to light a cigarette, and watched a white motor cruiser pass by on the canal. Now that Easter was over, there would be a lot more pleasure craft on the canal, and Doug reminded himself that he had promised the family a holiday on one of those long boats before the kids grew up and wanted a holiday on their own. Get the kids to work all those locks while he steered the boat. Stop for the night next to a pub and get lots of fresh air to work up a good appetite.

"Oh well! Maybe next year," he said, moving the digger into the bushes on the slope of the dip. He worked steadily for half an hour, ripping up bushes and small trees, while his crew dragged them off in dumper trucks. He reached the bottom of a depression covered in brambles, pushing and clearing them to one side before digging deep into the soil and leaf mould. He repeated this movement several times when an object caught his attention. It was caught on one of the spikes of the digger. He looked round for assistance, but his crew was loading a truck. He jumped down from the cab to see for himself.

Doug picked up the object and wiped the soil away. A human skull grinned back at him and a long red worm, whose home had been disturbed, wriggled out of one of the eye sockets.

"Oh! Bloody hell!" he gasped, turned his head and vomited.

****

"Dental records have identified the skeleton in the wood," said the detective sergeant, handing the papers to his superior, who put down his cup of coffee to read the contents.

"Well, I'll be damned!" said Chief Inspector Milner. "Tom Raggett! I wondered what happened to that little toe-rag."

"Did you know him?" asked the sergeant.

"I knew him alright and his boss. They gave me quite a lot of grief when I was a sergeant in Birmingham."

"Forensics reckon he's been buried there for fifteen to twenty years."

"Really! I suppose it would have been around '62 when I last had dealings with him. Him and his two mates did a big job robbing that old queer Lord Crantock. I pulled one of 'em, but Raggett and his mate Vince Rothwell got away with it. The last I heard of Rothwell, he was living on the Costa Del Sol and owned half a dozen English bars – you know, the sort of place where you can buy a pint of bitter with your shish kebab. I thought Raggett was probably out there as well. It was around that time a body was washed up riddled with bullets down the Costa Del Sol, but it turned out to be a mate of Tom Raggett's brother, another bloke with canal boat connections. That murder is still unsolved, but we thought at the time that Rothwell and Raggett might have been involved. Maybe we should open that one up again."

"Shall I get the papers, sir?"

"Yes, do that Sergeant. The details are probably with the Spanish police in Malaga. I seem to remember them making a bit of a fuss at the time about British crooks using their patch as a battleground."

"Does this mean you are going to take on this case personally, sir?"

"Too true, sergeant. After all Tom Raggett may have been a complete shite-hawk, but someone did him in and solving this murder could be an appropriate swan song to my career. There are some theories that Rothwell could have been involved in the big train robbery. They reckon that two or even three blokes got away. Could Tom Raggett, of all people, have been one of 'em?"

"I can see you do have a special interest, sir."

"Yes, sergeant, I certainly do have a personal interest in those gentlemen," Milner replied and thought, "Yes, it was those bastards that were responsible for breaking up my first marriage."

****

Brightly painted canal boats were moored in herringbone lines between wooden jetties. Sapling trees, planted when the marina first opened, had grown into mature specimens and formed an attractive green perimeter to the lagoon. A boat club had its headquarters in a newly-constructed building next to the moorings, and the marina's offices, workshops and chandlery were housed in a large building by the entrance.

Chief Inspector Milner stopped his car by the entrance and looked at a signboard, which stated in large red lettering, 'Hill's Marina – moorings, dry dock, chandlery, boat-building and repairs, all boating facilities'.

He parked his car and looked at the boats, before entering the building where there was an unmanned reception desk. The reception's walls were covered with maps of the canals and a large, framed, aerial photograph of the marina adorned the space behind the desk. Milner leaned over the desk and picked up one of the company's letter-headings. At the foot of the page was the list of proprietors: George Hill, Terry Hill, Raymond Hill.

"Can I help you?" Milner turned to see an attractive well-dressed lady standing behind him.

He replaced the letter-heading. "I'm sorry, old policeman's habits die hard." He produced his warrant card, "Chief Inspector Milner, and you are...?"

"Pauline Hill – Mrs Pauline Hill. Raymond Hill is my husband."

"It's Mister Terry Hill I want to speak to – is he in?"

"He's around here somewhere. If you wait there, I'll go and find him."

Milner looked carefully at an enlarged photograph pinned on the wall. It was taken at the time the marina was opened. Two tall men wearing mechanic's overalls flanked a short, stocky man with thinning ginger hair, who was wearing a smart brown suit. They all held what appeared to be glasses of champagne and looked pleased with themselves. He guessed that these were the three owners of the marina.

He heard muffled voices and the sounds of footsteps climbing the outside stairs. The lady returned and showed the inspector to an office on the first floor. A burly man with long, greying, greasy hair sat behind an untidy desk. Milner recognised him as one of the men in overalls in the photograph.

He stood up and offered a large oil-stained hand. "Pauline said you're a policeman."

Milner thought the man looked distinctly uneasy and said, "Yes, sir, I'm Chief Inspector Milner. Would you be Terry Hill?"

"That's right. What can I do for you?"

"Terry Hill, sometimes known as Ocker Hill?"

"That's what they call me."

Milner sat down opposite the desk and looked around the room, while Ocker looked apprehensively at his visitor. He felt as if he was sitting in the inspector's office rather than in his own. Suddenly, he didn't know what to do with his hands, so he stuffed them into his pockets and sat hunched in his chair.

Milner watched him carefully and, after a short silence, said quietly, "Well, now, Mister Hill, I need to ask you a few questions. I understand you once knew a man called Tom Raggett?"

Ocker felt the roof of his mouth become dry. He licked his lips and cleared his throat. "Well, I once knew him way back when we were kids, but we were never friends. I haven't seen him for years. They say he went to live abroad."

"I understand your sister lived with him for a time back in the sixties. Doesn't she know what happened to him?"

"Not as far as I know."

"She really has no idea what happened to him?"

"No, he went out one day with a suitcase full of clothes and never came back."

"Didn't she try to find him?"

"I don't know what she did."

"You must give me her address."

"She won't like you asking questions about Tom Raggett after all these years. She's married with a husband and three kids now."

"You mean she won't want me digging up the past?"

"What do you mean by that?" Ocker said, nervously.

"Oh! Just a turn of phrase," Milner replied.

"There seems to be another mystery connected with your family. Your brother-in-law's sudden death on the Costa Del Sol, back in 1963, was never solved."

"Corky got mixed up with some crooks in London, but we never found out what happened."

"It's not every day your brother-in-law is shot dead. Your wife must have been very upset."

"She was upset, even more so when her mother died soon after hearing the news. We had two funerals to arrange."

"That must have been expensive, especially bringing back a body from Spain," Milner said, carefully watching Ocker's reaction.

Ocker paused and then replied, "My cousin George paid for it. At the time he was in the motor trade."

"And now he is a partner in this fine marina," Milner said, with a smile. "How times change!"

Ocker didn't reply. He only wished this policeman with the penetrating stare would go away.

Milner looked at a framed photograph on the wall behind Ocker. It was of a young man, standing on the stern of a boat with one hand on the tiller, broadly grinning at the camera. "Good-looking boy, is he one of your sons?"

Ocker turned to look and answered, "Yeah, that's my lad, Alan. I've only got one son – me and his mother separated years ago."

"I hope he hasn't got into trouble like his uncle."

Ocker flushed with anger. At that moment Pauline entered with two mugs of tea on a tray and placed them on the desk. Ocker spooned sugar into his mug, then offered the sugar to Milner, who declined.

Milner sipped his tea and continued, "Would it be a surprise to you if I told you Tom Raggett was one of the train robbers?"

Ocker pulled his face into what he hoped was an expression of surprise, shook his head and then nodded in affirmation.

"And what's more, we think your brother-in-law might have been involved in that robbery because he was friendly with Tom Raggett's brother, Ronnie."

"Why don't you ask Ronnie?"

"We would if we could find him."

"Mebbe he went abroad as well."

Milner sighed, "Well, we know some of the robbers went to Spain and we thought that's where Tom Raggett was, hence the connection with your brother-in-law. Now we know that isn't true because we don't think Tom ever left the country."

Ocker said nothing and Milner continued, "You see, Tom Raggett or rather what's left of him, was recently dug up in some old woodland next to the canal near Milton Keynes."

Ocker tried to look surprised. His mouth felt dry again, so he picked up the mug of tea with a shaky hand and hoped Milner hadn't noticed.

"We're fairly certain that Tom and his mate Rothwell double-crossed the rest of the gang immediately after the robbery and made off with more than their share of the loot. We believe they had a canal boat waiting for them and they dumped the money into the boat and made off to the north, away from London."

Milner sipped his tea, but his eyes were fixed on Ocker's face as he continued, "Quite an ingenious idea to escape in a canal boat, when all the police forces would be watching airports and blocking the main roads. Now this is where your brother-in-law and Tom's brother, Ronnie, might have been involved, but we're not sure. What we do know is that Rothwell took off from a private airfield later that day and landed in France. We have the evidence from the pilot that no-one but Rothwell and a lot of money went on that plane. It seems that Tom Raggett carried on northwards with a canal boat full of money, until someone killed him and buried him in that woodland. We want to know what happened on that day. Who killed Tom Raggett and what happened to all that money? After all, it's unlikely but not impossible that he was killed by his brother, Ronnie."

Milner's penetrating gaze seemed to burn through Ocker's skull, but he a took a deep breath and said, "What's all this gotta do with me?"

Milner finished his tea, carefully placed the mug back on the tray and leaned back in his chair. "I've been talking to some canal people, especially those who were active at the time of the robbery. I spoke to an old boy called Ben Barnwell, who told me in some detail all about the feuding and vendettas that went on with the boating families. I understand from Mister Barnwell that your father was crushed to death in a lock by a boat steered by Tom Raggett and there had been bad blood between your families for generations."

"That's correct, the Hills and the Raggetts never got on with each other," said Ocker.

"I also learned that you were still a working boatman at the time of the robbery and regularly used the route where Tom Raggett's body has been found." Milner looked inquisitively at Ocker, "So it could easily have been you, not Raggett's brother, and your brother-in-law who helped Tom Raggett. That's just an assumption, of course – after all, what was your brother-in-law doing in Spain if he didn't have Tom's robbery money?"

Ocker shrugged, finished his mug of tea and glanced at Milner, who had a sardonic smile on his face. Milner said, "Now we have two unsolved murders that may be connected. After all, we still don't know who killed your brother-in-law, Corky, out in Spain."

"Did you ever catch that other bloke, who got away on the plane?" Ocker asked.

"Ah! The elusive Mister Rothwell. We believe he is still around somewhere in the south of Spain. I'd give half my pension for an interview with that gentleman." Milner smiled, then added, "Well, I'll not take up any more of your time, Mister Hill. I'm sure you are a busy man. This marina must take a lot of looking after."

"We keep busy."

"I'm sure. If anything should occur to you that you think I should know about, here is my number." Milner took out a card and put it on the desk. "Thanks for the tea, Mister Hill, and no doubt we'll be seeing each other again as the enquiries progress."

Ocker stood up and said, "I'll see you out."

"That's alright, Mister Hill, I'll see myself off your premises."

Ocker watched him leave the building and walk towards the car park. He saw Milner's car disappear up the drive towards the marina's entrance. Only then did Ocker run down the stairs, bellowing, "Pauline, where's George? I need to speak to him urgently."

Other books by this author

Canals in Colour, Blandford Press, 1974
  (Anthony Burton with photos by Derek Pratt)

Canal, David & Charles, 1976
  (Anthony Burton with photos by Derek Pratt)

Discovering London's Canals, Shire, 1977, 1981 & 1987

Southern Inland Waterways, Ian Allan, 1982

The Waterways of Britain, Collins Willow, 1983
  (Anthony Burton with photos by Derek Pratt)

The Grand Union Canal Walk, Aurum Press, 1993
  (Burton & Curtis with photos by Derek Pratt)

The Anatomy of Canals, The Early Years, Tempus, 2001
  (Anthony Burton with photos by Derek Pratt)

The Anatomy of Canals, The Mania Years, Tempus, 2002
  (Anthony Burton with photos by Derek Pratt)

The Anatomy of Canals, Decline & Renewal, Tempus, 2003
  (Anthony Burton with photos by Derek Pratt)

London's Canals, Shire, 2004

The Architecture of Canals, Shire, 2005